My Life as a Whore

My Life as a Whore

The Biography of
Madam Laura Evens
1871–1953

Tracy Beach

BOWER
HOUSE

DENVER

BowerHouseBooks.com

Cover design by Margaret McCullough
Text design and composition by D.K. Luraas

Printed in Canada

Library of Congress Control Number: 2015939490
Paperback ISBN: 978-1-55566-462-6
Ebook ISBN: 978-1-55566-484-8

10 9 8 7 6

Contents

Acknowledgments

I'd like to thank my wonderful husband, Doug, for helping me fill our house with photos of vintage nudes and historical artifacts. To my children, Airick and India, for all their help with the piles of interviews I needed to organize. To Tracee Bruce for being my biggest cheerleader and always giving me ideas when I got stuck. To Jeff Donlan, from the Salida Regional Library, for giving me the original idea and helping me with photographs. To Dick Leppard, Laura Evens' great-grandson, for sharing his family's history and Laura's private photographs and diaries. And a special thanks to Bob McCormick from the Monarch Shriners for allowing me to tour Laura's parlor house not once, but three times, and for giving me historical paperwork regarding the house.

Introduction

Inside the basement of the Salida, Colorado, library sat a small cardboard box. The librarian handed it to me with a smile. "Nobody has ever written a book about her ... it's time someone did."

I placed the box on a table and after wiping off the dust I opened it. Inside I discovered a pile of papers, seven old photos, and two small paperback books.

"Fred Mazzulla interviewed her from the late 1940s and up until weeks before her death in 1953. He wrote these two books on prostitution. One covers Denver and barely mentions her and the other covers prostitution all around the United States," he said, as he held up the two small books. He then carelessly tossed them back into the box with an annoyed huff.

As I took the papers out of the box, I saw the photos—an old woman rolling a cigarette, a lady on a donkey, a group of women standing next to a bar. Which was Laura Evens?

I was raised in Salida, but had never heard her story. I never knew that Sackett Street, down near the park, had once been the town's red light district ... or that my town even had a red light district. After filling the library's copy machine with dimes, I copied every paper and photo in the box.

Five minutes later I found myself parked on Sackett Street and looking at it in a way I had never seen it before. What was once just a street that held cheap apartments now held a story. I got out of my truck and slowly walked past each building, as though seeing them for the first time, and in a way, I was. Walking to the end of the block, I stopped at the two-story building that I only knew as the Shriners building.

The familiar "Mon-Ark Shrine Club" sign above the red painted front door now seemed out of place. The copy of the photo that I held in my hand showed an older woman pointing to a small white sign on that same door, which read "No Girls." As I walked slowly around the building, I noticed something odd ... except for a small circular window,

1

too high for an average person to look through, the first floor no longer had any windows.

Through the stucco, which covered the building, the outlines of the old window frames could be seen peeking out. Eager to start my research on this woman who had captured my interest, I contacted the Mon-Ark Shriners.

After leaving a message, I headed back to work. I had been working at the Starbucks inside the Salida Safeway. Being a small kiosk, each employee worked alone for most of his or her shift, which came in handy for what I was about to do ... interview every single person who bought coffee.

As the months continued, I was able to find people who had not only heard of Laura Evens ... but had known her. I found myself spending my free time interviewing elderly residents of my town and hearing amazing stories of a woman I was only beginning to understand. I visited the local nursing home and spent hours with people who were thrilled that their lives were once again being thought of as useful.

The Shriners, happy to share their building's history, allowed me to have a tour. As we walked around, they explained how the original staircase that led up to the second floor had been moved over to the far corner. A newly created trap door sealed off the second floor from sight. All people could see now was an oddly placed staircase that stopped at the ceiling.

As we continued the tour of the first floor, they explained how they had torn the bedroom, which had belonged to Laura Evens, off the side of the building. The back of the building, which originally held a bathroom, kitchen, and large screened-in porch, was torn apart and only the kitchen remained.

The second floor, which was accessible after the trap door was unlocked, held the best treasure. The girls' original rooms had been left untouched ... but the years had not been kind. The roof of the building had leaked terribly over the years. The walls and ceiling were collapsing and years of old water stains had rotted the wallpaper. As I walked from room to room, I was faced with the challenge of ducking under 2x4 braces in order to tour each room.

The rooms still contained the original flowered wallpaper, and you could see where a small sink had been mounted to the wall, an area for a small wood stove, and what appeared to be a very large walk-in closet.

In a time when most homes used an armoire, it was an odd find. Was this small room used for something else? A writing desk? A small sitting room?

After taking photos of every room and writing down everything I was told, I left the building with an increased sense of curiosity. But how do I find out more than what was written in the small stack of interviews? Luckily, my questions were about to be answered—this time, by a large envelope and a secret promise.

As I stood at work making coffees, a familiar face approached me. With a finger to his lips, he handed me a large envelope. As I slid the paper out, I saw my next clue to this amazing woman ... her daughter's death certificate.

"As you can see, the paper lists her grandson's name and address ... which is Laura Evens great-grandson," he pointed out with a smile. "Dick Leppard, Salt Lake City, Utah."

As soon as I got home, I typed up a letter and mailed it off. Short and sweet. I gave him all my contact information and hoped he would respond ... and five days later he did. After a week of emails and phone calls, my kids and I were in the truck headed for Salt Lake City, a twelve-hour drive.

The family was amazing. Being devout Mormons, they took us for a tour of the Temple grounds and then out to lunch. We then spent the evening going through boxes of Dick's grandmother's things—diaries, letters, and photos of Laura and her girls. He explained that his grandma, Laura's only child, was ashamed of her mother. But as the years went by, the family became curious about her and they showed me things they had collected ... including one of the missing windows from the front of the parlor house!

"My brother bought it at auction. The Shriners removed all the first floor windows and sold them, I'm not sure why," Dick explained, as he showed me a photo of the window. After photocopying all his papers, we then spent two hours at Walmart scanning his box of photos. With a smile and a hug, my kids and I piled back into the truck and headed home.

Back at work making coffee, I was greeted once again by someone who was offering me information about Laura. I had already interviewed a man who had been a football player at the high school in the 1930s, who told me about how Laura paid for their fancy satin uniforms. I interviewed another man whose uncle sold Laura her car that she paid for with silver dollars. And with this new tip I had a chance to collect more information on Laura, in the form of a woman named Norma Friend.

After a quick phone call, I found myself in the very neat and tidy house of this elderly woman. She explained to me that she touted herself as the town's historian and had heard that I wanted to write a book about Laura. She led me into her back bedroom, where I was faced with a wall of filing cabinets. As I looked around the room I saw maps of Salida, photos of old trains, and shelves filled with books on Colorado history.

"The files are right here. I'm glad you can make use of them, I just never found the time to write her story," she explained, as she piled folder after folder on her work table. "I have her obituary and the story the *Denver Post* did after her death. I even interviewed people like you're doing," she said with a smile. She then handed me the folders and wished me luck.

As my collection of information was growing, more of Laura's story was taking shape. As the months continued, as did my interviews, I was informed of an interesting twist to my research. It seems that the Denver History Museum had more of the Laura Evens interview and a large collection of photos! Unfortunately, I would now be hitting a road-block that would last three years.

Upon contacting the museum, I was informed that the collection was in storage until April 2012. A new museum was being built and everything was packed up until the grand opening.

As the years flew by, I spent the time researching my book, *The Tunnels Under Our Feet: Colorado's Forgotten Hollow Sidewalks* (Johnson Books/Big Earth, July 2014). Finally, the new History Colorado Center re-opened and I was able to read the rest of the Laura Evens interview and collect more of her personal photos.

As I read through these new interviews, I noticed something interesting ... Laura was giving dialog. Fred Mazzulla had promised her a book about her life and she was giving him complete conversations to use. Like a high school girl gossiping about what happened in school, Laura had given each side of the conversations she had been part of.

I was able to read what Winfield Stratton said to Laura in Leadville when she got a new dress at the post office, I found out why Diamond Dick Valentine committed suicide, and what Laura talked about to Lou Bunch in Central City when they met for the first time.

A page from the transcript of the interviews that Fred Mazzulla had with Laura.

As I continued to look through the Mazzulla interviews, the librarian from the History Colorado Center brought out a new box and set it on the table next to me. "Are you aware that Fred Mazzulla also interviewed two of Laura's girls?" she asked, as she handed me a pile of folders. Shocked, I opened them to see not only more information on Laura, but more conversations.

With all the interviews in hand, and more photos copied, I was finally able to piece together the life of this amazing woman.

The title of my biography of Laura comes into question by many people. The answer is simple—this is how she described herself. In one of the interviews I did, it was explained to me. People would refer to Laura as a soiled dove or painted lady, but she corrected them. "I am not a soiled dove or a lady of the evening ... I'm a whore. Call me what I am."

So I did.

✢ 1 ✢

The sweet taste of candy
and the white fur coat

| 1895 |

On the stage stood twenty-three young girls. Seeing that there was quite a turnout, Doctor Moxsom could chose to be picky. None of the girls knew what to expect, but they were all there for the same reason. They were all willing to become prostitutes.

Laura stood quietly on the stage and watched as the group of girls was asked to turn around, show their teeth, and were judged like you would a horse. Within fifteen minutes, the group dwindled down to just seventeen.

Laura had been brought to this skin auction by a man she had met in Cripple Creek by the name of Pete Peterson. He was one of her regulars at the Albert and Burns Saloon, where she worked as a blackjack dealer. She made good money there—a dollar an hour. But Pete had lured her here with the promise of much more.[1]

Doctor Moxsom, pleased with his selection, announced to the remaining girls that they would now have to show themselves to the prospective madams. They would judge for themselves if any of the girls would be a good addition to their houses. The girls watched as an all-Negro band walked over to the corner of the stage and sat down with their instruments. As the men began to play, Doctor Moxsom motioned for maids to come and assist the girls with the removal of their dresses. At this, Laura got up and left the stage. She had never undressed in front of anyone before, including her husband, and she was not about to start by undressing in front of a group of Negros.

Laura saw Pete sitting at a table near the stage, enjoying the show, and sat down with him. She thought that she would be having a private

Denver, Colorado, in the 1890s. Courtesy History Colorado, Fred Mazzulla Collection, #10049687.

audition with Madam Jennie Rogers, who owned the famed House of Mirrors. There, she was told, she could make $1 from each customer she serviced. The thought of what she would have to do to earn the money disgusted her, but at the same time, it was also too good to pass up.

As Laura poured herself a glass of champagne, she watched as eight more girls refused to get undressed and leave the stage. The remaining nine girls, bare as the day they were born, nervously tried to cover their naked bodies by crossing their arms and hiding behind each other. Curious to see what the girls would have to go through, Laura quietly continued to watch.

Doctor Moxsom, satisfied that no other girls would be leaving the stage, picked up a small, blue metal box that had been lying on a nearby table. As he approached the nervous girls, he opened the box to reveal an assortment of hard candies and silver dollars. He handed each girl a hard candy and then looked over at Laura, who was still sitting in a nearby chair, and offered her one. She politely refused.

With a sly laugh, he turned his attention back to the girls and paired them into groups of two. The odd girl out would have to wait her turn. With a nod from the madams, Doctor Moxsom proceeded. "Ladies," he announced in a firm, but comforting voice, "in this box I have enough silver dollars for each of you to get five … but only if you are willing to play a game." The girls all began to whisper and some even started to stand a little straighter. "I need each of you to put that sweet candy in your beautiful little thing, while the other girl will eat it out … and eat it all."

Laura was stunned. "Holy God! Is this what it takes to be a sporting woman?" she asked Pete, as she quickly jumped up out of her chair and grabbed her cloak. "I quit! I'm going upstairs to pack my trunk!"

Pete, with a nervous smile, quickly followed after her and offered to buy her a bottle of wine if she would at least promise to sit in the parlor with him. Never one to turn down a free bottle of wine, she agreed.

After only a few sips from her freshly poured glass of wine, Laura noticed Doctor Moxsom enter the parlor room and it appeared that he was looking for someone. And he was. "Ah, there you are young lady, I was hoping you were still here. Are you ready to join the party?" Laura turned away from him and took a long drink from her wine glass.

"I'm sure you are liquored up enough to let everyone see that beautiful little thing of yours now," Doctor Moxsom teased.

"Beautiful little thing? It looks more like a dead hog's eye!" Laura replied, still refusing to face him. Doctor Moxom laughed. He sat the small, blue metal box on a nearby table and pulled out five silver dollars. He jingled them in his hand as he offered her a second chance to earn them.

"Why don't you just show yourself to us," he asked in his nicest tone, "I won't even offer you a candy." Laura grabbed her fur cloak off the back of the chair before she turned to face him.

"I quit! All those men? My God! You even have a mirror laying on the stage where everyone can see ... you know." She paused to take a quick drink before slamming her empty glass down to get her point across. "And you have five niggers up there and you want me to strip naked? I quit!"

As Laura stormed off, she didn't notice Doctor Moxsom and Pete exchange glances. Pete ran after her and tried to coax her back to the parlor. "Well, come on," Pete pleaded, "let's just go see what they are doing. Maybe you can just sing them a song. The Negro band played very well tonight. What do you say?" He added, "Let's show them what a lady you really are."

Laura stopped and thought for a moment. "Maybe you're right. I should show them how a real lady acts." With a smile on his face, and an approving nod from Doctor Moxsom, Pete led Laura back into the ballroom.

Seeing that Laura had changed her mind, Pete nodded to the band, who quickly pleaded with her to sing. "Oh Laura, come on," they said, "let's practice a song, won't you?" Laura had a beautiful singing voice. Her father had paid many a dollar for singing lessons when she was younger. She thought for a minute, and then instructed the band to play the music from the popular Vaudeville song, "The Sidewalks of New York."

As they started to play, she noticed movement off to her right and the sound of bottles popping. Three of the girls who had been up on the stage earlier were running toward her and started spraying her with champagne. Unable to get away, Laura was soon soaked and wringing wet.

"Don't any of you undertake to take this dress off me!" Laura snarled, as she quickly wrapped the train of her dress around herself and slowly backed up toward the parlor room.

A girl named Jenny dropped the empty champagne bottle she was holding and walked over to Laura with a disgusted look. "You high-classed bitch!" she screamed. With that, Laura dropped the train of her dress and quickly removed her slipper. In an instant she had knocked Jenny to the floor and was savagely beating her with all the built-up anger she had from this terrible night. It took a combined effort to pry her off the girl she would forever refer to as "Big-mouthed Jen."

Pete ran over to Laura and offered to take her upstairs. She yelled at him for ruining her dress and for tricking her into coming there in the first place. Pete replied, "I saved you."

Laura looked at him and screamed, "No, by God ... you didn't! Look at my beautiful dress! Chances are it's ruined! Champagne will spot you know!"

Pete smiled at her and said, "Well, I will send it down. If it's spoiled I'll take you down to Daniels and Fisher and buy you a new one."

Satisfied with his offer, Laura replied, "I have to go up and change. And now where am I going to take a bath? Have you ever tried to wash champagne out of your hair?"

After calming her down a little, Pete led Laura upstairs to her room. He called for a maid to come in and gave her five dollars to rub Laura down and wash the champagne out of her hair.[2]

The next morning Laura met Pete downstairs for breakfast, but she was still plenty mad at him. The only thing that kept her pleasant was the promise he had made the night before to buy her a new dress. Pete told Laura that he actually admired her for her independence. She replied, "You're an educated man. Why would you come down and ask a civilized person to go through what those women did in that ballroom with the candies ... and encourage them? I don't know if I want to join this lifestyle or not."

As Laura and Pete sat drinking their coffee, a woman came up to the table and asked if she could join them. She introduced herself as Jennie Rogers.

Jennie was a very beautiful woman and stood almost six feet tall, which made her very intimidating. She had dark brown hair piled up in a large bun, and wore sparkling emerald earrings. These earrings were her trademark, and she was never seen without them.[3] As the waiter poured her a cup of coffee, Jennie told Laura, with a mischievous smile, how she would like to offer a place in her parlor house to the girl who beat the hell out of Jenny the night before. With the ice broken, Pete politely excused himself and the two women started to discuss business.

Jennie Rogers had opened her parlor house in 1889 and named it the House of Mirrors, after the many mirrors she had used to decorate the walls and ceilings. She explained that she had actually given up on her parlor house in 1892, only four years after she opened it, and had leased it to a madam named Ella Wellington. Jennie thought that a move out of state would calm down her husband, Jack, and curb his drinking and gambling, but it didn't.

On July 28, 1894, Jennie received an urgent telegram from one of the inmates at the House of Mirrors. It seemed that Ella had shot herself in the head the night before and the girls were very upset. Jennie decided to leave her husband to his drinking and quickly headed back to Denver.

Jennie Rogers, madam of the House of Mirrors, Denver. Courtesy History Colorado, Fred Mazzulla Collection, #10025165.

When Jennie arrived, she found that the maids had already cleaned up the blood and that the police had closed the brothel, waiting for her return. The girls sat down with Jennie and explained what had happened.

Ella had been married to a man named Fred Bowse and they had adopted two children. Soon after, she decided that she didn't enjoy being a mother and left her family for a man named Sam Cross. In 1889, she and Sam had parted ways and she took a train to Denver to become a prostitute, which is when Jennie had met her.

The night of the shooting was just like any other night. Ella was dressed in a beautiful silk gown adorned with a $2,000 necklace. On her fingers she wore several ruby and diamond rings and was enjoying the company of her boyfriend, Frederick Sturges, while the parlor house's nightly party was in full swing. The parlor house had a well-respected restaurant on the first floor and that night Ella was summoned to the dining table of a familiar couple from her past.

The husband and wife had been friends of Ella's and her now ex-husband Fred. She sat with them as they told her how happy Fred and the children were with his new wife. Ella became enraged and started to babble, "Oh, I am so happy, oh so happy!" Her boyfriend Frederick excused Ella and led her upstairs to rest. The girls said that as she walked to her room they heard her scream, "Oh I am so happy, so happy! I think I'll just blow my goddamn brains out!" Later that night, after everyone had gone to bed, the girls heard a gunshot. Ella's boyfriend Frederick was asleep in the bed next to her.

Jennie explained to Laura that this was actually common with inmates of parlor houses, except most of them used poison to end their lives. Chloroform, morphine, and laudanum were the most popular, since they were easy to purchase. Jennie then added that poor Frederick was so upset that he slept on top of Ella's grave for the next four nights. He bought the plot next to hers and within three weeks he was found dead of a morphine overdose. In his pocket was a photo of Ella and a note that read, "Bury this picture of my own dear Ella beside me."[4]

Jennie let the story sink in as she quietly finished her coffee. Laura thought a minute, then asked about the pay. Pleased that Laura was still interested after her cautionary tale, she continued.

"All the girls that apply for a job at the House of Mirrors have to be top notch, know the ways of a man, and how to get them off good and fast ... because time is money. Some men will buy a girl for the whole night and even sleep over. That will earn you up to two hundred and fifty dollars, where a regular date will earn you around a dollar. All of the girls get trained by my partner, Miss Glenn, in a brothel I own in Leadville. If you decide you like Leadville, like many of the girls do, you are welcome to stay." Jennie added, "I get paid either way.[5]

"So," Jennie said, as she put down her empty coffee cup, "ready to join my world?" Laura smiled and with a handshake agreed to meet Jennie at the House of Mirrors the next afternoon. But for right now, she had to get some things in order. Especially when it came to her daughter Lucille.

Laura returned to her rented Denver hotel room at the Imperial Hotel at 314 14th Street.[6] As the trolley stopped in front of the five-story hotel, she thought about how she was going to break the news to her landlady, Carrie Ward. Carrie had been caring for Lucille while Laura had worked as a clerk at 1100 Larimer[7] and then later when she found a better paying job in Cripple Creek. But now she needed to know if she would continue to watch Lucille while she tried out this new job in Leadville.

Carrie Ward was originally from Denmark. She started working as a landlady after becoming a widow only three years earlier. She had been married less than three years and caring for Lucille helped take her mind off her late husband and the children they would never be able to have together.[8]

Laura sat down with Carrie and decided that the truth would be best. She explained meeting with Jennie Rogers, the strange interview from the night before, and that the job offer would be taking her to Leadville for an internship. Carrie had seen many of her tenants turn to prostitution, so she wasn't surprised. After discussing Lucille's living arrangements, Carrie only had one more question. "Are you going to use your birth name or continue using the name Laura?"

Laura Evens had been born Alice Chapel Reed on May 31, 1871. After leaving her husband, John Cooper Evens, Jr., back in Missouri, she decided to re-invent herself. She no longer wanted the name that her father had given her. He had destroyed her marriage to John and she wanted to start over. A new life and a new name ... well, not entirely new. Her husband's younger sister's name was Laura Andrews Evens. It was such a pretty name. When John's sister married, she became Laura Andrews McAndrew, which always made Laura laugh.

Laura had brought her infant daughter with her from St. Louis in 1892, to start her life over in Denver. She had been seventeen when she married her thirty-year-old husband. Their only child, Lucille Vista Evens, was born on October 3, 1891.

John's father, John Cooper Evens Sr., had been one of the wealthiest men in St. Louis, Missouri. Along with his business partner, R.J. Howard, they formed the Evens and Howard Fire and Brick Company. John Jr. worked as an accountant for his father's company and was able to supply his wife with all the luxuries that he himself had enjoyed his entire life.

Laura had been raised on a farm in Mobile, Alabama—quite a different world than the luxury apartment that John had been raised in. Laura had left home when she was thirteen to live with her older brother, George, and his wife in St. Louis. Her father, who was originally from St. Louis, wanted her to attend a Catholic seminary school to continue her education. When she was fifteen she was introduced to John at a dinner party hosted by her brother's company.

After John's father's death in 1867, his mother Elizabeth had married a man named Ellis Leeds on January 31, 1871. Laura was loved and accepted into the family's social circle and quickly adapted to a lifestyle full of parties, beautiful clothes, and servants for her every need.

But all of this had come crashing down days after the birth of her daughter. Her parents came by train to meet their newest grandchild and after a couple of drinks following dinner, her father revealed a devastating family secret.

Laura's father, Hugh Reed, had been a private in the Civil War, on the Confederate side. This did not sit well with Ellis Leeds, who had been raised in Missouri, which fought for the Union side. To add fuel to the fire, Hugh proceeded to enlighten the family and all of their high-society dinner guests with stories of his involvement with the Ku Klux Klan. He gave them details of how he had been a Grand Cyclops and head of the Mobile, Alabama, chapter. Ellis Leeds had enough, and had Laura's parents removed from his house.

Laura was devastated. On the carriage ride home Laura told John the whole story of her father's past. "I wish to God that I'd ..." Laura took a deep breath, and tried to calm down. "It's true. My father was the head of the Ku Klux Klan. I've heard stories of his Civil War days. There were just seven left out of his old army regiment that were part of the Klan and they used to come every Sunday for dinner. I'd go upstairs to the second story front room ... you know and to see those weird pictures. Where they had 'em taken by a campfire. Burning! You see? He was a terror!"

Unfortunately, the damage was done. The dinner guests had spread the story and it took off like wildfire. In order to save the family's reputation, John Evens was fired from his job and disowned.

John was unable to find work in St. Louis because of the gossip, so he moved Laura and his new baby daughter to Kansas City, Missouri. There they decided to wait until the firestorm had cooled down. They wouldn't have to wait long.

On January 8, 1892, seventy-eight-year-old Ellis Leeds died. John, Laura, and Lucille attended the funeral. The baby was only three months old. To avoid any conflict, they kept to themselves. After the funeral, they attended the reading of the will. Baby Lucille had inherited stock in the company, but John and Laura had been disinherited. He was broke.[9]

Carrie Ward sat fascinated by Laura's story. After she regained herself, she asked, "But why did you leave him, didn't you love him?"

Laura shrugged her shoulders and said, "I'm not going back ... he's broke and I'm tired of him. I'm not used to poverty."[10]

"So you're keeping the name Laura then?" Carrie asked.

Laura smiled and thought a minute. "Yeah, I think I will. That was the first name that came to me. I resemble John's sister, so I might just as well take her name ... she was a lovely girl. Besides, John doesn't know where we are and he will be looking for Alice ... not Laura."

In regards to Lucille, Carrie agreed to watch her as long as Laura continued to pay for Lucille's care. This all worked out best for Laura. She never really knew what to do with the baby or how to care for her.

As Laura watched Lucille toddle around the parlor, she asked Carrie if she had ever noticed anything odd about the child. "Some of John's family died of water on the brain. That was what I was afraid would happen to Lucille."[11]

Carrie laughed at the thought. The condition, called hydrocephalus, is an abnormal accumulation of fluid in the brain. This results in a large head size, seizures, vomiting, and causes the child's eyes to eventually face downward, due to the pressure. "Lucille's fine," Carrie reassured her. "She is two. We would have seen something by now."

"I have just always been so worried and nervous around her. Up until I got on that train with Lucille, I had never taken care of the baby." Laura added, "I had a nurse to take care of her and I had never done it before. I didn't know what to do when the baby cried. I didn't know whether to feed it or what."

Carrie smiled. She had seen this with a lot of the privileged ladies. They have so many nannies and maids that they lose their natural mothering instincts. "She's in good hands with me, don't you worry," promised Carrie.[12]

As Carrie took Lucille out of the parlor room for her nap, Laura was left alone to think about everything Jennie Rogers had told her that morning. As she sat, she noticed a young woman enter the lobby. She was wearing an elegant blue dress with a matching hat covered in long beautiful feathers. She wore a floor-length white fur coat and Laura was sure it was fox. She used to dress like that before John lost all his money and she missed it. Working at Cripple Creek dealing blackjack wasn't going to earn her that fur coat, but working with Jennie Rogers would.

⇥ 2 ⇤

A mirrored ceiling and the crystal chandelier

1895   At 11:30 a.m. the next morning, Laura received a call that there was a carriage waiting for her downstairs. Her first reaction was fear. She had always been afraid that John would hire someone to find her and force her back to St. Louis to face the problems her father had caused. Make her rebuild a life with a man she didn't want to be with anymore. As she poured herself a glass of wine to relax, she heard a knock at her door. It was Carrie Ward, with Lucille in tow. "Laura," she said, with an approving smile, "it looks like Jennie Rogers has sent you a first-class carriage for your meeting today." Laura let out a loud sigh. She was never so relieved.

Arriving in the lobby, Laura saw a beautiful white carriage with a matching team of black horses waiting for her outside. A fine looking coachman held the door open and helped her inside, where she saw two other young women who looked just as nervous as she was. The three women sat silently as the carriage started off. Since Laura wasn't sure if either of these women had helped pour champagne on her the night before, starting a conversation seemed out of place.

After just a couple of blocks of awkward silence, the carriage stopped in front of a run-down boarding house. A young woman wearing an old cloth jacket and a faded dress stepped up to the carriage before the coachman even had a chance to open the door. "I can get the door myself, Sweetie," she said, as she winked seductively at him. The coachman smiled, but continued to hold the door for her as she climbed inside. "What's with all this balderdash? You would think somebody just died!" Laura quickly looked at her new carriage companion.

"Name's Jessie, but I'm thinking a whore name like "Feather Legs" or "Sweet Fanny" will sound better. Get all the whoremongers to pony up." After just a few seconds of shocked silence, all three women started to laugh. The ice had been broken.

As the carriage ride continued, the talk turned not to sex, but to the different boarding houses the women were living in. After seeing the boarding house that Jessie lived in, and not knowing where the other two girls were boarding, Laura was reluctant to talk about the brand new eighty-five-room hotel she was boarding at. The Tuscan-styled, red sandstone building with not one, but two elevators. Every room had a tiled and carved fireplace and hand-woven Turkish rugs. Each night she could play in the casino or relax on the roof garden after dinner. She had already been called a "high-classed bitch" the night before, and she wanted to make friends with as many of the women as she could.

Jessie described her boarding house as a nightmare to live in. The main floor had originally been a bowling alley, and the lanes were still intact, as well as the ball returns. She described how the other boarders would use them as a dumping ground for trash, coats, and umbrellas. She even mentioned how a wild cat had a litter of kittens in one of the ball returns and how she would bring them scraps. Her room was small and had only an old chair, washstand, and a small mirror. She had to make a bed out of whatever she could find. Laura stayed quiet. Her room not only had a luxurious bedroom set, but a private bathroom.

Luckily for Laura, the carriage pulled up to the House of Mirrors before anyone even thought to ask her where she was boarding. As the women stepped out of the carriage, Laura looked up at the building. It looked like a basic row house made of beige stone and had what appeared to be a restaurant attached to the left side. The brothel itself was three stories tall and had a large arched window on the first floor. An illuminated sign advertising a good time hung in the window above a half curtain.

Along the front of the building she saw some elaborate stone carvings and up on the third floor she noticed stone carvings of human faces. As she continued to look, Jessie came up behind her and said, "I've heard those stone heads are the people she blackmailed to build this place." Before Laura could respond, Joy, another girl from the carriage, chimed in. "I think that's just a ghost story. They are probably just meant to look like pretty girls." Laura smiled at Jessie. She had also heard the blackmail story.

The front door was opened by a well-dressed Negro doorman, who smiled and motioned for them to head into the parlor, which was off to their right. As they entered the foyer, Laura quickly noticed that the doorposts were very elaborately carved. As she looked closer, she could see that they were actually an intricate collection of carved penises. Slightly embarrassed and not wanting anyone to notice her staring, she quickly turned her attention to the carved newel posts at the bottom of the staircase. Looking closer, she could see that the stairs were covered with elaborate, oriental carpeting. The walls were covered in floral wallpaper, and every square inch leading up to the second floor was covered in framed mirrors of all shapes and sizes. As they stepped into the parlor, Laura quickly realized how the house got its name.

The parlor was covered, from floor to ceiling, with large plate-glass mirrors framed in birdseye maple. The floors were parquet and covered in beautiful oriental rugs. The women just stared at the room. None of them had ever seen a ceiling covered in framed mirrors before. A large

The House of Mirrors and its attached original restaurant. Author's personal collection.

crystal chandelier, made from hundreds of glass-faceted prisms, hung from the center of an eight-foot by eight-foot square of mirrored ceiling located in the middle of the large room, while the rest of the ceiling was covered in two-foot by two-foot framed mirrors. It gave the room a shimmering beauty that reflected onto the golden harp and rich brocade chairs.

As the girls continued to walk around the parlor, Jennie Rogers entered the room unnoticed, wearing a deep blue velvet dress and her signature emerald earrings. "Ladies," she announced, "would any of you like a tour?" Quickly the four girls composed themselves and stood at attention. In all, the house had twenty-seven rooms that included a kitchen, a ballroom with gold chairs lining the walls, four parlors, a wine room, and sixteen bedrooms. The parlor house also had only two bathrooms, each with a tub.

One of the parlors in the House of Mirrors before it was dismantled and turned into a Buddhist temple. Courtesy History Colorado, Fred Mazzulla Collection, #10025163.

Jennie explained that the first floor was where the girls would meet their guests in what she called the viewing room. Up on the second and third floors were the girls' rooms. The smaller rooms, without a wood stove, were around 9x7 feet, and a man would pay 75 cents for a lay. In the rooms with a wood stove, which were slightly larger, a man paid $2 for a lay. Each bedroom had a nice bed, a private toilet with a small sink, a rocker, a chair, and a writing desk. The windows were decorated with lace curtains. One feature that Laura did not like was the Murphy-style bed that, when lowered, blocked the door.

Jennie explained that each room was designed to make the men feel more secure. The act of lowering the bed was like an extra lock on the bedroom door. This way a high-profile client could relax and not worry about being "caught in the act." But Laura wasn't buying it—it also had a major drawback. Laura had met many prostitutes while she worked in Cripple Creek and they told her how a "date" normally went.

It seemed that once a man entered the bedroom, he normally lost his manners. He considered the woman fair game and felt that he could do anything he wished. With the bed blocking the door, there would be no way that anyone could save her if she was being robbed, beaten, or God forbid ... murdered. Laura thought long and hard about this as she finished the tour. If she were to work here one day, she would have to re-arrange the bedroom.

As the girls walked back down the stairs to the first floor, they were introduced to a large Negro man named James. He had a huge smile and beautiful white teeth. Jennie explained that he was one of four bouncers that worked for her. Seeing the size of James definitely made Laura feel more at ease.

As they stepped off the staircase and turned to the right, they entered into the restaurant. Inside they had a piano player, bartenders, and in the back corner were gambling tables. Laura asked Jennie if she had problems with the police. Jennie laughed. "Laura," she said, "my husband Jack Wood is a cop. I once shot him after catching him with another woman and I didn't even get arrested for it. I told the police that I shot him because I loved him, and that was good enough for them ... and besides, as long as I give them part of my take, I can pretty much do whatever I want."

Once back in the parlor, Jennie started to talk business. She explained that as a madam, she was charged a monthly "fine" by the city

The staircase in the House of Mirrors that led up to the girls' rooms. The door to the restaurant is on the left. Courtesy History Colorado, Fred Mazzulla Collection, #10049685.

of Denver, costing around ten to twenty dollars a month for running a brothel. Each girl was charged between two and eight dollars a month. On top of that, each girl had to have a health checkup by a doctor, who came to the house once a month. This would cost an additional two dollars, unless he had to do a procedure.

She went on to explain that the doctor also treated venereal diseases and would perform an abortion if needed. Jennie stopped talking when she saw the shocked looks on the women's faces.

"Sweeties, don't worry about that too much," she added, with a reassuring smile. "We will teach you how to use petroleum jelly when you're with a man. Always remember—a greased egg doesn't hatch."

After what seemed like hours, the girls were finally able to step outside for some much needed fresh air. The parlor house smelled of stale perfume, cigar smoke, and sweat. Laura understood that the windows had to stay closed most of the time to prevent anyone from getting a freebie, but maybe they could hire the bouncers to just guard the open windows once in a while. The whole house just smelled so stale.[13]

As the girls waited for the carriage to take them home, they decided this would be a good chance to walk around the neighborhood. None of them had ever dared to come to this part of town before.

As they walked around, they could see that for three blocks it was nothing but parlor houses, saloons, and gambling houses. Women hung out of windows, barely dressed, while yelling very vulgar things to get attention, and it seemed that every fifth person was handing out business cards that advertised the area's entertainment. Laura and Jessie grabbed a couple of these cards and shared them with the other two girls. One advertised that they were the "Friendliest house in town," while another stated, "Men taken in and done for." This job was going to be very interesting.

☙ 3 ❧

Fuzzy burros and the bottle of Listerine

895 | It was a cold February morning when Laura watched her trunks being loaded into the wagon bound for Leadville. She had already talked to Jennie Rogers about her desire to stop by Cripple Creek along the way in order to tie up some loose ends. Eager for an adventure, Jessie decided to join her. She had never been to Cripple Creek before, but had heard it was a hoot.

Laura and Jessie heard the train whistle as they arrived at Union Station. Their tickets were for the 8:35 a.m. Santa Fe heading to Victor. From there, they would have to take a stagecoach on to Cripple Creek, which would hopefully put them there before dark.[14]

As soon as the two women got settled into their seats, they immediately started to gossip about the House of Mirrors and the stories surrounding the carved stone faces on the third story of the brothel.

In 1887, Jennie Rogers decided that she wanted to open up a brothel on Market Street, but didn't have the money to open the type of house she wanted. Then along came Jack Wood. Seems that Jack, being a Denver police officer, had insider information on a local millionaire that he could exploit. As he and Jennie became lovers, the idea took root.

The word was that this man had a young wife who mysteriously disappeared and was never seen or heard from again. Soon after, he married his boss's wife and became quite wealthy. The story was full of questions, suspicions, and opportunities.

As a police officer, Jack Wood had access to many things, including the skeletal remains of a female murder victim that had recently been discovered. Jack stole the corpse from the morgue and buried it in the backyard of the house the man had shared with his missing wife. Jack then obtained a search warrant and "found" the body. When he questioned the man, Jack told him that this could all go away ... for a price. Rumor had it that Jack received $17,000, which Jennie then used to build her parlor house.

As Laura and Jessie continued to talk, they were unaware that the man sitting across from them had been eavesdropping. "Excuse my intrusion," the man interjected, "but I've heard that Mrs. Rogers got the money after having a secret child with this man. The child was sent away and the money was to keep Mrs. Rogers from telling the man's wife."

Before Laura could say a word, the woman sitting behind her leaned forward and added, "He just gave her that money as an investment. There's a lot of money to be had in investing in a good parlor house." At that, the two strangers began to argue, which Laura and Jessie found quite comical.[15]

The train pulled into the Victor station right on time. The ladies had their trunks put into storage and simply had a small bag to take with them to Cripple Creek, as they were only planning on staying the night.

The stagecoach ride to Cripple Creek was extremely rough. Small wooden bridges had been built along the way to allow the stagecoach to cross over small ravines, but it seemed that it was more of a trail than an actual road. After they arrived in Cripple Creek, they quickly ran into the stage stop to dust themselves off from the trip. It was amazing how much dust could cover your clothes, despite being only 7 degrees outside.

Leaving the stage stop, Laura and Jessie took a carriage over to the National Hotel to get a room for the night. When Laura had worked in Cripple Creek, she stayed at a boarding house on Bennett Avenue. The rooms didn't have any real walls, just small, creaky beds separated by a blanket strung up by a rope. At the time, she saw no reason to waste money on a fancy room when she was already paying a hefty fee to keep Lucille in the lap of luxury at the Imperial Hotel back in Denver. But with this being Laura's last night in Cripple Creek, she decided she had earned the right to stay in a room that at least had real walls.

After finding suitable rooms for the night, the two women headed over to the Albert and Burns Saloon. Laura had worked there for over a year dealing blackjack and wanted to ask her boss if he would hold her job for her, in case she couldn't stomach being a whore. There was no

Bennett Ave, Cripple Creek, Col.

Cripple Creek, Colorado, in the 1890s. Courtesy History Colorado, Fred Mazzulla Collection, #10049123.

point in making up a silly excuse of why she was leaving, since she was sure that Pete Peterson had already spread rumors all over town about her meeting with Jennie Rogers. Her boss seemed happy to see her, and after just a short discussion, he agreed to hold her job if she chose to return.[16]

With her old job secured, Laura and Jessie decided to take a look at the dance halls and parlor houses on Myers Avenue—maybe they could get some useful advice.

As they walked, Laura entertained Jessie with stories of how the variety theaters would set up bands on the streets and parade show-girls up and down to drum up business. The bands would play the song "There'll Be a Hot Time in the Old Town Tonight." Shame it was too cold for that right now, as she had always enjoyed it.

As they got closer to Myers Avenue, Jessie noticed people coming in and out of small buildings that were located in the alley. "Oh those?" said Laura, as Jessie stopped to take a peek. "You don't ever want to be seen in there. That's where all the hop joints are … the opium dens." As they passed by the Union Theater on Third Street, Laura told Jessie the story of Cleo the Egyptian belly dancer. The theater, being the hottest burlesque theater in town, was forced to fire her after people complained that her show was too indecent. With a nudge against Jessie's shoulder, Laura added, "I'm sure no man objected."

As the women continued to walk, Laura told Jesse about the silly little burros. When she had first started to work in Cripple Creek, she was used to seeing horses and donkeys, but had never seen a burro before. "I was so drunk one night I actually fell backwards over one. He was standing right behind me and I didn't even see him, he was so small." Laura kept her eye out as they walked, and soon was able to point out quite a few burros eating out of a hay bin. As the women petted the fuzzy animals, Laura explained how a burro is really just a small donkey. The babies are quite fuzzy and as adults they continue to grow their furry coats back in the winter, which is why they are so popular with the miners.

As the girls continued to brave the cold, they walked past the parlor houses—Sunny Rest, The White Leaf, The Chicken Ranch, The Harem Club, The Place, The Old Homestead, and The Library. Laura joked how she always loved the name "The Library." She could just see men telling their wives, "I was just at the library last night."

Despite the cold, or maybe because of it, the parlor houses seemed to overflow with customers. Bright lights and piano music streamed down the streets as the nightly parties were just getting started. As they continued to walk farther down Myers Avenue, they started to dance along with the piano music in an attempt to keep warm. Not paying any real attention to what they were doing, Laura suddenly realized that they had wandered too far down. They now found themselves in Poverty Gulch.[17]

Poverty Gulch held the one-woman cribs. These were flimsy, two-roomed frame houses with tiny windows. They didn't have numbers, just a woman's name painted above the door.

Looking for a little adventure, the women decided to take a peek at where old, used up parlor house girls sell their wares.

Kitty, Rosy, Eva, Doll, Dot ... as the girls continued to read the names above the doors, a woman came out of her shack to question them. As Laura turned toward the woman, she noticed the name Frankie above the door.

"What are a couple of fancy girlies like you doing slumming down here for?" the woman asked, as she held a thick coat tightly against her body in an attempt to keep warm. Eager for advice, Laura quickly explained why they were there. With a smile and a nod, the woman motioned for them to come inside.

The crib was quite small, but seemed well kept. The woman motioned for them to sit in the only two chairs the front room held, as she offered them coffee. As she looked around, Laura noticed that the crib was actually two rooms. The front room, where they were sitting, held a bed, a

1890s prostitute "Frankie." Courtesy of Legends of America.

table, the two chairs they were sitting on, and a heating stove. The room was decorated with pretty flowered wallpaper, fancy lace curtains, and framed pictures of children, dogs, and naked women hung on the walls. The back room held a small kitchen, along with a small wooden table and two chairs.

"If you don't mind me asking," Laura inquired, as she looked around the room and gave a curious, little sniff, "what is that smell?"

The woman grabbed a bottle of a brown liquid off a shelf and handed it to her. "It's Listerine. Great stuff. Cleans the floors, walls, and even cleans your quim," she said with a smile.

"Your what?" asked Jessie, as she looked around for something that fit that description.

"You girls have a lot to learn," Frankie joked. "A quim? An oyster catcher? A pussy?" With a startled look, Laura suddenly realized what the woman was saying. "Yeah, now you're getting it. It also works great for the clap. Cleans you right out."

Laura and Jessie sat quietly as the woman poured the coffee. In an attempt to change the subject, Laura asked about the red light district.

Frankie started out by explaining the cribs. Poverty Gulch held around thirty shacks that stretched for about a quarter mile down Myers Avenue. They held all types of girls, but not all of them could charge the same. The preference was French, American, Mexican, Indian, Negro, and then Chinese ... in that order. A French woman could charge $1 and men would travel all night just to get the chance to be with a French girl because the rumor was that they were amazing lays.

When it comes to a white woman, the fairer and the whiter the skin, the better. You just have to stay out of the sun if you want to get $1, if not then you only get around 75 cents for a lay. If a woman has red hair, she could charge more because men thought that they were firecrackers in bed. To earn more money, a lot of the girls dye their hair red.

Frankie quickly took a sip of coffee and filled them in on a secret. "Now, if a woman wants to look real white, she just gets hooked on laudanum. That's an opiate. It gives the girls real pale skin and glassy-looking eyes. It also makes the lays easier. It takes you away from what you're doing."

"Now ..." she continued, "when it came to the Negro, Mexican, and Indian, they only earn around fifty cents for a lay. The Chinese also earn fifty cents, but they are the least popular. The miners don't like the competition they have with the Chinese men. They are willing to work longer hours for less pay, and that makes things look bad for the rest of them. But on pay day, when the lines get too long, the men will fuck anyone, so the Chinese get their share."

"What about you?" asked Jessie. "Do you earn a dollar?" Frankie smiled, as she nodded that she did.

"Now, since you girls are thinking of joining the world's oldest profession, I'll tell you how a parlor house really works. I used to work in a parlor house and earned two dollars a lay, plus tips. But they like to shuffle their whores around and get in fresh meat for the customers to pick from. They don't want the selection to get stale. I've worked at all the top parlor houses around here, but I got stale and now I'm down here." Frankie let out a loud sigh, as she looked around the room. "Yeah, once you're washed up, you either have to leave town and start over or become a crib girl. I'm just saving my money so I have something to live on once my body is worn out."

Laura was captivated. "What are the ages of the girls?" Laura asked, as she sipped her coffee.

Frankie explained that the girls range from around fifteen to thirty years old. Some girls start as young as ten, but those are normally orphans. Laura was stunned. She couldn't believe that a man would want to defile a child so young.

"How do you advertise all the way down here?" asked Jessie, seeing that Laura had gotten quiet. "I hope you don't take offense, but wouldn't the men prefer to visit the parlor houses?"

Frankie smiled as she stirred her coffee. She explained that a lot of the parlor houses only except a certain type of clientele. They only want the rich men or the mine owners who can throw a lot of money around. Some even offer a fancy dinner and imported wines to get their men all liquored up. The idea is to not let a customer leave with a dime left in their pocket. The regular miners can't afford that, so they come down here. "When it comes to advertising, that's not too hard. On payday the men swarm the cribs and all that the ladies have to do is get them to notice them. They hang out of their doorways, show their bosoms or a little leg. A lot of them scream vulgarities to the men to make them look their way."

She poured some more coffee before taking a sip. "Yeah," she sighed, as she leaned back in her chair, "I normally service around twenty men a day. They come at all hours, due to different shifts at the mines. But on payday, whew … I can fuck around seventy-five men."

Laura and Jessie both set down their coffee cups and just stared at the woman. "Now the hardest part about all of it," Frankie added, oblivious to the reaction she just got from her last statement, "isn't the fucking … it's keeping your crib clean. Nothing will lose you a customer faster than a dirty crib." Looking over at her guests, Frankie suddenly realized that they were staring at her in total disbelief.

Still stuck on her last statement, Frankie just shrugged her shoulders and continued. "See … your customers are in a real hurry to get off, so they leave their clothes on. They just pull down their pants just enough to get the job done. Oh, and remember … the most important thing." She took a pause to sip her coffee. "Always lay a rain slicker or an oil mat across the bottom of your bed."

At this, Jessie snapped out of her trance. "The most important thing is an oil mat on the bed?" she asked, with a confused look on her face.

"Well, you don't want the men's boots to ruin your covers, do ya?" asked Frankie, with a roll of her eyes. "Some men have spurs on their boots." After taking another sip of coffee, she quickly remembered another important point. "Oh … before I forget … always make a man take off his hat. It's respectful. It reminds him he is with a lady."

Laura looked at Jessie, before looking back at Frankie. "His hat? Removing his hat makes him respect you?"

Just then, the girls heard a noise outside on the street. Getting up, they looked out the small window to see a naked woman stumbling down the road. "I own this town!" yelled the woman, as she took a swig from the bottle she was holding. "I'm queen of the row!"

"There she goes, all fired up again," Frankie said, as she quickly put on her coat. As she left to catch the woman, Laura and Jessie followed her in case she needed help. And she did. It took all three women to calm the naked woman down enough to convince her to go back to her crib and warm up. There they noticed that, despite the freezing temperatures, she didn't even have her stove lit. A thin layer of ice had formed over the inside of her windows. This crib had been cold for quite a while.

"Leo? Leo? Calm down, Honey," pleaded Frankie, as she quickly covered her up with every blanket she could find. Leo in turn, struggled against her attempts. Being covered in ice cold blankets was not what she wanted. Trying to be useful, Laura and Jessie quickly started a fire in the stove in an attempt to warm up the shack. Looking around, they noticed that the place was very bare and covered in trash. There was an old bed in one corner covered in a ripped and stained quilt, and empty liquor bottles littered the floor. Upon seeing this, Jessie whispered to Laura as she pointed to the bed, "Look, look … she didn't use her oil mat."

"She used to be a madam," Frankie explained, as she tried once again to cover the struggling woman. "They called her Leo the Lion, because she was so tough. We just call her Leo now. She doesn't get many customers anymore and it makes her drink." As Frankie started a pot of coffee on the warming stove, she explained how a lot of the women turned to drugs or drank too heavily. "They think it will make everything better … but it doesn't. The women don't even have to leave their cribs to get a fix. They hand the money and a playing card to one of the little paperboys, who runs down to the nearby drugstore. The druggist knows what the cards mean and gives the boy the bag—laudanum, morphine, whiskey. Some don't even care anymore."

As Leo started to calm down, Frankie was able to replace the whiskey bottle she had a tight grip on with a fresh, hot cup of coffee. As she started to drink it, Frankie decided that now would be a good time for a cautionary tale. As she wrapped the blanket tighter around Leo, Frankie told the women about Ruth Davenport.

It was just that past January. Being a working girl at almost 10,000 feet, combined with the harsh winters, could really be deadly. "Down on Myers Avenue there is a dance hall called Mernie's. The rooms on the second floor are rented out by working girls, who all tend to look out for each other. But pneumonia doesn't care if you have a lot of friends or how old you are."

Ruth was only nineteen. Her family had no idea she was in Cripple Creek. They had no idea she was a prostitute. Her friends did the best they could to care for her when she got sick. They kept her room warm, brought her food, and used the only medicine they could get their hands on—libradol. This soft, greenish ointment is rubbed on the chest to help with breathing. No doctor would come to her room to see her and Ruth was too weak to get down the stairs. After just a week, the undertaker's wagon removed her body.

"Pneumonia is a very real threat up here girls, and Leadville will be no different. Hell ... it might even be worse. When you get there, always remember to air out your rooms and keep them clean. I think the Listerine has helped me stay alive." The women then turned their attention back to Leo, who had fallen asleep. Now that the crib had warmed up a little, Laura noticed that it smelled like sour milk and whiskey.[18]

⇝ 4 ⇜

The salmon in the sandpit

895 It was almost 9:00 p.m. on an icy February evening when Laura's and Jessie's train pulled into the station in Leadville. Their backs were stiff and their legs had been going numb from sitting for so long. They had tried walking up and down the train cars to stretch their legs, but it didn't help much. At least Frankie had given them a lot to talk about during the ride. It was a sad thought that while one woman could be living it up in one parlor house, another could be quietly dying in another.

A man was already loading their trunks into the back of a carriage when they took their first steps outside. The frigid air took their breath away. "Draft!" exclaimed Laura, as she quickly placed her hands over her chest. "I think my lungs are frozen!"

With a smile, the coachman quickly opened the carriage door and helped the freezing women inside. Once they were seated, he quickly covered them up with big buffalo fur blankets that were lying on the seats across from them. Large gallon-size jugs of boiling water sat at their feet. Before closing the carriage door, the coachman looked inside and laughed at the shivering women. "What's wrong?" he teased. "It's only twenty-five below outside, it's like springtime."[19]

As the carriage traveled down Harrison Avenue, the women got their first look at Leadville. It was similar to Cripple Creek, but the streets were just a little wider. They also appeared empty. As Laura looked out the windows, she noticed a strange haze around the gas streetlights. "What's that haze I'm seeing?" Laura asked the coachman, as she leaned forward, being careful to stay wrapped in the blanket as much as possible.

"That's sulphur from the smelters," the driver yelled back. "It's a blackish-yellow color during the day. You can actually predict the weather by how the smoke behaves. If it rises straight up the stacks, the weather will be good. If it slides back down the stacks and over the roof tops, then we are going to get a storm." Laura looked around and could see that the haze was lying around the streets and buildings.

"It seems that the haze is doing that now," Laura replied back. "Are we having a storm right now?"

The driver laughed and said, "No ma'am, this is just normal February weather up here in Cloud City. The storm should hit by morning."

Laura sat back and looked over at Jessie. "It's going to get colder. Colder than minus twenty-five degrees."

The driver soon pulled up to a simple wooden house at 118 West Fifth Street.[20] The lights were on and there appeared to be a party going on inside. As the coachman was helping the women out of the carriage, an argument caught their attention. They turned around just in time to see a man getting thrown into the street. "Come back when you have some money, you worthless drunk!" screamed an older lady in a blue dress. Laura and Jessie stepped back a little to avoid the man, before looking back up toward the house.

The house appeared to be just an average, two-story house. It wasn't fancy like the House of Mirrors, but not many places were. "Girls!" the woman hollered, while holding out her arms for a hug. "Welcome! We have been waiting for you. Come on in. Come in." The girls started to head into the house, when they heard the sound of the man vomiting in the street. "Get away from my house!" the woman yelled again. She stared up at the sky and shook her head. "I hope this storm comes in to-night. It will help cover over all this mess." She then turned back toward the man. "Yes! I'm talking to you! Get the hell out of here!" When the older woman noticed that he wasn't moving as fast as she wanted him to, she picked up a handful of snow, made a snowball, and threw it at him. Laura and Jessie smiled at each other. They both liked her already.

The woman introduced herself as Miss Glenn. She appeared to be in her late fifties and was wearing a satin, off the shoulder dress that came to the floor. Around her neck she wore a diamond necklace. As they walked inside, they could see a number of men sitting on velvet couches while a young Negro maid wearing a simple white-aproned dress served them drinks. A second Negro was playing the piano, while women tried to coax the men on the couches to dance with them. Laura noticed that Della and Joy, whom she had met during the House of Mirrors tour, were among the women.

The parlor was decorated with a patterned carpet and covered over with elegant Turkish rugs. The walls were covered in floral wallpaper and framed paintings of naked women engaging in sex acts. The furniture all appeared to be covered in velvet, with handmade doilies draped over all the arms.[21]

Nobody seemed to notice their arrival into the house, until the coachman set down the first of their trunks. The sound of the heavy trunk hitting the wooden floor sounded like an explosion and the whole house seemed to go silent. Laura noticed that the men had turned away from their current female interests and were gaping at her and Jessie with wild looks. She felt like a canary that had just stumbled into a room full of cats. The women, on the other hand, were trying their hardest to get the men to turn back toward them.

"Ma'am, which of the rooms would you like these trunks put?" the coachman asked.

"Upstairs, down the hall, and to the left," Miss Glenn instructed, oblivious to the scene in the parlor. "Laura goes in the pink room and Jessie in the green."

Laura's room at the Leadville parlor house. Courtesy History Colorado, Fred Mazzulla Collection, #10039976.

The women followed the coachman and Laura was relieved to see that her bed did not fall out of the wall to block the door, like the beds at the House of Mirrors. Her room had a double-sized brass bed, two dressers, three chairs, a chamber pot, and a washstand. As she walked around, she noticed the patterned carpets covered in more Turkish rugs. "Tomorrow, after you rest up, you can decorate your room with all the leftovers in the basement. We have piles and piles of sheets, blankets, and pillows." Miss Glenn stopped and thought for a minute, then added, "I think there might be a couple of trunks of dresses down there from when Dottie was here ... you seem to be about her size. Take as much as you want ... oh, and the bathroom is down the hall on the left." She then left Laura alone and turned her attention to Jessie's room down the hall. Laura looked around her room and smiled.[22]

The next morning Laura quietly got dressed and snuck out of her room in her stocking feet, while carrying her slippers. She had heard the party going on until the wee hours and didn't want to wake anybody with her noisy shoes. Reaching the parlor, she could smell food cooking and the sound of singing coming from the back of the house. She quietly followed the sound, and found an older Negro woman rolling biscuits. "Good morning ma'am," said Laura, as she looked around the kitchen. The woman smiled and introduced herself as Prudence. She explained that the women didn't eat until around 11:30 a.m., due to their late hours.

"Miss Glenn mentioned a basement with sheets and trunks of clothes, where would I find that?" asked Laura politely, as she snuck a cookie off the counter.

Prudence wiped her hands on her apron and led Laura down the back hall to a small door. "Just pull the chain at the bottom of the stairs, Sugar, and watch for the spider webs," she instructed. As she went back to her baking, Laura headed down to see what treasures she could find.

It was almost three hours before Jessie came looking for Laura. "I think the men stayed until the sun came up ... don't they have jobs?" she whined, as she flopped down on the bed, rubbing her temples. Flipping over onto her stomach, she quickly noticed that Laura was shaking out a black silk evening gown. "Hey, I want one!" she joked, as she lazily reached for it.

"You have to brave the spiders if you want one," teased Laura, as she held it up to her body and swung it around.

The sound of footsteps in the hallway caught both women's attention. Jessie sat up just as Miss Glenn came up to the bedroom door. "Knock, knock," she said with a smile. "Are you girls ready for breakfast?" Knowing that this meant the other women were now awake, Laura slid on her shoes.

Downstairs, Laura saw Joy and Della, whom she already knew, and was introduced to Nora and Spuddy. "Why Spuddy?" asked Laura, as she sat down to breakfast.

1890s prostitute "Spuddy." Courtesy of Legends of America.

Shrugging her shoulders, the young woman replied with a thick Irish accent, which took Laura and Jessie by complete surprise. "It just sounded better than Gobdaw or Biddy," she replied, as she took a bite of her breakfast. "I'm as weak as a salmon in a sandpit this morning. My box is so fucking sore."

With a confused look, Jessie asked, "Your what is sore?"

Spuddy thought for a moment and tried to find the right word. "My box? My growler? My … ummm quim?" replied Spuddy, with an unsure look on her face.

"A quim! I know what a quim is!" Jessie proudly announced with a little too much excitement. With that, the whole table burst out laughing.

Seeing that Jessie was a little embarrassed, Della leaned over and whispered to her, "Don't feel bad, nobody else knows what the hell she says either. We just nod our heads and smile."

"Hey! Ara be whist!" joked Spuddy. "I'm just trying to teach you the correct way to talk. Besides, I have the biggest diddies in this house, don't you forget it." With that, the women all smiled and nodded. Spuddy just rolled her eyes and let out a loud huff, as she finished her eggs.

Portrait of Della taken in Leadville, Colorado. Courtesy History Colorado, Fred Mazzulla Collection, #10049670.

After breakfast, Miss Glenn announced that she was taking Laura and Jessie shopping for new clothes. Nora asked if she could tag along, saying she needed to pick up some more embroidery thread. As the girls were bundling up against the cold that they knew was waiting for them outside, Miss Glenn explained how this was now free time. The girls had the entire day off to do as they pleased, since clients didn't tend to arrive until 6:00 or 7:00 p.m. Being wintertime, the girls normally stayed inside and occupied themselves with their needlepoint, reading, or taking a well-deserved nap. Sundays, she explained, were completely free. Nobody worked on Sundays.

The women quickly piled into the carriage and headed toward Harrison Avenue. Now that it was daylight, Laura could get a good look at Leadville. It looked like any other small town—wide dirt roads, gas streetlights on the corners, wide wooden sidewalks, and shops offering anything your heart desired. She even saw a "Justice of the Peace." Miss Glenn saw Laura looking and said, "I've lost a lot of good girls to that damn building!"

The carriage stopped in front of Madam Frank's Emporium, between Fourth and Fifth Streets. The small, two-story brick building was what she was expecting, but not what she was used to. She was used to shopping at Daniels and Fisher in Denver, which was a huge, three-story monstrosity of a building, but it was a beautiful thing to see. They sold everything you could ever imagine—fabrics, ribbons, crystal, furniture, lamps, rugs, and the most wonderful clothes and shoes. They even had a room set aside for the newest French styles and beautiful furs from Europe. On the first floor they had their own greenhouses where they raised roses and chrysanthemums. A small wagon delivered these flowers all over Denver.

1890s Leadville, down Harrison Avenue. Courtesy Salida Regional Library.

Daniels and Fisher store, Denver, Colorado. Courtesy Denver Public Library, Western History Collection, #X-2281113.

The four women entered the clothing store and when the saleslady saw Miss Glenn, she lit up like June bug. She quickly took the ladies into the back room to show them the "better dresses." Full-length gowns with wonderful long trains. High necklines adorned with lace, sequins, and pearls. Some of the dresses had "leg o'mutton" sleeves. Women normally stuffed these types of sleeves with tissues to make them as large as possible—the bigger the better.

Miss Glenn explained that the basic crib girls wore very short dresses that only went down to their knees. The women would then swish the skirt so it rustled and then sway in their doorways to attract a customer. But that's not what a proper parlor house girl did. A proper woman did not show her legs, or her ankles, to a man ... unless he paid good money to see them.

The gowns that Laura and Jessie chose were between $100 and $150 each. Laura also chose heavy black stockings embroidered with pink roses. Miss Glenn explained that the cost would be taken out of their pay, a little at a time, until they were paid off. Laura wasn't even listening ... she was in love with her new dresses.

When she lived in Cripple Creek, she would buy used clothing. Once she bought a $150 gown for only $25, and she still had it. The dress was of black silk with big, jet nailhead glass beads all down the front and sides. A wonderful long train hung from the back. Laura loved the fact that the high society ladies would only wear a gown once. The whores they vowed to hate were the same ones who wore their old clothes.

While Laura and Jessie continued to look around the store, Nora busied herself with the embroidery thread. She was comparing four different shades of pink when Laura glanced over and decided she needed help.

"What's the name of the color you're looking for?" asked Laura.

"It's pink, but like a darker pink. I don't remember the name," Nora replied nervously, as she turned away.

Before Laura could reply, Miss Glenn called her over to the other side of the store. "Nora can't read," Miss Glenn whispered. "I've offered to teach her, but she's too proud." Laura thought a minute, and then went back over to Nora.

"Did you buy your pillow pattern here?" Laura asked. Surprised by her question, Nora replied that she had. With that, Laura simply asked the saleslady to pull down the same kit off the shelf. After looking over the supply list, the women were able to find the exact color. Nora didn't say anything, but Laura understood the smile she got in return.[23]

Soon all the women were finished with their shopping. Miss Glenn had placed her order for the house and all the dresses and hats had been wrapped up in brown paper. As the women piled back into the carriage, she announced, "Now ladies … all that's left is to get down to business."

1890s prostitute "Nora." Courtesy of Legends of America.

→ 5 ←

Arse bandits and dickey dazzlers

1895 | After an early dinner, Miss Glenn led Laura and Jessie back to their rooms to talk business. She showed each of them the secret drawer they had, located inside a small table near their beds. Inside the drawer was a small wooden box with a lock on one side and a small slit on the top. The box was nailed to the inside of the drawer so it couldn't be removed. Miss Glenn explained that when the men come into the parlor house, they buy a small metal coin called a brass check. When the man chooses the girl he wants to be with, he gives her the brass check. When they enter her bedroom, the brass check is placed inside the locked box. The box is nailed to the inside of the drawer so the man can't steal it back. The next morning after breakfast, all of the boxes are unlocked by the madam and the girls get paid.

When it comes to liquor, the women are not allowed to get drunk, but are allowed to drink just enough to get them loosened up. They are encouraged to get the men to drink, and every drink the women have is to be paid for by the men. There is never a reason for a woman to pay for her own drink. Miss Glenn explained that a glass of beer at the local saloon was around 5 cents. In the parlor house it was $1. At the end of the night, the girls get a cut of the liquor profits.[24]

When it came to talking about the sex act itself, Miss Glenn took the women back into the parlor room and asked the housemaid to bring them some coffee. This attracted the attention of the other girls, and soon the whole parlor room was full of stories. When the coffee was served, so was a wooden box full of bottles, jars, and boxes. As Laura peeked into the box, she even saw a rubber penis.

"Really? Why would a woman need a fake dick when she has a whole house full of dicks?" Jessie asked, as she flopped the dildo back and forth. Laura couldn't stop laughing, even after Jessie threw the rubber dick at her.

"Ewww, yuck! I don't want that thing!" Laura then threw it at Nora, who pretended to put it in her mouth.

"Oh girls! You know that's not for us," teased Spuddy, as she took a sip of her coffee. "It's for the arse bandits."

"It's for who?' Nora asked, as she continued to flop the dildo around.

Spuddy thought a minute and then added, "It's for the dickey dazzlers? ... ummm, a Mary? What do you call men who fuck other men?" With that Nora threw the dildo back in the box and went to the kitchen sink to spit and wash her hands. Despite the gagging noises coming from the kitchen, the women couldn't stop laughing.

"Okay, I just have to ask ... where does it go?" asked Nora, as she sat back down and wiped her mouth and hands with a napkin.

Spuddy set down her coffee cup, grabbed the dildo and demonstrated it with her hands. "They like it in their arse. Just take a handful of Vaseline and it slides right in."

Laura shook with fake shivers at the thought of it. "I don't care how much that pays," she said, "you can have those."

As the women calmed down, Miss Glenn started to talk about birth control. She explained that, despite the 1873 Comstock Act, birth control was still available. The Comstock Act defined any contraception as obscene and made it illegal to sell any medicine that prevented pregnancy. The Comstock Act was based on its creator's own personal tragedy.

Morals crusader Anthony Comstock and his wife, Maggie, were only able to conceive one child, a little girl, who died within the year. Mrs. Comstock was never able to get pregnant again. This knowledge infuriated Mr. Comstock and he decided, right then and there, that nobody should be allowed to prevent a child from being born.

This did not stop the sale of birth control devices. To help stop their use, doctors tried to scare their patients by telling them that contraceptives caused cancer, sterility, deranged bladders, and even insanity. Nicholas Cooke, who wrote the 1870 book, *Satan in Society,* taught that if a man withdrew from a woman before ejaculating he could die. Cooke explained how it caused diseases in the brain and spinal marrow, functional disorders, diseases of the heart and kidneys, wasting of the muscles, blindness, and impotence.

To avoid arrest, companies simply changed the description of their products. They were referred to as "security and reliability for the married woman," and given names like uterine elevators, ladies' shields, protectors, womb veils, and the married woman's friend.

"So what type of uterine elevators will we be using?' joked Laura, as she sipped her coffee.

"Well, an elevator *does* go up and down," teased Nora, as she nudged Laura in the shoulder.

With that, Jessie grabbed the dildo back out of the box and started to make the sounds of an elevator. "First floor, housewares; second floor, furniture; third floor, women's undergarments … come off!" she joked.

Trying to get back on track, Miss Glenn took the dildo away from Jessie and pulled the rest of the supplies out of the box. She explained that the best way to not get pregnant was to use Vaseline mixed with 4-5 grams of salicylic acid. Mr. Colgate himself invented it back in the late 1870s.

"Did he get arrested for it?" asked Jessie, as she motioned the housemaid for more coffee.

"No, he was clever. He sold the supplies and the directions on how to mix it, but didn't sell it ready to use. Besides, who is going to arrest a rich businessman?" Miss Glenn joked.

"Now, you can sell a rubber to a customer if you like," she added. "I have supplied a box in each room. These are to prevent the clap."

Nora sighed and rolled her eyes. "They never want to use them. I don't even know why we even bother. They would rather risk a disease than wear one."[25] Spuddy nodded her head in agreement, as Nora continued. "I heard that to treat a man for the clap, they inject pills of mercury right up his pee hole twice a day. They keep doing it until he starts to foam at the mouth."

Laura made a disgusted face at Nora. "Yuck! That just sounds so painful."

Nora continued, nodding her head in agreement. "They also rub an ointment made of mercury on their sores to try to burn off the disease."[26]

"Now, Laura and Jessie, listen up. This is for the two of you and it's very important," instructed Miss Glenn. She went on to explain how to check a man for a venereal disease. "After the man undresses and exposes himself, you need to clean him up with an antiseptic containing potassium permanganate. I've left three bottles in each of your rooms. Then you let him see you clean yourself up with the same antiseptic, but a different washcloth of course. This will keep him from telling people he caught anything from you."

Miss Glenn took a sip of her coffee, and realizing it had gone cold, motioned for the housemaid to give her a new cup before continuing. "Now, if a man undresses and then asks to wash himself up … he has the clap. He doesn't want you to see that he's dripping with disease. You need to tell him to go."

"What if he won't go? What if he makes an excuse and says I'm lying?" asked Laura, disgusted with the thought of laying with a diseased man.

At this, Nora spoke up. "That's why we have the bell. Ring the bell and someone will come in."[27]

Nodding in agreement, Spuddy quickly added, "And that's why you don't lock your door until you have looked at his gooter. You can twist it and clean it at the same time."

Laura and Jessie now turned their full attention to Spuddy. "A gooter?" asked Laura, with a quizzical look on her face. "I'm guessing a gooter is a penis?"

Rolling her eyes Spuddy answered, "Yes, a penis. You twist it and clean it at the same time."

Seeing that she was having a hard time explaining the twist and clean motion, Nora threw the dildo at her.

"Okay, let's start from the beginning. Nora, come be my fuck," Spuddy joked, handing the dildo back to Nora, who quickly jumped up and held it in front of herself. Her dress had so many pleats that she had to fold some of them over just to find a flat spot. "Okay, first you pour the antiseptic into the hot water. You want to make sure he sees you do this. Then you take a dry washcloth and dunk it in the water. Okay class, why do we use a dry wash cloth?" Spuddy said in a comically stern voice.

"Because it shows the lay that the wash cloth is clean," answered Nora proudly, with a wave of her arms.

Spuddy smiled and said, "Yes, you're correct. And men don't remove their gooters when they talk with their hands." All the women began to laugh.

"Now, after the fuck has placed his gooter back its correct place …" Nora quickly smoothed her pleats back down and re-positioned the dildo. "You need to do the wash and twist. This will allow you to clean him and check for discharge and sores. You simply take the hot wash-cloth and wrap the entire thing around the bottom of the shaft, so it is snug. Then, quickly twist your hand back and forth toward the head. Don't forget to press your thumb up the bottom seam of the gooter as you do so. Any discharge will spill out the top. Any questions?"

Laura thought a minute, and then with a disgusted look, she asked, "How much disease will come out?"

Spuddy quickly grabbed the dildo away from Nora, who gave a pained look as she held the spot where the dildo had been. "I will never pee again," she whined, as she comically fell onto the couch.

"It depends on if the lay has tried to clean himself up before he tried to lay with you, but it can be a tablespoon or more. Now keep in mind, the disease comes in three different colors," explained Spuddy, as she tried not to laugh at Nora, who was still moaning on the couch begging for her penis back. "It starts off white, then yellow, and finally green. Any of the colors can be mixed with blood. The head and shaft can also be covered in pustules and the pee hole can be red and sore."

Laura and Jessie turned to make faces at each other. Jessie grabbed her throat and made gagging sounds, which sent Laura into a cough-ing fit.

Nora sat up quickly and added, "Hey, I know why they call it the clap. You wanna know?" Seeing that she had all the women's attention, Nora continued, proud that she could add to the conversation. "So, you know that the clap is also called gonorrhea ... right?" she started, "but, the reason it's called the clap is because of a trick to help a man pee. See, the clap causes a blockage of pus in the pee hole. To unblock it, the man has to clap both sides of his dick at the same time."[28]

Seeing the shocked looks on the women's faces, Nora stood up with a smile and hung both of her hands in front of her ... and then loudly clapped them together. "And that, ladies, is ... the clap." After a round of applause and a dramatic bow, Jessie started to throw rubbers at her.

As the women sat and finished their coffee, Miss Glenn looked up at the clock and noticed the time. "Okay ladies, time to stop cackling like hens. The men will be here soon."

Laura put a hand on her chest and with a long nervous sigh, she looked over at Jessie. "Oh, it's going to be fine," Jessie said with a smile. "It's just a dick. It will be over in one shake of a lamb's tail." Laura started to laugh as Jessie shook her bottom. "Baa, Baa," she teased. "Now let's go herd some sheep."

→6←

The pony ride

895 Laura heard the men start to arrive before she even finished getting dressed. She just wasn't sure what to wear. She had beautiful gowns embroidered with pearls, glass beads, and sequins, but she hated the thought of a man tearing one off of her. The other women had told her stories of how every man will want to lay with her the first night, because she was one of the new girls. She looked through her clothes and finally decided on a simple black-sequined blouse with a matching skirt. This way she didn't have to bother with too many eye hooks—easy on, easy off. With a quick look in the mirror, she took a deep breath and headed into the parlor.

Once in the parlor, Laura was quickly snatched up by Miss Glenn, who led her over to one of the couches on the far side of the room. There she saw Joy, Jessie, and Della. "We are getting our picture taken," Jessie announced with a smile, as she pointed to the empty spot next to Joy.

"Where are Spuddy and Nora?" Laura asked, as she looked around the room.

"Oh, they already had their pictures taken months ago. This is just to show off the new girls," Miss Glenn answered, as she positioned herself against the white lace curtains that led into the dining room.

From her view point, Laura could see the men sitting in the front of the parlor smoking their cigars and getting served drinks from the young Negro maid that she had seen the night before. As the maid walked away, Laura could see the men stare at the young girl's body.

Miss Glenn called the Negro piano player over and handed him a small brown Kodak camera. This new type of camera came pre-filled with one hundred exposures and cost around $25. After all the photos had been taken, the customer had to ship the entire camera back to the

First night in the Leadville parlor house. From left to right: Joy, Laura Evens, Miss Glenn, Jessie, and Della. Courtesy of Dick Leppard.

factory in New York. For an additional $10, the factory shipped back the developed pictures and re-filled the camera.[29]

As Miss Glenn instructed the girls on how she wanted them to pose, men started to approach Laura and Jessie and force brass checks into their hands. Laura was shocked as some men even threw the checks at them when they found that they couldn't squeeze past the other eager men. As the men argued about who was going to break in the new girls first, Miss Glenn shooed them away.

"Gentlemen, we are having our photo taken. Please don't make me throw you outside in the snow," she said with a tense, fake smile. None of the men even flinched until Miss Glenn stood up and glared at them. "I said *now*, gentlemen." The men turned and looked at her with a shocked expression, before taking a few steps back.

"I'm still getting first crack at the one in the black dress," demanded an older man with a large moustache, as he banged on his chest with his fists. He appeared to be around sixty years old and his voice boomed when he talked. Laura looked around at the other girls and with a shiver, suddenly realized that she was the only one wearing black.[30]

As soon as the last of the pictures were taken, the men ascended on the women. Some stood off to the side, trying to start a pointless conversation, while others wanted to get right to business. The older man with the moustache quickly approached Laura, but made no attempt to talk to her. He pushed past three other men who were standing nearby and grabbed her by the wrist. "You already have my check ... let's go Chickie," the man instructed with a harsh tone. "My boner needs polished."

Laura tried to pull away from the man, but he was much bigger than she was. As he continued to pull on her, she could hear the sleeve of her blouse start to rip away at the shoulder. Just as she thought she would scream, a large glass of water was splashed in the man's face. As he released his grip on Laura's wrist, she was grabbed by an unseen hand and whisked through the parlor and down the hall into the bathroom. As her captor quickly locked the door, Laura looked around for any type of weapon she could find. She quickly spied Joy's hand mirror and swung it at the man's head.

"Ouch, hey ... that hurt," the man said, as he rubbed his head. "So, this is what I get for saving the damsel in distress?" Laura suddenly felt a little guilty.

"Let me see it," instructed Laura, as she tried her hardest not laugh. As she led him over to sit on the toilet, she could see that it was bleeding just a little. She took a small towel and had him hold it to his head, which made him wince a little.

As she stepped back, she was finally able to get a good look at him. He appeared to be in his mid-thirties and was quite striking to look at. He had a head full of dark brown, wavy hair and dark eyes.

"Name's Laura," she said, as she held out her hand.

"Clark," the man replied, as he tried to smile. Before they could even try to start a conversation, there was a loud banging on the bathroom door.

"I paid for that whore and I'm not leaving until I break that pony in!" the man yelled.

Clark looked back at Laura and asked for the man's check. He then quickly slid it under the door. "This little pony is going to the stables with me tonight, big man. Go find yourself another mare to ride." After a couple more choice words, the older man left in a huff.

"Sounds like you plan on breaking me in?" Laura asked, slightly embarrassed at the proposal.

Clark stood up and smiled. "Yes ma'am."

He checked the towel to see if his head was still bleeding before he opened the bathroom door and peeked into the hallway. Luckily, the older man was nowhere to be seen. Laura quickly led Clark to her room and locked the door.

"Oh, I'm supposed to leave the door unlocked until I check you for the clap," Laura announced, more to herself than him. She then started to wander around her room talking to herself. "Oh, and his brass check. Yeah, that goes in the box. Where's the box?" she asked herself as she wandered around the room. "It's inside a table. Yeah ... now which table?"

Clark slowly walked over to her and carefully slipped the brass check into her hand, then turned her shoulders toward the small table next to the bed. She just stood there, not moving. He then gently walked her to the table and slowly opened the drawer. Seeing the small token box, Laura snapped out of her trance. "There's the box!" she announced proudly.

Clark sat himself on the bed and watched her for a minute before he started to remove his clothes. She was laying out washcloths, towels, and pouring water into the wash basin like she was measuring out ingredients.

"Have you ever been with a man before?" he asked, with a curious look.

"Ever?" Laura stopped what she was doing and turned to look at him. He was sitting completely naked on her quilt, wearing nothing but a confused smile. "Well, of course I have. I was married for a while," Laura explained, with a quizzical look and a roll of her eyes, as she turned back toward her bottle of antiseptic in an attempt to read the directions.

Clark finally decided that if he didn't show her, they would be there all night. He got up and held his hand out. "Can I have the bottle?" he asked, with a pleading smile. With the patience of a saint, Clark spent the next ten minutes showing Laura how to measure out the antiseptic, how to perform the "clean and twist," and how to check for sores. Laura was so intrigued that she almost forgot the real purpose for them being in the room together.

"Now," Clark purred, "we move on to the next step." He slowly un-fastened the eye hooks on the front of Laura's blouse before carefully removing it and placing it on the nearby chair. He could feel her body tense up with every movement, so he continued to undress her as slowly as possible. His head still stung from getting smacked with a metal hand mirror earlier, and he had no desire to spook her again.

The sex act went better than Laura expected. She had been told that kissing was not allowed because it made the act itself too intimate, but she was thankful for it. After he rolled off her and caught his breath, he got up and showed Laura how to clean him and then herself. He finished his lesson by helping her change the sheets for the next customer.

As Laura began to get dressed, Clark looked around the room and decided he would dump the water from the washbasin outside. As he opened the bedroom window, he was spotted by a passing couple walking their dog. "Good evening," announced Clark, as he stood there in all his glory, "lovely night."

The woman gasped as her husband led her and the dog quickly past the house. Laura couldn't stop laughing.

As they both dressed, he informed Laura that for her to wear undergarments was a waste of time. "Once you get back out to the parlor, I'll guarantee that there will be a line of men waiting for you. Some of them won't even want you to undress. They will just bend you over the bed and have their way." Seeing Laura's shocked expression, he smiled, tilted her face up to his and gave her a quick kiss. "Have fun, my little pony. I'll see you next week."

The next morning, Laura woke up to the sound of someone knocking at her bedroom door. As she sat up, she discovered that her whole body ached and that the room had a stale odor. It reminded her of the terrible smell in the House of Mirrors. "Come in," instructed Laura with a sleepy voice, as she wrinkled up her nose at the smell and rubbed her eyes. "As long as you're not a man," she added.

As she slowly turned, she saw the smiling face of Miss Glenn. "Rough first night?" she asked, with a concerned smile.

"I feel like I got hit by a train," Laura explained, as she pushed the blankets off. "But at least most of them are quick." Laura slowly climbed out of bed and opened the windows.

"It's cold outside, Sweetie. You sure you want to do that?" Miss Glenn asked with a concerned look.

"Just until I go downstairs. The room smells rancid," Laura answered, as she waved the fresh, cold air into the room.

When Laura left her room and entered the parlor, she was comforted by the smell of Prudence's wonderful biscuits. She could see that some of the other girls were already sitting at the dining room table and quickly took a seat next to Spuddy. Out of nowhere, Jessie ran up to Laura and punched her in the shoulder. "You are so mean to me! "Jessie announced with a high pitch. "You ran off with that young, handsome man and I had to lay with the old man with the fuzzy moustache!"

Before Laura could answer, Spuddy and Nora began to laugh. "He called me a pony!" Jessie whined, as she crossed her arms in front of her and pouted.

Laura stood back up and gave her friend a hug. "If it makes you feel any better, I cracked my lay over the head with Joy's hand mirror." Nora laughed so hard she almost choked.

As the girls began to eat their breakfast, Laura looked around and noticed that someone was missing. "Where's Joy? Is she still in bed?" Miss Glenn got a quizzical look on her face and got up to check. Within five minutes they had their answer.

"She's gone," announced Miss Glenn. "Her trunk is gone too. She must have carried it out when we were all sleeping." The women all got quiet. Miss Glenn explained that a lot of men came to the high-classed parlor houses looking for wives. The newer girls are more sought after since they haven't been too spoiled yet.

"But now what is Laura going to hit our customers with? I'm sure Joy took her hand mirror," joked Spuddy, as she ripped a chunk of biscuit off seductively with her teeth and growled.

➤←

As the winter continued, Laura and Jessie fell into a routine. During the day, the girls would have their singing lessons, read, or embroider. At night they would entertain the men. Laura was thankful that Clark had kept his promise and continued to visit her once a week. With all her lays being as romantic as washing dirt off her shoes, she welcomed the chance to kiss someone and experience true affection. She was also thankful that Clark was married. This assured that he wouldn't want to whisk her away like Joy had been, since she had no desire to be anyone's wife again.

After months of being cooped up in a musty house, Laura was never so happy to see spring arrive. She had heard that it took longer to reach Leadville, but now that it was finally here she couldn't stand being inside. Every day after breakfast she and the other girls would dress in their best outfits and walk around town. They visited all the stores and even handed out cards to solicit lays. Laura and Jessie even found a store that sold poodles, which they found quite comical.

No high society woman would ever own a poodle, or any kind of small dog. Since the little dogs could be carried from town to town, in a bag or under a coat, the working girls could easily take them when they moved on. Laura, Jessie, and Nora decided that they would all own one before their internship was over the following January.

Unfortunately, their happiness was short lived. Spring soon turned to summer and the sunshine couldn't stop the past from creeping up and destroying whatever it touched.

On a warm Thursday night in July, the parlor house was full of laughter, dancing, and drinking, as was the nightly schedule. Nora was standing next to the Negro piano player singing a song, while the men enjoyed their cigars. Nobody noticed when a young, blond-haired man walked in through the front door. He was well dressed and carried a mahogany cane with a silver, eagle-face handle. He wandered around the parlor and even paid for a drink from the young Negro maid who worked in the evenings. Nobody noticed anything different about him, except for Della.

Della was sitting on the lap of a prospective lay when the man attacked her with his cane. In a split second, he had swung the metal tip of the cane again, striking her in the same spot he had hit before. The eagle's hooked beak had left a deep gash in her temple and she was badly bleeding. After the second swing of his cane, he stood back just long enough for her to see him—it was her brother, Walter.

He quickly grabbed her up off the velvet couch and threw her to the floor. The man she was sitting with, not wanting to risk spilling his drink, got up and walked away. Walter kicked her and screamed that she was a disgrace and how she would go to hell for ruining the family name. At this, Miss Glenn ran into the room and with the help of the piano player, pulled the man away from Della. Nora and Jessie, the only two women not busy with a lay, grabbed Della and started to pull her into the dining room.

Walter, not willing to give up on his mission, wiggled loose, pulled out a small handgun and within a split second, fired off four shots. The first hit Nora, the second hit the mirror on the back wall, the third went through the wall into the kitchen ... and the fourth hit Della. At the sound of gunfire, the men who were busy with Laura and Spuddy came running out of the back bedrooms with guns drawn. Walter was dead before he hit the floor.

It was quite a sight. Three grown men stood near the back wall and had ignored the attack on the young woman, who now lay convulsing on the parlor carpet. Two grown men, naked as the day they were born, stood over the dead man's body holding smoking guns. Laura and Spuddy ran out of their rooms, dressed only in light dressing gowns, to find their two friends bleeding from gunshot wounds. Miss Glenn called for the maid to grab towels to stop the bleeding.

Laura threw herself to the floor and held Della's bloodied head in her lap as she took her last breath. Nora lay gasping next to her, as Jessie and Spuddy ripped off her shirt to find where the bullet had entered.

The two men, guns still in hand, ran back into the bedrooms and quickly got dressed. As they re-entered the parlor, the men threw their suit coats onto a nearby couch and quickly ran over to check on the two women. First, they checked Della. Laura pleaded with them to help her, but they couldn't find a pulse. Laura's lay shook his head as he reached down and gently closed Della's eyes, before going over to Nora.

Nora was lying on the parlor floor trying not to panic. Jessie and Spuddy had found the bullet hole and were pressing towels against the wound, as Nora stared at Della's lifeless body lying next to her. She was relieved when the men came over to her. The two men introduced themselves as George and Thomas and asked how she was feeling as they took a peek beneath the blood-soaked towels. Despite the pain, Nora found it funny how the women would lay with these men, week after week, and didn't even know most of their names.

George grabbed a clean towel and wrapped it around Nora to keep her modest, since her shirt had been torn in the attempt to find the wound. With that, he carefully picked her up, while Thomas grabbed their suit coats and opened the front door.

In a split second they were gone. As Laura continued to cradle Della's lifeless body against her own, she realized that she might lose two friends tonight.[31]

→ 7 ←

Chocolate teapots and
an ancient forest

895–96 Within the hour, the undertaker had removed Della's body and the customers who had stood and watched her die were asked to leave. If they ever returned, Miss Glenn promised them each a bullet of their own.

Nobody knew if Nora was even still alive, so the night was spent cleaning up the blood from the carpet as they waited to hear back from their two heroes. The piano player and Jessie had dragged Della's brother's body out of the house and had thrown him into the street. He didn't deserve respect or to be near his sister. The undertaker nodded his understanding as he loaded Walter's body into the wagon. Where he had gently set Della's body into the wagon, wrapped in a sheet, Walter's body was simply thrown in uncovered. Finally, as the sun began to rise, everyone quietly went to bed. There was nothing left to do.

Prudence arrived around 9:00 a.m. to start cooking breakfast for the girls, completely unaware of what had happened just hours earlier. She quickly realized that something was terribly wrong when she discovered freshly washed laundry hanging on the line. The parlor room carpet was wet and all the furniture had been moved into the dining room, along with Miss Glenn's large silver mirror, which normally hung in the parlor. Upon inspection, Prudence could see that it no longer had its glass and was on the floor, propped up against the wall.

Everyone slept later than usual. The first of the women came into the dining room around 1:00 p.m., just as the cookies were coming out of the oven. Prudence looked up to see Jessie, who was very quiet and pale. Desperate for answers, Prudence brought her a cup of coffee and sat down next to her at the table. Very quietly and slowly, Jessie told her the whole story. She stayed calm and didn't cry, until she mentioned Nora.

By 2:00 p.m., all the women had gotten up and eaten breakfast. The house was so quiet, Laura decided she needed some fresh air and a change of scenery. Sitting in the house watching the carpet dry was just too upsetting. As she got up and opened the front door, she saw a familiar carriage pull up. One of the lays from the night before jumped down from the seat and opened the door to take hold of someone. As he turned around, Laura could see that he had Nora in his arms!

Nora was dressed in her bloodied clothes from the night before, but it looked as though someone had tried to wash them out the best they could. She winced just a little as she was carried into the house and gently placed on the couch in the parlor. She had a sling wrapped around her shoulder to keep her arm still and padding and gauze could be seen sticking out from the side of her shirt. All the women gathered around Nora, as the lay grabbed a small stool and carefully put her feet up.

Nora told how the two lays had whisked her off to the hospital and had startled the poor nuns who ran it when they carried her in. She then looked over at her rescuer and nodded for him to finish telling the story, while she took a deep breath. Talking made her shoulder hurt.

"Thomas held the towels against Nora inside the coach and I carried her into the hospital. The poor nuns had no idea who the victim was because we were all covered in blood," George explained with a smile. "Luckily, the bullet went straight through her shoulder, so it was a clean wound. They gave her some stitches and wrapped her up. They kept her until today to make sure the bleeding stopped."

"They didn't judge me," Nora added, with a smile. "They could tell by my fancy dress that I was a whore, but they didn't judge me."[32]

St. Vincent Hospital was founded by The Sisters of Charity of Leavenworth in 1879. Three of the sisters had arrived in Leadville a few days after Christmas in 1878 to plan a hospital. Horance A.W. Tabor, who was mayor at the time, started a fund-raising campaign with a donation of $500. Within a month, all the funds needed were raised. W.H. Stevens, a successful miner, had donated the land.

The hospital was a two-story frame building with two wings, four wards, and twelve private rooms. In total the hospital had around fifty beds.[33]

With Nora home, now Della's burial could be planned. Since it was obvious from her brother's actions the night before, there was no need to try to locate her parents. It would be a simple burial in the potter's field, but it would still be done with respect.

At 7:00 p.m. that night, the customers came into the parlor house completely unaware of what had happened the night before. Thomas was not from Leadville, so no one had spread any stories and a dead prostitute was not normally discussed in proper conversation. It raised too many suspicions and people would ask unwanted questions.

Laura, Jessie, and Spuddy had a busy night, as Nora sat on the couch and told her story to all the sympathetic men as they waited their turn with the only three available girls in the house. Miss Glenn had already been on the phone with Jennie Rogers and had sent for two more girls.

Four days later, the women piled into the carriage along with Miss Glenn to met the new girls at the train station. A second carriage was waiting to load up their trunks. Laura remembered how cold it had been the night that she and Jessie had arrived and how tired they were. She was glad that the train was coming in the afternoon. It gave the girls a reason to go on a carriage ride and get some fresh air. She also knew that both of these girls would get all the business the next couple of days. She, Jessie, and Spuddy could really use a break.

The new girls were Clara and Brady. Clara was new to the business, but Brady had worked for a small parlor house before joining Jennie Rogers. Despite being eager to join the party, they both seemed very relieved to hear that they had the night off to rest after their long train ride.

"I am so glad to see you girls," Spuddy exclaimed, her Irish accent as strong as ever. "My quim is as useless as a chocolate teapot! And the painters are coming in the next couple of days and I'll be banjaxed."

The women stared at Spuddy with mouths wide open, as the other girls laughed so much they could hardly breathe. Spuddy rolled her eyes and smacked Laura on the shoulder. "You're being such a little muzzy," Spuddy joked, "I feel like I'm in a carriage with a bunch of muppets."

The laughing continued until the carriage pulled up to the parlor house. As the men carried the trunks into the house, the new women still looked confused. "What the hell was she saying? Why are painters coming to visit her?" Clara quietly asked Jessie, as they walked into the house.

1890s prostitute "Brady." Courtesy of Legends of America.

1890s prostitute "Clara." Courtesy of Legends of America.

"Well ... it means that she is going to be riding the cotton pony," answered Jessie, as she took off her coat.

Laura looked over and saw that Clara still looked confused. "She is getting her red wings? ... ummm ... She's on the rag?" Laura added, while looking to see if Clara finally understood.

"Oh," Clara replied, with a relieved look, "she's getting her monthly." Laura smiled and gave a satisfying sigh ... but she still liked Spuddy's description better.

Within a week, everything felt back to normal. Nora's shoulder had healed and the new girls hadn't run off and married any of the lays. Laura even had a new beau. Despite the fact that Clark still visited her when he was in town, she had met a new man who even took her out on the town on her day off. He was a mining operator and made pretty good money—enough to pay for a lay with Laura and still take her out to dinner on Sundays.

➤←

As summer ended and fall approached, the town started to gossip about a palace made of ice. Many of the parlor house customers were men of high society, and when they drank … they talked. One of their regulars was Mayor Samuel Danford Nicholson. He had a bad habit of biting the girls on their thighs when he drank. The first time Laura laid with him, he had bit her so hard on the thigh that she hauled off and punched him. He ended up with a black eye and later she had to go to the hospital and have the bite cauterized.

Samuel Nicholson was mayor of Leadville from 1893 to 1897, ran for Colorado governor, and then became a Colorado senator. He died in 1923 of liver cancer while still in office. When he was with the girls, he loved to brag about being the president of the Western Mining Company and discovering a zinc ore that he named after himself—Nicholsonite.[34]

As the gossip about the palace of ice grew stronger, the newspapers started to print stories to stop all the guessing. It seemed the original price the town was planning on spending was $5,000, but it had swelled to $20,000. On November 12, 1895, the newspaper reported, "Director General Wood is moving heaven and earth and the remains of the ancient forest that stood on Capitol Hill to make room for the Ice Palace."

November 28 marked the first day of construction. Eighteen teams of horses and wagons hauled ice to the site, which employed over two hundred and fifty men who were paid between $2.50 and $3.00 a day. A total of 182,000 feet of lumber was used to build the skeleton, but the wood would not rest on the ice. The wooden skeleton would be free-standing so the structure could be used all year.

The ice blocks were laid, one on top of another, and frozen together by pouring hot water over them. When it was completed, the Ice Palace measured 420 feet long and over 5,000 tons of ice had been used. The main tower reached 90 feet high by 40 feet wide and the palace covered five acres. An ice sculpture of "Lady Leadville" stood in the front of the Ice Palace to welcome the guests. She was 19 feet tall and stood on a 12-foot tall pedestal.

Scheduled to open Christmas day, the Ice Palace finally opened on January 1, 1896. A huge parade was held on January 3. Governor McIntire, Lieutenant Governor Brush, Mayor McMurray from Denver, and Mayor Nicholson from Leadville opened the parade. There were bands from all over Colorado and people dressed in colorful costumes waved at the onlookers. The men who helped construct the Ice Palace proudly carried a banner that read, "We helped build the Ice Palace," while they carried the tools they used to show to the crowd. The city of Pueblo even gifted a large bass drum to Leadville, which was carried by four donkeys.

The most popular attraction was the toboggan slides. There were two courses and a total of one hundred toboggans were used, as each was launched every thirty seconds.

The first course was located at the Ice Palace site and went down Seventh Street at a length of 900 feet. The second course was located on the south side of Seventh Street from Harrison Avenue, and was a total of 1,200 feet long. Both courses turned south on Spruce Street and were equipped with a 50-foot ramp to give each toboggan a good start.

To light up the courses at night, 2,000 candle-powered lights were installed at 100-foot intervals. Each course was also equipped with

Leadville Ice Palace toboggan slide. Courtesy Denver Public Library, Western History Collection, #X-256.

comfortable waiting rooms and lunch counters. The cost to make both courses and to purchase the toboggans cost the city around $2,500.[35]

Laura and the other girls joined in on all the fun. The parlor house didn't open until the evening, so they had all day to play. Since it was bitter cold outside, the girls bought toboggan suits. These were one-piece hooded, padded snowsuits, with elastic around the wrists and ankles. Ruffles were added to make the suits more feminine, but as Laura and the girls walked up to the toboggan slides, they got a lot of unwanted attention.

It seemed that the "proper" women didn't like that the sporting women were wearing the toboggan suits without skirts over them. They felt it was indecent for any woman to show her shape in public and felt it was advertising and vile. As the town's women protested, Laura decided to put an end to it all. "Look ladies," Laura said, as she and the other girls piled onto a toboggan and handed the man six bits, "we aren't showing anything indecent. If you don't like our outfits, then go tell the manufacturer not to make them. We have as much right to wear them as anyone else."

Seeing that her comment didn't calm down the women, Laura rolled her eyes and took a deep breath of annoyance. The women kept insisting that a decent woman would wear a skirt over the toboggan suit and that they should cover up for the sake of the children.

Laura had enough. As the toboggan was ready to head down the hill, she yelled at the ladies one last time. "We look like fucking stuffed teddy bears, for crying out loud! How the hell is that advertising?"[36]

On January 16, Leadville held a press day to advertise the Ice Palace. Around fifty newspaper and magazine reporters attended, many from other states. A parade of sorts was held on Harrison Avenue. People walked up and down the street showing off lavish costumes they were planning on wearing that night to the Grand Masquerade Ball at the Ice Palace. Despite being a Thursday night, the parlor house was closed to allow all the girls to attend.

Press day went from 2:00 to 10:00 p.m. and the mayor passed a law that anyone on the streets not wearing a mask, costume, or fancy dress would be arrested. He believed that the success of the carnival depended on people wearing some type of costume. He also asked people to use mouth horns, sleigh bells, or anything else that would make a lot of noise.

The mayor also felt that the toboggans were a huge part of making the carnival a success. On press day he had two large barrels of ham fat brought up to both toboggan runs and had them greased.[37]

Whenever a masquerade ball was held, a costumer would come to town to rent out costumes. Unfortunately, Laura and Brady got there too late. They were so busy riding the toboggans that they forgot. Brady had intended on going as a princess, so her costume was easy. Laura was planning on going as a knight, so she had some work to do.

Laura got hold of her beau Nick and borrowed two suits of his long underwear for her tights. She discovered he had pink silk ones, which she paired up with some high black boots. She then added a velvet opera cape and a large hat with a huge feathered plume. The only problem was that Nick's silk underwear was too big, and with two layers on to keep warm, Laura had a lot of bunched-up fabric under her outfit. When she and Brady finally got to the ball, the man at the door questioned what her costume was.

"Okay, so I know what the little girl is supposed to be. But what the hell is that big one?" asked the doorman, as he stared at Laura with a quizzical look. Laura thought a minute before she grabbed at the knots of fabric under her outfit.

"They are muscles. I'm a ballet dancer and these are my muscles." With a shrug of his shoulders, he accepted their 50 cents and let them in.[38]

A season pass to the Ice Palace, which covered three months or 180 admissions, was $25. A pass for only January was $15, or you could simply pay the daily admission of 50 cents. Children were 25 cents.

The inside of the Ice Palace was amazing. Electric lights were everywhere and gave off a wonderful glow. Upon entering, one could see roses, wildflowers, fruit, and trout frozen inside the ice. The walls held displays of taxidermied animals and ice sculptures showing the life of a prospector.

After walking up a large, impressive staircase made of wide wooden planks, you came upon the ice rink. Located in the center of the Ice Palace, the ice rink was 190 feet by 80 feet, with a beautiful wood-beamed ceiling. Ice pillars, five feet around and set 15 feet apart, framed the ice rink.

On each side of the ice rink were the ballrooms, both 50 feet by 80 feet. Each of these rooms also included the restrooms and heated lounge areas, which were glass enclosed to allow people to watch the skaters while staying warm.[39]

Looking around for a drink, Laura noticed that in order to get a drink they had to sit at tables, set off to the side. Once seated, the bartender brought over a teapot full of beer and two teacups with saucers. When they wanted a refill, the man would pour a bottle of beer into the teapot to refill it.

The weeks continued with trips to the Ice Palace to ice skate, watch the horse shows, or attend one of the many functions held daily. There were gymnasts, trapeze artists, and even bike shows on the ice.

On February 14, the Ice Palace hosted the Shriners circus. As part of the show, they put ice skates on the camels and had them skate around the rink. Watching the camels on the ice gave Laura an idea. If a camel can skate on the ice ... why can't a horse?

The next day Laura and the girls decided to ride the toboggans again and as usual, they brought Laura's horse, Charlie. Since the toboggan ride went nine blocks, people had to either walk back up to ride again or get swindled and pay $2 for a sleigh ride back up the hill. Laura simply hooked a sleigh to Charlie and would pull the girls back up the hill. But after a couple of beers, she decided to try something different.

Charlie was a very good horse, even though he had a crooked tail, Laura could do anything with that horse. Once she even walked him straight into a bar, ordered a drink, and then backed Charlie right out. So she knew he could do this.

After the girls finished their toboggan ride, Laura had Charlie pull the sleigh back up the hill to the Ice Palace, but instead of stopping at the top ... she walked him toward a side door. As the horse entered the Ice Palace, he started to get nervous. She calmed him down long enough to get the horse and entire sleigh into the building before he slipped on the ice and panicked. Charlie spun around and flipped over the sleigh in his attempt to leave the building, and in the process he kicked one of the shafts loose on the sleigh, which spun it around and knocked over a four-by-four-foot ice display.

The horse, now loose, ran out of the Ice Palace. The broken sleigh, lying on its side, was covered in broken chunks of ice, frozen chickens, wild birds, and a deer, which had been incased in the ice display.

A couple of men ran over to the girls, still dressed in their toboggan suits, and helped them up, while others started to remove the sleigh from the Ice Palace. Laura walked outside to find Charlie, who was standing next to the horse barn. Expecting to be thrown out, Laura walked

Leadville Ice Palace skating rink. Courtesy Denver Public Library, Western History Collection, #Z-15579.

Leadville Ice Palace interior arches. Courtesy Denver Public Library, Western History Collection, #Z-15599.

Leadville Ice Palace. Courtesy History Colorado, Fred Mazzulla Collection, #10025101.

back inside to see that people were simply picking up the knocked over displays, pushing the broken chunks of ice outside, and acting like this happened all the time.

Laura looked over at the girls and said, "Well, while we're here, why don't we get a pot of tea."

Clara, still brushing small chunks of ice off her suit, glared at Laura and said, "What in the hell do I want tea for? And what the hell were you thinking? Charlie is a horse, not a penguin!"

Laura smiled, grabbed her by the arm and led her over to a small table. "Oh, come on. You will like their tea."

The girls all sat down, as the bartender brought over the teapot, cups, and saucers. As Laura poured the tea for Clara, she saw the foam in her cup. "Is this some kind of joke?" Clara asked Laura, as she took a slow, suspicious sip.

"Nope," Laura replied, "this is just Ice Palace tea."[40]

By the end of February, warm weather started to threaten the Ice Palace. Director General Wood spent $5,000 of his own money to cover the ice with muslin in an attempt to save it, but to no avail.

The Ice Palace closed on March 28, 1896. The newspaper wrote, "The Crystal Palace is fast fleeting away back to earth. It will soon live but in a memory, as in a child's fairytale, as a castle built in air."[41]

→ 8 ←

Canaries and
diamond garter buckles

896 | With the Ice Palace closed, it was now time for the girls to head back to Denver. Their one-year internship was long overdue and a new group of interns was heading to Leadville to take their place. Laura, Jessie, and Nora packed their trunks, but Spuddy decided to stay in Leadville. She had found a place to rent and was going to try working for herself.

The train back to Denver took them through the small town of Salida. Laura and Jessie had stopped there on the way to Leadville the year before, and had found it promising.

When the train stopped in Salida, they got off to have another quick look around and to stretch their legs before heading on to Denver. The town was about the size of Leadville and had their red light district down Sackett Avenue, only a block from the train depot, which was very convenient. The town didn't seem as wild as Leadville, but as they walked around, they could see that there was no shortage of customers.

It was evening before the train finally pulled into Union Station in Denver, and the girls were tired. Jennie Rogers had sent a man to pick up their trunks and had set them up in rooms down the street from the House of Mirrors, at 2009 Market Street. Since the girls had brought their horses with them, they simply followed the carriage on horseback and set them up in the stables next door.

The next morning the girls walked over to the House of Mirrors and had a meeting with Jennie Rogers. They spent the day talking about Leadville, the Ice Palace, and poor Della's murder. Jennie told the girls that she had no rooms available in the House of Mirrors, but the rooms

Denver parlor house at 2009 Market Street where Laura stayed (building on right with awning over the front door). Courtesy History Colorado, Fred Mazzulla Collection, #10039975.

down the street, from the night before, were available. She went on to mention that she had some exciting trips planned for them.

Jennie explained that she was planning on sending some of her girls to Honolulu, in the Republic of Hawaii, and another group of girls to China. As the three women screamed and hugged each other, Jennie stopped them long enough to tell them that it wouldn't be until July ... but that didn't stop the celebrating. Being only the beginning of April, the women did not mind waiting.

Laura, Jessie, and Nora settled right into to life in Denver. They had new men to lay with and new parties to attend. Laura had even run into Pete Peterson, who had brought her to Jennie Rogers the year before. He was attending a party at the House of Mirrors and they sat and talked. Pete always had a soft spot for Laura because she resembled his dead wife. He started to call at her boarding house and take her out to lunch, followed by a bath in champagne.[42]

Nora had also attracted the attention of a new beau named Henry Owens, and he showered her with diamonds and new dresses. Unlike Laura and Jessie, Nora worked as a whore to support her family, which was very poor and none of them, including Nora, could read or write.

Laura would write letters for Nora and help her to send money to her family every week. Being with Henry allowed her to send more money to her family and to also have things for herself.

On April 26, Laura got a phone call from Pete Peterson about a fire in Cripple Creek. Knowing she had a soft spot for the town, he rushed over, newspaper in hand, to read her the headlines.

It seemed that a bartender, who worked at the Central Dance Hall, started a fight with his girlfriend, who was a taxi dancer. A taxi dancer was a woman who charged money for the luxury of a dance. For ten cents, a man would get one dance to a single song. Sometimes the women were also called "nickel hoppers," since they only earned five cents out of every ten. Not one to put up with being slapped, the girl charged at him with a Bowie knife. As he fell over backward in an attempt to get away from her, he kicked over a lighted kerosene heater and started the room on fire. In three hours, the fire had spread and burned down much of the business district of the town and left fifteen hundred people homeless.

On April 29, a second fire started in Cripple Creek, this time in the kitchen of the Portland Hotel. A pan of grease spilled onto a hot stove and set the hotel on fire. This time the wind was blowing and the fire spread fast. To add to the hysteria, The Palace Hotel's boilers exploded and seven hundred pounds of dynamite went off in a grocery store.

Seeing that Cripple Creek once again needed help, James Ferguson Burns, president of the Portland Gold Mining Company, sent out an emergency phone call before the phone wires burned. He called Colorado Springs Mayor J.C. Plumb, who in turn called Winfield Scott Stratton.

Mr. Stratton was Cripple Creek's first millionaire and he was eager to help the town that made him rich. Stratton immediately drove to the Colorado Midland Depot, ordered a special train, and filled two boxcars full of supplies. He purchased: twenty cases of canned beef, six cases of beans, six cases of condensed milk, twelve crates of crackers, and a thousand loaves of bread. He then called all the department stores and bought out their entire supply of blankets, which added up to over 500. He also bought 750 diapers, 165 eight-person tents, and one tabernacle tent—the only one he could find.

By 9:00 p.m. the train pulled into what was left of Cripple Creek, which was not much. St. Peter's Church had survived, and Father Volpe was using it to house the babies and small children. As soon as the first train had left Colorado Springs, Stratton was already loading up a second train, which left at 2:00 a.m. the next morning. He would not let Cripple Creek go without. In total, he spent $50,000.[43]

As Laura read the headlines, day after day, she promised herself that if she ever met Mr. Stratton, that she would thank him and shake his hand.

➤◆

The months quickly went by, and soon it was July. Jennie Rogers had instructed Laura, Jessie, and Nora to attend a briefing at the House of Mirrors to learn about the trip to China. When they arrived, they saw four big men guarding the doors. "What are all these great, big, barefooted Chinks doing here?" whispered Laura, as they entered the restaurant.

"Maybe we are supposed to fuck them," Jessie answered, with a shrug of her shoulders.

As the girls waited, a group of around two hundred women entered the room and took a seat. They were dressed in beautiful gowns, furs, and wore so many diamonds that the room had a sparkle to it. Laura recognized one of the girls as Lola Livingston, from Cripple Creek. She worked for Pearl DeVere at The Old Homestead parlor house. As Laura looked at all the beautiful gowns, many with an Asian flavor, she wondered how Lola felt about Cripple Creek burning down, or if she even knew.

The man who was in charge of the evening explained that any girl who chose to go would only go for a six-month visit. They didn't want the "merchandise to go stale" he said, with a snide laugh. He went on to explain that the girls would not get a dime of their money until they arrived back in the United States, then they would give it to them in a little box.

Laura, Jessie, and Nora had already decided that they wanted to go before they had even entered the room, so they wasted no time signing up. As they finished, a lady came over and explained that all of their things, such as their trunks, pets, and even their horses, would be taken care of for a fee of $30 a month. They just needed to have their things packed and a man would come pick them up and put them in storage.

After all the women had signed up, the man explained that they were to meet again that night at the Markham Hotel at 8:00 p.m. From there they would board a train to Cheyenne, Wyoming.

At that, Nora looked over at Laura and said, "I have to go see Henry. I have to say goodbye."

Laura looked at the clock and said, "Nora, it's already five o'clock. Are you sure you will have time?"

Nora smiled as she headed out the door. "I'll meet you at the hotel—Seventeenth and Lawrence."

Laura and Jessie walked back to their boarding house and packed up their things. Nora had moved into a hotel on Larimer Street that Laura was not too fond of. She had gone there a couple of times and found the place to be run down and dirty. Nora had kept her room clean, but the hotel had cockroaches. After a couple of visits, Laura told Nora that she would just sit in the lobby and wait for her when she visited. She didn't want any of the cockroaches coming home with her.

Laura and Jessie nervously sat in the lobby of the Markham Hotel waiting for Nora. It was after 7:00 p.m. and the lobby was quickly filling up. The man who was running the tour had already checked Laura and Jessie in and given them their train tickets.

When 8:00 p.m. came, the tour guide walked around and looked for any of the women who had not checked in yet … which included Nora.

As Laura took another look around, she heard her name being called. She glanced over to see a uniformed detective scanning the crowd of women and calling her name. As she walked up to him, he asked, "I'm looking for a Laura Evens. Are you Laura Evens?" With a nervous nod, she answered that she was. The detective then pulled out a small notebook and said, "Do you know a Nora Kirk?"

Laura suddenly felt very cold and could feel her stomach start to knot up. She reached out to the first girl she knew in the lobby, grabbed her arm and said, "Can you please go get Jessie?"

Once again the detective asked if she knew Nora, and when she answered that she did, he asked a question that made her almost lose her footing. "Would you be able to come down to the morgue and identify her?" With that, Laura must have gone pale, because the detective grabbed her arm and helped her into a nearby chair. Jessie saw what was happening as she walked up and quickly asked the detective what was going on. When she had her answer, she excused herself for a minute, removed Laura's train ticket from her hand and walked back over to the man who was hosting the tour. With a deep sigh and almost in tears … Jessie turned in their train tickets.

After canceling their trip, Jessie and Laura got into the detective's coach and headed for the morgue. On the way, the officer explained that they had a man named Henry Owens in custody and that it was he who had told the detectives where to find Laura. It seems that a neighbor had called authorities when they heard an argument and a woman scream. The detectives found Nora dead and had discovered that Henry had tried to commit suicide, but had failed. He was arrested wearing nothing but his nightshirt.

In the morgue, Laura and Jessie saw poor Nora laid out on a cold metal table. She was covered in blood and they could see that Henry had cut her open. The detective asked if Laura could positively identify her. She thought a minute, and then realized that she could. She explained that Nora had a scar on her left shoulder from a bullet wound she received the previous year in Leadville. As the mortician proceeded to remove her blouse, Laura started to ramble. She told the men about Della's death and how Nora had gotten shot trying to save her. When the detective saw the scar, he nodded to the mortician that he had a positive identification.

In an outside room, Laura asked the detective if he had seen Nora's jacket or her parasol in Henry's room. Laura explained that soiled doves didn't normally put their money in banks, but instead bought jewelry and loose diamonds. The jewelry was either worn or hidden in pockets that were sewn into the lining of jackets or hats, and the loose diamonds were hidden inside parasol handles. The detective agreed to take Laura and Jessie back to Henry's apartment to look for Nora's things.

Before they left, the mortician asked who was going to bury her. Laura looked at the man and said, "I will take care of it." She quickly unfastened a diamond broach she had on her jacket and handed it to him. "I'll come by tomorrow and make arrangements."

The two women found Nora's coat and parasol at Henry's apartment, but no diamonds or jewelry of any kind. The door to Henry's apartment had been left slightly open by the police and the nervous looks on the other tenants' faces quickly explained the missing items. Laura and Jessie called for a coach to take them to Nora's apartment. Hopefully, Laura could find something of value there to send back to Nora's family.

Nora usually kept her diamonds hidden in a small towel in her clothes hamper, but they were nowhere to be found. Luckily, Jessie found Nora's diamonds hidden in her clothes and in the handles of her numerous parasols.

Laura and Jessie spent the night going through Nora's things and deciding what was going to be sent back to her family. They found diamond earrings, slipper buckles, garter buckles, bracelets, necklaces, and a rose broach with two carats of diamonds. Even her watch was studded with diamonds. Diamonds were a pretty cheap way to invest their money. The girls could get a full carat diamond for only $100.

Laura packed Nora's trunks with her best clothes, her umbrellas, and all of her diamonds and put them on a train to her parents the next morning. She also included a letter explaining what had happened and that she was being buried in Denver. The rest of Nora's clothes, and her canaries, came back with Laura to her boarding house. She didn't really think the canaries would like the long train ride.[44]

The next day Jennie Rogers called Laura and Jessie to the House of Mirrors to talk about what had happened the night before. Realizing that the girls had to miss their trip to China, she tried to cheer them up by reminding them of the upcoming trip to the Republic of Hawaii.

Two weeks later the girls were invited back to the House of Mirrors to meet the other women who had been invited to go on the tour. There were about fifty girls and Laura recognized a girl named Annie. She lived in the same boarding house as she and Jessie.

After everything was decided, all the girls went back to their rooms to pack for the trip. Laura found that she was actually a little excited and that this trip might be just what she needed. Unfortunately, history has a bad habit of repeating itself.

The next morning, as the women were sitting down to breakfast, they learned that Annie had been murdered just hours before. It seems that she went to see her beau to tell him that she was leaving for Honolulu … and he had killed her.

According to the detective, who stopped by later in the afternoon, Annie's beau tried to make it look like self-defense, but the detective wasn't buying it. It seems that her beau had clipped off his own ear and blamed it on her. Laura looked over at Jessie and they both nodded in agreement—they weren't going to Honolulu either.[45]

After the detective finished his questioning, Laura and Jessie went back up to their rooms to pack. Laura didn't want to stay in Denver anymore. All these murders reminded her too much of the Jack the Ripper killings, back when she first moved to Colorado.

In November 1894, while Laura was living between Cripple Creek and Denver, the killing started on Market Street. Originally known as the Denver Strangler, the newspapers quickly changed his name to Jack the Ripper because all the murders were similar to the ones committed in London. Market Street became known as "Stranglers Row," and the parlor houses started to install bars on their windows and hire bodyguards.

By November 13, three prostitutes had been strangled—Lena Tapper, Marie Coantasoit, and Kiku Oyama. Detectives stated that a towel or cord had been used.

A man named Richard Demandy was arrested and charged with the murders. His sister, Madame Fouchett, went insane after her brother's arrest and had to be committed. She claimed that the ghosts of the strangled women appeared to her and tormented her.[46]

Laura and Jessie didn't want to stay in Denver anymore, not without Nora. They had seen to it that she was buried with respect and they had given her canaries to Jennie Rogers. That way the birds could enjoy the fancy parties.

With one last look around Union Station, the two women loaded their trunks and Laura's horse onto the train and headed back to Leadville.

→ 9 ←

A toothy grin and the gray jumpsuit

896 | The train ride back to Leadville was a quiet one. Laura had a lot to
think about. She had visited her daughter Lucille while she was in
Denver right before she left, and saw how fast her only child was growing up. She admitted to herself that she had no desire to give up her
lifestyle to raise Lucille herself, but did want her closer so she could be
in her life … but at a distance.

As the train stopped at the station in Salida, as it always did, she took
another look around—a real serious look. Could this be a town that she
could work in? Could this be a town that her daughter could be raised
in? Leadville was nice, but far too wild for her daughter. So was Denver.
Too many ways for a young girl to get into trouble.

Before getting back on the train, Laura picked up some flyers on
Salida, along with a map of the area. As the train pulled out of the station, Laura smiled as she watched Salida disappear out her train window. As she sat back in her seat, getting comfortable for the long ride to
Leadville, she thought to herself, yes … Salida is perfect.

The train pulled into the Leadville station after dark, and Laura and
Jessie could feel that fall was in the air. The temperature was only around
35 degrees, but it gave the women a chance to wear their furs.

As the women walked outside they were greeted by a wonderful
white carriage drawn by black horses. Seeing that their trunks were being loaded, and Laura's horse Charlie was safely tied to the side of the
carriage, the women quickly entered their evening's transportation and
snuggled beneath the familiar buffalo fur blankets. Jennie Rogers had set
them up in a new boarding house, and they were ready for a hot meal
and a good night's sleep.

Arriving at the boarding house, they were greeted by a woman named Rene Broroned. She introduced herself as the landlady and gave each of the women a quick hug before taking them into the parlor. They could see that the nightly party was just getting started, but they were too tired from their trip to care. As the house's customers approached them, the women just smiled and shrugged them off. Not tonight.

The next morning, Laura and Jessie headed downstairs for breakfast and to get a good look around. The other inmates were sleeping, so they had the house to themselves. The house was a typical two-story with Turkish rugs, wood-trimmed walls, and the familiar smell of cigar smoke and lust. Taking a peek around first, Laura opened a couple of the windows to let in some fresh air. All she wanted to smell this morning was fresh mountain air and the biscuits baking in the oven.

As Laura and Jessie were looking around, they heard the front door open and a tall man with a large mustache walked in. The man was nicely dressed and was obviously not a working man. He quickly came over, and with a sly smile, introduced himself. "Good morning, ladies," he said, as he removed his hat and gave a quick bow. "I don't think we have had the pleasure, or at least … not yet." He gave a dramatic pause and a quick wink, before he continued. "The name's Arthur Nichols, but you call me Nick," he said, with a large, toothy grin. For added effect, he tilted his head just a little to the side, as though posing for an unseen photographer.

Laura and Jessie, with bored looks on their faces, just stared at the man. Laura crossed her arms and switched her weight to her right hip, while Jessie let out a loud huff and added an eye roll for a dramatic touch of annoyance.

Seeing that these new inmates were not easily impressed, he quickly cleared his throat and continued. "Being new here, I'm sure you are not aware that I am in charge of all of Mr. Moffat's holdings … and I mean *all* of them." He added another wink and flashed his toothy smile once more, as he waited for the familiar swoon he was sure to come. As he straightened up his jacket to add to the appearance of importance, Laura and Jessie turned around and walked out of the room.

Hearing the two women laughing in the adjoining room, he quickly ran after them. "Are you ladies even familiar with David Moffat?" he asked, as he caught up with them. Jessie turned around and faced him.

Hands on her hips and with a sarcastic tone to her voice, she responded, "I'm guessing that Mr. Moffat is just one of the many millionaires around Leadville. I'm sure we will fuck him sooner or later. As long as I get paid, I don't really care who he is." Seeing the shocked look on the man's face, Jessie added, with a sharp poke of her right index finger to his chest, "Or ... who you are."

As the two women headed into the kitchen, Laura and Jessie gave an overly dramatic shake of their hind ends as they continued laughing. Nick stood back and watched as the two ladies mocked him and smiled. He liked them already.[47]

As Laura and Jessie were sitting in the kitchen drinking their morning coffee, their landlady, Mrs. Broroned, walked in and joined them. Finally able to be properly introduced, the three ladies sat and discussed their lives and what types of things were going on in Leadville since they had left. Unfortunately, Mrs. Broroned had bad news.

In May of 1896, just a month after Laura and Jessie had left for Denver, the Western Federation of Miners had succeeded in forming a union called the Cloud City Miners Union Local #33. A lot of the miners had joined up, but there wasn't really anything the union needed to do. Around 70 percent of the miners were making a healthy wage, but the union was worried they would lose their newly acquired dues if they didn't throw their weight around.

To keep their new members hooked, the union proceeded to spread a false rumor that the mine owners were going to drop the wages by 50 cents a day. Frantic over the news, the miners contacted the union and insisted that they do something. Happy to see that their rumor was believed, the union arranged a meeting with the mine owners.

Desperate to make a good impression, they tried to force all the mine owners to pay their miners 50 cents more than they were already making. Some of the mine owners agreed, considering that the miners pay had been cut by 50 cents back in 1893, due to the Depression. But some of the smaller mines refused. They claimed that since the Depression, they hadn't made a dime in profit. Happy that their lie was getting more miners to join the union, a strike was called on July 6, 1896.

Now, being the middle of August, the mines were being run, not by the miners, but by scabs from Denver who crossed the picket line. These men were not mining ore, but simply keeping the pumps running. Leadville's mines were constantly filling up with water, and if the pumps were turned off, it could be years before they could be drained enough to be re-opened.[48]

Laura and Jessie quietly sat and listened to Mrs. Broroned as she explained how the strike was being handled on their side. "We still are getting customers. Since Mr. Moffat owns this boarding house, and a couple of others in town, he is sending all his rich friends over to have a good time. He gets a cut of our profits, so it helps out everyone involved."

"So, the mines are all closed?" asked Jessie, with a concerned look. "Then what are we doing up here? How are we going to make any money?"

"Well," Mrs. Broroned continued, "you can either work the house like the other girls or if you're adventurous … you can visit the scabs in the mines. They are too scared to come up to the surface, too scared they will get shot at, so some of the girls have been going to them."

"You mean … actually go into a mine? Down the shaft?" asked Laura, with an adventurous smile. Then her look changed, as she thought about it a minute. "How do we get paid if the men are stuck down in the mines? How are they getting their pay?"

Jessie chimed in before Mrs. Broroned could answer, "I'm not fucking anyone for free … or for credit." She made sure to cross her arms and add a slight pout for added effect.

Mrs. Broroned laughed. "They are still getting paid … they just can't leave the mine. The owners are afraid the scabs won't be allowed back into the mines, which is what the union wants. If the mines flood, the union feels they will win. But if the mines flood, every miner will be out of a job."

Seeing that the women where showing a bit of interest, she added, "Now you have to understand that in order to visit the scabs inside the mines … you have to cross the picket lines." Taking a dramatic pause, Mrs. Broroned added, "You might get shot at."

Mr. Moffat owned five mines in Leadville: The Breece Iron Mine, The Maid of Erin, The Henriette, The Resurrection, and The Little Pittsburg. He also had stock in many other mines, such as The Little Johnny Gold Mine. Being the owner of the boarding house, Mr. Moffat made sure that his right-hand man, Arthur Nichols, found girls willing to keep his scabs happy so they would stay in the mines. He couldn't afford to have his mines flood.

Laura and Jessie were still thinking it over as night fell and customers started to file into the boarding house. The fear of being shot at made them nervous, so the girls decided to try their luck with the regular clientele for a couple of nights, but quickly saw that pickings were slim. Too many girls and not enough men to lay with.

As Laura was sitting alone on a blue velvet sofa sipping on her glass of red wine and scanning the room for available men, she caught the eye of Arthur Nichols.

Sitting down on the far side of the couch he decided to re-introduce himself. "Slow night isn't it," he started, with a slightly nervous tone to his voice. "Shame about the strike. We used to have a full house every night."

Laura turned and gave him a slight smile before offering her hand to him. "Name's Laura."

With a relieved sigh, he replied, "Nick."

The two of them spent the rest of the night talking. He told her about how he ran all of Mr. Moffat's holdings and she talked about the trips she had missed out on back in Denver. By the end of the night Nick had given her a brass check, and they went up to her room for the rest of the evening.

Laura quickly became Nick's favorite girl. He was impressed by her business sense and turned her into his private secretary. Laura was eager to learn anything she could about running a boarding house. Nick allowed her to make deposits and showed her how to keep the palms greased of the local officials so they would turn a blind eye to the boarding houses' business ventures.

After many slow boring nights, Laura and Jessie decided to take the risk and visit the scabs in the mines. Nick showed the women on a local map what trails to take to sneak in the back way to the mines and gave them hints on how to act if they were caught by the striking miners or any union officials.

"Act stupid, that's all there is to it … act stupid. Say you were picking berries, looking for your dog, or picking wildflowers." Taking a step back, Nick looked over Laura and Jessie and realized one more piece of advice. "And you can't wear those fancy dresses, either. You have to look like a regular housewife or a barmaid."

The women looked at each other, and started to laugh. "We get to go slumming!"

The next afternoon, Laura and Jessie dressed in their plainest dresses and worn-out shoes. As Nick looked them over approvingly, he pulled out two small envelopes and asked the women to hold up their shirts to expose their stomachs. "This is the week's pay for the mine," he explained, as he strapped the first envelope around Jessie's waist. "I've divided their pay into two envelopes, just in case."

"Just in case ... what?" asked Laura, as Nick started to strap on her package.

With a loud sigh, Nick admitted the dark truth. "In case you both don't make it."

Climbing up onto their horses, the two women got some last minute advice from Nick. "Okay girls, now the Little Johnny mine is down past the end of East Fifth Street. In order to avoid any trouble, you need to go up Harrison Avenue to East Seventh Street and take that out of town. If you don't see anyone, then you can cut across Little Stray Horse Gulch, off to your right. If you do see anyone, go up the hill a little farther and take Stray Horse Ridge. It's a little out of the way, but it's safer." With a quick kiss for Laura and a concerned smile for Jessie, Nick stepped out of their way as the girls headed up Harrison Avenue.

The trip up to the mine was actually easier than they expected. Laura smiled as she and Jessie reached the back side of the Little Johnny mine. As they tied up their horses and dusted themselves off, they were approached by armed men who tried to look tough, but instead just looked tired.

"What can we help you lovely ladies with this afternoon," asked the first man, as he balanced his rifle up on his shoulder to show he meant them no harm. Laura looked over at Jessie and gave a nod, as she pulled up her shirt to reveal the pay envelope strapped to her stomach.

"Well, I was hoping one of you strong miner types would help me get this terribly heavy package off my delicate skin."

The men gave her and Jessie approving smiles, as they lowered their guns. "Right this way ladies, we've been waiting for ya."

Laura and Jessie had never been inside any of the mines before. When they first walked in, they discovered that everything was covered in a fine, shiny powder and the pumps were very noisy and smelled like cooking oil and kerosene.

"Afternoon, ladies, name's Jacob. Is this your first time to the Johnny?" Laura turned to see a good-looking young man who was trying his best to tilt his hard hat to be polite, despite it being strapped onto his head. He was practically screaming at them, just so they could hear him over the pumps.

"Yes," Laura yelled back. "So, who collects the pay?" Laura pulled up her shirt and removed the envelope. Knowing that Jessie couldn't hear her, she nudged her in the shoulder and held up the envelope for her to see. Nodding in understanding, Jessie quickly removed her envelope and handed it to Laura. The young man smiled and led them into a private office, where they met a man who introduced himself as the foreman. He closed the office door, which helped a little with the noise.

"You ladies took quite a risk coming here. Did you have any trouble?"

Laura smiled and said, "No. It's pretty quiet outside right now. So ..." she added with a sultry tone to her voice and a twinkle in her eye "how do we do this?"

The foreman gave her an approving look and led her and Jessie into a room full of lockers and hooks. He looked each of the women over for size, and then handed them each a thick, grayish jumpsuit, boots, gloves, hardhat, and a rubber overcoat. "You can hang up your dresses right over here on these hooks. Sorry it's not too clean in here, but we do our best."

"Why are we taking off our dresses?" asked Jessie, as she sat down on a wooden bench to remove her shoes.

"Nobody goes into the mine with their civilian clothes on," the foreman answered, with a serious tone. "Everyone undresses completely in front of these here guards. That way nobody can put any ore in their pockets. Men have been known to put gold ore into secret holes in their shoes and even in their beards. Men still do swallow the small pieces of gold ore, but we can't really stop that."

"I thought the mines weren't working right now. I thought your men were just keeping the pumps running," Laura said, as she started to unhook her blouse.

Breaking his trance, the foreman looked back up to her face and answered, "You are right, ma'am, we are just keeping the pumps running, but there is still ore laying on the ground."

As the women finished undressing, they noticed that the foreman and the guards had gotten quiet. Jessie nudged Laura, who suddenly took notice of the audience they had attracted. Jessie stood up in all her glory and walked over to the foreman. As she slowly ran her index finger down the front of the man's jumpsuit, she stared up into his eyes and said, "If you would be so kind as to hand these men their pay, we can get started."

Laura and Jessie didn't leave the mine until almost morning. After the men had enjoyed the women's company, they sat and questioned the gals about the strike and any gossip they had heard about the union's plans. As they headed back to the boarding house, they talked about how visiting the scabs was the best deal going.[49]

On September 14, the union released an offer to the mine owners. The miners were getting hungry and nervous that they would lose their jobs forever to the scabs that were keeping the pumps running, and were pestering the union to get them their jobs back. The union offered to lease all the mines from the mine owners and pay them a 25 percent royalty on all the ore. The union would then hire all the miners back at $3 a day… the same as they were making before the strike. The mine owners refused, and instead, sent for scabs from Missouri to run their mines and men from the Colorado Militia to help guard them.

Around midnight on September 20, Laura was jolted by a loud explosion that shook her bedroom. She ran to the window to see the streets full of striking miners holding torches. They were setting the mines on fire.

As Laura and the other inmates of the house got dressed, they could hear people banging on the boarding house door screaming for everyone to get out of town. Instead, Laura, Jessie, and some of the other inmates climbed up onto the boarding house roof to get a better look.

The Coronado Mine and The Penrose Mine were on fire and Laura could hear explosions coming from down the street, as well as gunfire and the sound of men fighting. The firemen were trying to put out the fires, but a wall of striking miners was blocking their way. The firemen started to push back against the striking miners and proceeded to hook up the fire hoses. In a show of force, Fire Chief Jerry O'Keefe was shot in the head and killed. The other firemen put down their hoses to help their friend, only to be attacked by the striking miners. In a twist, the striking miners were then fought off by the townspeople who were not happy with their favorite fire chief being killed.

As the striking miners continued their fight, the fire was spreading to businesses and people's homes. Seeing that their actions had gotten out of hand, the striking miners backed off and allowed the homeowners to help the firemen save as many houses as possible. In a twist of fate, most of the homes lost belonged to the striking miners.

As the firemen worked on one area of town, the striking miners went across town and set fire to The Emmet and The Maid of Erin mines. Luckily, the scabs that lived at the mines put the fires out quickly and shot many of the striking miners to stop the attacks.

At 3:00 a.m., the angry strikers once again attacked The Emmet. The scabs were ready and quickly put out the fires. Bombs were thrown at The Emmet, but luckily none exploded. After forty-five minutes the strikers gave up and went home.

The next morning after things had quieted down a bit, Nick came over to the boarding house to check on the inmates. As he entered, he could see that some were packing their trunks and others were crying. Nick told Laura that he was heading out to check on Mr. Moffat's interests and offered to take her along.

As they rode along in the carriage, Laura was shocked by the destruction she saw. Buildings had been burned and debris was everywhere. People were quietly walking around, trying to pick up the pieces. Nick explained that most of the mine owners and even the superintendents had already left town and the banks were starting to close. Seems the striking miners were storming the banks and threatened to blow up the buildings if they didn't get their money.

As promised, the first trainload of new scabs from Missouri showed up on September 21 and were safely escorted to The Emmet mine by the Colorado Militia. As more scabs arrived, more mines re-opened under the protection of the militia.

The historic motto of why Missouri is called "The Show Me State" is said to have started during the strike. The miners from Missouri, not understanding how Leadville's system of mining worked, were shown how to run the mines. It is reported that the men from Missouri had to be shown so many times, over and over, that the motto stuck.[50]

Returning to the boarding house, Nick could see that the remaining inmates were very concerned about their ability to make any money. He calmed them down and explained that Mr. Moffat would make sure that they were all taken care of. As he turned away, his fake smile of reassurance was gone and his look of uncertainty returned. His first priority was to make sure that there were enough inmates left in Leadville to keep the Missouri miners happy, but it wasn't looking good.

Out of the original five hundred ladies of the evening that normally worked in Leadville, only a handful was left. The town had closed the saloons, most of the banks, and people were scared to walk the streets.

Bodies lay in alleys and nobody wanted to talk on the telephones, due to the rumor that the phones were bugged.

The strike and the fires did chase the mine owners out of Leadville, but it also attracted sightseers. Mr. Moffat's partners were very interested in what was going on in Leadville and decided to see for themselves. One of the partners who wanted to check on his holdings was Eben Smith.

Eben Smith, originally from Erie, Pennsylvania, had been a partner of Moffat's for many years. He had originally teamed up with Moffat, Jerome Chaffee, and Horace Tabor to purchase The Little Pittsburg mine in Leadville. But when the mine dried up and the stock began to fall, Smith was warned by his fellow investors to sell quickly and get out, but he refused. That decision cost him everything and he was left almost penniless.

Not ones to let a friend down, Moffat and Chaffee allowed him to take charge of the interests in The Maid of Erin mine, The Henrietta, and The Louisville. With this opportunity, he was able to rebuild his fortune and once again become an investor. When he heard that The Maid of Erin mine had been a target during the September 20th fires, he wanted to check on his holdings himself. He was not going to lose his fortune again.[51]

Mr. Smith brought four other investors with him to Leadville to check out the damage. To Nick's relief, the men spent their evenings at Mr. Moffat's boarding house.

Laura, Jessie, and the remaining inmates put on their best dresses and a small band was put together. Nick wanted to make a good impression, not for the investor's benefit, but Mr. Moffat's. He knew that anything that happened here would be reported back to him.

Working for Mr. Moffat, Nick made $500 a month plus 10 percent on the profit from the boarding houses. He lived well, and had no plans on that changing anytime soon. Strike or no strike.

The evening started, not with frolicking or dancing, but with the talk of business over brandy and cigars. As more brandy was served, the more the men talked. Eben Smith was in a very talkative mood, and shared his view of the strike with whoever would listen.

"The strikers got the worst of it in the raid on The Coronado and Emmet," Mr. Smith began. "There were around ten or twelve killed and a great number wounded. They take care of their wounded the same as the Indians, but every now and then a fellow turns up that the rats have been eating and we know another one got shot."

Jessie, who had been listening intently, leaned toward him and asked," Do you think they will close all the mines?"

Mr. Smith laughed as he took a quick sip of his brandy. "Not unless lightning strikes and kills off all the Irish!"[52]

With their talking finished, it was time to get down to more personal business. The inmates made their usual small talk as they tried to lure in a lay. Mr. Smith wasn't too sure about his choices, and asked Nick about the women. He particularly had his eye on Laura.

"So, Nick ... tell me," Mr. Smith asked, with a puff off his cigar, "how much is this long-legged beauty worth?"

Not wanting to show favoritism, Nick responded with an uncaring attitude. "Oh, about two-fifty or three dollars." Without even making eye contact with Laura, Nick thought a minute. "Actually, you don't even have to pay for this one's entertainment."

Before Mr. Smith could say a word, Laura jumped up, hiked up her dress, and ran toward Nick. Laura had wrestled him to the floor and punched him in the face before he even realized what was happening.

"Get this crazy bitch off me!" Nick screamed, as he wiggled loose from Laura's grasp. Laura, not willing to let Nick humiliate her in front of anyone, chased after Nick and cornered him in the parlor. As he stood up against the parlor room window, he held up his hands and motioned for her to calm down. Instead, Laura held up her skirt and ran toward him again, this time pushing him until he was against the glass door. With one last shove, she threw her entire body weight against his, which caused the glass to break. Together they both fell onto the front steps.

"Help me!" yelled Nick, as he held his hands up to his head. "This crazy bitch is trying to kill me!" Laura got up and grabbed a small piece of broken glass and held it to his throat. With a slight motion, she quickly made a small gash before throwing the glass into the yard. Happy to see that Nick was bleeding, and seeing that her revenge was complete, Laura brushed the broken glass off her dress and walked back inside with her head held high.

Mr. Smith was so impressed that he bought Laura's company for the entire weekend. To Laura's surprise, the sixty-four-year-old was quiet frisky in the bedroom and a little rough. To show her displeasure, Laura clawed at her weekend lay and left deep scratches on his scalp.

The next morning, Mr. Smith was treated by Doctor Meers for his wounds. When Laura came downstairs and saw the sight, she couldn't help but laugh. Mr. Smith glared over at Laura and with a pointed finger, motioned over to her. "That lascivious bitch has quail claws!"

Despite his wounds, Mr. Smith was determined to tame her. He took her to a gambling hall down Harrison Avenue and they spent the day rolling dice and counting cards. Being a former blackjack dealer, Laura had the upper hand and Mr. Smith won $242. He shoved $16 down Laura's dress and headed back to the boarding house, where he begged Laura to sing his favorite song, "After the Ball."

With a wicked smile, she agreed. Unbeknownst to Mr. Smith, Laura had learned a parody of the song and chose to sing that instead. The original chorus was:

After the ball was over, after the break of morn,
After the dancers' leaving, after the stars are gone;
Many a heart is aching, if you could read them all;
Many the hopes that have vanished, after the ball.

Instead, Laura sang:

After the ball was over, Bonnie took out her glass eye,
Put her false teeth in the water, hung up her wig to dry;
Placed her false arm on the table, laid her false leg on the chair;
After the party was over, Bonnie was only half there!

When the weekend finally came to an end, Mr. Smith walked over to Nick, shook his hand, and thanked him for a wonderful weekend. "I would have you know my boy ... that hand-painted bitch didn't even leave me two bits to go buy a drink. Cleaned me out!"

With his conscience finally coming to the surface, Nick went upstairs to find Laura, who was sitting by the window with her embroidery. Feeling ashamed of how he had treated her, he sat down next to her and offered to buy her dinner. Laura turned toward him and coldly said, "And a new dress. That sixty-dollar one I've seen at the Emporium."[53]

With the weekend behind them, and her new dress in hand, Laura and Jessie could focus on sneaking up to the mines to lay with the scabs. They enjoyed the adventure and the money was too good to pass up.

Despite the strike and the union causing trouble at every turn, the militia was able to get the pay to each mine, except The Maid of Erin. The scabs from Missouri were getting rowdy due to the lack of pay, but nobody wanted to take the pay up. Every time anyone tried, they were shot at. Something had to be done, and fast.

✦ 10 ✦

$25,000 and a
shot between the ears

1896 | Nick had tried sending every militiaman he could find to deliver the pay to The Maid of Erin mine, and none succeeded. Most were stopped and threatened before they could even get out of town, while the ones who did get close to the mine were shot. If the pay didn't make it up to the Missouri miners soon, they were threatening to turn off the pumps.

Laura sat with Nick in his cabin on East Fourth Street with a group of the Colorado Militia as they discussed the options left to them. Tired of hearing a bunch of grown men complain and point fingers at each other, Laura decided to end the childishness.

"The problem with you damn militiamen is you think you are all real soldiers! You come here from Fort Logan, down in Denver, and think you all know how to fight tough old miners." Pausing for a second, Laura leaned toward the men and said with a snear, "You can hardly lick a postage stamp!"

After a shocked pause, one of the militia members looked at Laura and presented her with a challenge. "If you think you can do better little lady … then you go! I'll even buy you a drink if you make it back!" Nick quickly looked over at Laura and placed his hand on her arm to keep her calm. He knew how she could get.

Before Laura could answer, another man in the room threw out a promise of payment if she succeeded. "I'll do better than that … I'll give you ten dollars if you make it back."

"Fine!" answered Laura, as she pulled her arm away from Nick's grasp. "How much am I taking up?"

Nick didn't like this at all, but it was the only plan they hadn't tried. Nick looked over at Laura, and with a whisper said, "It's twenty-five thousand dollars."

Shocked, Laura looked around at all the militiamen before looking back at Nick. "That's a large bundle. Why so much?"

Nick went on to explain that each time the militiamen got stopped, another day had gone by, and then a week and now … it had been too long.

"Well, no wonder the Missouri-ites are mad!" Laura responded, with a shocked tone to her voice. Nick walked over to a cabinet and took out a bundle wrapped in paper and handed it to her. She held it in her hands to feel the weight before she unwrapped it. Flipping through the money, she noticed that there were a lot of small bills. "Is there any way to reduce this? Maybe throw some thousand-dollar bills in here to cut down on the weight." As Nick watched Laura divide the bills into small piles, he smiled. This might actually work.

Knowing that the men were anxious to know what she was thinking, she looked over at them and grabbed her breasts. "See these? These are fake … they are just cotton tits to fill out my dress. My rear end is also just stuffed with paper." Nick sat back and smiled a proud smile as Laura continued describing her plan. "If they stop me, they won't find anything. They will search my saddle bags, but they won't search my tits."

Satisfied with the plan, the militiamen said their goodbyes and left Nick and Laura alone. Nick didn't want anyone to know more than they needed to.

"You do realize that I can't take the money with me now, I won't make it down the street before those militiamen jump me," Laura explained to Nick, as they sat and talked. "You should never have shown them the money."

Realizing his mistake, it was decided that the money would be transferred in small quantities to the hardware store.

The following afternoon, Laura, Jessie, and a couple of the other inmates walked to the hardware store, and to give the appearance that it was just a normal day, picked up a couple of things for the boarding house. As the striking miners looked through the ladies' bags, the $25,000 was tucked safely inside the lining of Laura's coat.

Finally returning to the boarding house, Laura made a quick trip up to her room, took off her coat, and pulled the money out of it. Looking around for a good hiding spot, she finally just threw it in the bottom of her laundry hamper and covered it over. She sat on her bed with a relieved sigh. What had her temper gotten her into this time?

Looking around her room, she tried to decide which outfit to wear up to the mine. The housemaid dresses that she and Jessie normally wore to visit the scabs didn't have much decoration or anywhere to really hide anything. A fancy coat over a plain dress would draw too much attention. As she stood up and adjusted her skirt she felt the familiar lump of her bustle. With her hand still on her skirt, Laura stood still for a second as the idea took shape.

Quickly hiking up her skirt, she removed the bustle and threw it on the bed. After checking that her bedroom door was locked, she quietly removed the bundle of money from her clothes hamper and unwrapped the package. Just as promised, Nick had reduced the money down and she could see the $1,000 bills peeking out of

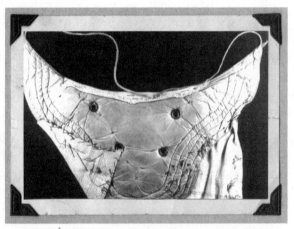

Laura's bustle used to sneak $25,000 up to The Maid of Erin mine in Leadville, Colorado, during the mining strike. Photo courtesy of Dick Leppard.

the pile of money. Taking a pair of embroidery scissors out of her sewing bag, Laura sat on the edge of the bed and started to rip out the seam of her bustle.

Laying the bustle open, Laura carefully laid out the money and arranged it inside, making sure to straighten it out so it was as flat as possible. Pleased, Laura sewed the bustle back up and laid it flat on the top of her dresser. Now, she needed to clean her rifle. She was not going up without it.

The next morning, Laura got dressed and headed down to breakfast. She didn't want to change her routine any, just in case a miner had come in for a lay the night before. After breakfast and some small talk, Laura slipped on her favorite jacket. It was a beautiful, gray corduroy riding habit with box pleats divided on the sides with buttons. If she was going to die today ... she was going out in style.

Without a word to anyone, Laura mounted her pony. She wasn't taking Charlie up today, as he wasn't too fond of gunfire. This little squaw pony had been trained just for a day like today. This was the pony Laura and Jessie took up in the mountains for target practice and trick shooting—it wasn't scared of much.

When she left the boarding house, Laura took Harrison Avenue and turned at 7th Street, as usual, but this time she went over the peak and got up as high as she could. She made sure to walk her pony through a stream, just in case the striking miners were using dogs today. She wasn't taking any chances. But it didn't work.

Just as Laura spotted the mine, a shot was fired and she saw the bullet kick up dirt right near her pony's feet. He didn't budge. Instead, he shook his head and ruffled his mane in annoyance. Patting the side of his neck, she knew she had brought the right horse.

Laura lifted her rifle up from the holster attached to her saddle. It was a model 1890 Winchester rifle with a repeating slide. She loved this gun. It only weighted six pounds and was easy to shoot. She laid the rifle on the top of the pony's head, right between his ears, and took aim.

The Maid of Erin mine, Leadville, Colorado. Courtesy Denver Public Library, Western History Collection, #X-60968.

She could see the striking miners hiding near the entrance of The Maid of Erin. She shot at the men's feet and succeeded in moving them away from the mine's entrance, but they simply ran behind a nearby building and returned fire.

Hearing the gunfire, the guards at the mine joined in and soon she had a clear path. She could see the guard up on a tower wave her down and point to a large side door. Taking a deep breath, she slowly edged her pony down the side of the hill. She made it a point to never run a horse down a hill. Once at the bottom, she was able to hide behind a mine building and wait for a second signal. While she waited, she put her hand behind her and felt for her bustle. Reassured it was still there, she flattened her jacket over it and gave it a last minute pat.

Across the yard she could see the guard up on a tower. He kept looking down at her and making a motion with his hands for her to stay where she was. Finally she heard a heavy metal door slowly creak open to her right. She turned to see a group of Missouri miners motioning for her to come toward them. She turned away and looked back up to the guard on the tower for a sign. He motioned for her to go and she slowly walked her pony in through the open door and heard it close safely behind her.

Once inside, Laura jumped down off her horse and asked for Ed Holloman, the foreman. The men quickly led her down a hallway and into a back office. Once inside, she closed the door and locked it. Still facing the door and without even turning around, she started to hike up her skirt so she could remove her bustle. Laura was surprised when she heard a man's voice speak to her in a harsh tone.

"What are you doing?" the man asked, with an added touch of annoyance. "You're not going to piss on my floor, are you!"

Laura turned around to face him. Without a word, she walked over to him and shoved her bustle up against his chest. "You're welcome," she said snidely, as she glared at him. She took a step back and with an annoyed smack of her hands, lowered her skirt and straightened up her jacket.

With a confused look, the foreman stared down at the bustle he was now holding, and then back at Laura. "You have your goddamn money," she hissed, as she walked back toward him and shoved her finger into the bustle. "Now get me the hell out of here!"

Laura quickly left the man's office and jumped back on her horse.

The miners already had the door slightly open, and had been giving signals to the guards up on the towers. One of the miners touched her on the leg to get her attention. "Laura," he said, with a sincere look, "if they hurt you, we are prepared to blow up the whole Maid of Erin hill they are standing on."

With a relieved smile, Laura touched his face and said, "Let's hope it doesn't come to that."

As the miners peeked out the door, the guard gave a signal that caused the miners to close the door and lock it. "What are you doing?" asked Laura, as a miner took the reins of her horse and turned it around.

"We are going out the back and heading you down the hill. The guards have the shooters concentrated at the front."

Laura was given an unexpected tour of the mine as she was led through the building. She could see the big brass engines that were running the pumps, which were so clean they gleamed. She gave a quick laugh as she watched the reflection of her and her horse in the shiny brass. She gave him a reassuring pat as they passed by the loud pumps and unfamiliar surroundings. She didn't need him getting spooked.

As they continued to walk, she saw miners wearing rubber overcoats as they were being loaded into elevators. The miner that was leading her horse noticed her interest. "The water is still sifting up from the top level," the miner yelled, "coming in at about a million cubic feet a minute, I reckon."

As her tour came to an end, the same miner leaned toward her and gave a bit of advice. "If you don't mind my saying, I'd think it better if you found a cabin or cave to hide low in before you head back into town. Those strikers are gonna be mighty annoyed with ya right about now." Laura nodded in agreement. She took a deep breath as the men opened the big metal door. With her rifle in place, between her pony's ears, she looked around as she slowly headed out.

Laura could hear gunfire as she headed toward Leadville. She saw a striker just over the hill with a bayonet on his rifle. When he took aim, he hesitated and she got her shot off first. She wasn't aiming at him, just near him, but the guards were not as considerate. As she took off in a full gallop, she kept her eyes out for the washer woman's little cabin she knew was just around the corner. She just hoped she could make it.

Coming over the first hill, she could see the sun reflecting off the metal wash basin and kicked at the pony to quicken his run. Arriving at the cabin, Laura quickly slid out of the saddle and led the pony into the barn and tied him to the far pole. Putting down her wash and drying off her hands, the washer woman walked over to see who had just made themselves at home in her barn.

"Laura? ... Laura, is that you?" the woman asked, as she opened the door to the barn. Laura quickly came into the light and put her finger to her lips to quiet the woman's normally loud voice. Running over to the door, she gently closed it and motioned for the woman to sit on a nearby stool. Grabbing her rifle, Laura stood up against the front wall and peeked through a slit in the wood.

"What kind of circumstance have you gotten yourself into now?" the woman asked, as she watched Laura peek through every split in the wood or hole in the barn she could find.

"Well, Margaret, I have gotten myself into quite a pickle." Laura paused for a moment, as she checked outside again. "I snuck the pay up to The Maid of Erin."

With a smile on her face, the older woman started to laugh. "Well girl, it's about time you did something worth a damn!"

Laura stayed in the barn, sharing her adventure, until dark. She didn't arrive back at the boarding house until 8:00 p.m.[54]

"Where have you been? Arthur's been burning up the phone lines!" exclaimed Mrs. Broroned, as Laura walked in and started to remove her coat. "Oh no, young lady. You need to leave your coat on and go pack a bag. You have a nine o'clock train ticket waiting for you at the station." As Laura headed up to her room, she heard the phone ring. She paused just a moment to see if it was Nick. Mrs. Broroned motioned for Laura to head back down to take the call.

"Where have you been? I heard you were shot! Did you deliver the package?" babbled Nick. Laura could hear the fear in his voice.

"Nick, I'll see you at the train station," Laura replied, as she hung up the phone with a touch of annoyance. He had been telling her stories of the phone lines being bugged since the strike began. She had just spent hours hiding in a barn to avoid being found, and now he could have just told the union officials where to find her. She had to hurry and get out of the building.[55]

Laura went upstairs and packed a small bag. Knowing she might be gone for a while, she packed her trunks and locked them tight. She couldn't risk taking them with her, as it would attract too much attention. She padded her coat and the inside lining of her bag with money, grabbed her favorite fur, and headed downstairs. After a quick talk with Mrs. Broroned and a note for Jessie, Laura headed out to the waiting carriage. She wouldn't feel safe until the train pulled out of the station.

The train left for Denver at 9:00 p.m. sharp. When Laura picked up her ticket, she was surprised when the conductor handed her a sealed envelope. She held it in her lap until the train pulled away and Leadville was behind her.

After a cautious look around, Laura opened the envelope.

Laura,
I hope this note finds you well. A room is waiting for you at the Rio Grande Hotel.
With deep regards,
Nick

Laura leaned back in her seat and smiled.

Nick arrived at the hotel the following afternoon and after a well-deserved meal, took her down to Daniels and Fisher to get her dolled up. He was taking her to meet Mr. Moffat.

The carriage pulled up to a magnificent mansion at 808 Grant Street. Laura had never been inside a millionaire's house before and just couldn't seem to get the smile off her face. As they walked up the front steps, Laura could see that there was a sunken garden full of all types of flowers. She had been in Leadville so long that she had forgotten how much she missed green grass and flowers.

As they walked into the house, she saw beautiful marble floors and an iron stairway with filigree railings. On the banister she noticed a marble statue of a naked woman holding up a chandelier with almost fifty electric lights in her hand. It was the most beautiful thing she had ever seen. As she climbed the stairs to get a closer look, she didn't notice Mr. Moffat walking up to her and Nick.

"So, is this our little heroin?" Mr. Moffat asked Nick, as Laura touched the statue and ran her fingers down the smooth marble.

"Yes sir, Mr. Moffat," he announced, as he grabbed Laura by the waist and quickly turned her around. Trying to keep her footing, Laura grabbed hold of Nick to steady herself. Turning toward him, she gave him a quick smack on the shoulder.

David H. Moffat Residence at 808 Grant Street in Denver. Courtesy Denver Public Library, Western History Collection, #MDD-3983.

"Jesus Christ! You could have killed me, Nick," she yelled, as she pushed his hand off her waist and angrily patted her jacket back down with a huff. Quietly Nick stared at Laura and made a motion with his eyes for her to look to her left. Suddenly aware that someone else was in the room, Laura slowly turned her head and caught the gaze of Mr. Moffat.

"I'm awfully proud to meet you, young lady," Mr. Moffat said, as he placed a folded-up bill in Laura's hand as he shook it. Too scared to peek at it, she smiled and just held it.

"Thank you, sir," Laura replied, as she gripped the gift in her hand. She desperately wanted to slide it into her purse, but she was afraid that if she opened her purse, she would pull out a cigarette.

As Mr. Moffat took them for a tour of his house, Laura finally reached her free hand into her purse and found a small handkerchief. She quickly pulled it out and wrapped the folded-up bill inside of it before stashing it in its new hiding spot.

Overstuffed high-backed chairs, beautiful carpets, parlor after parlor full of magnificent furnishings. As Laura walked into yet another parlor, she heard a voice come from a darkened corner. "Are you admiring anything, daughter?" the woman asked. Laura walked toward the voice and saw an older woman sitting in an overstuffed chair sewing something. It appeared to be a little white embroidered handkerchief and the woman motioned her to come closer. "Would you like a tour of my home?" the woman offered.

As Mrs. Moffat took Laura on a private tour, they eventually entered an elegant dining room with a buffet full of cut glass and silverware, but that's not what had Laura's attention. Covering a large window was the most amazing drapery she had ever seen.

As she found herself drawn to the window, she saw heavy, dark blue, velvet drapes separated by big, taxidermied lions' heads. The fabric hung from their open mouths, along with electric lights, tassels, and great big velvet cords. Next to them sat a baby grand piano. Eager to show off her home, Mrs. Moffat tore Laura away from the drapes and into the kitchen.

Laura had no use for a devilish kitchen. As Mrs. Moffat led her around and discussed how she cooked for her husband, all Laura could think about was having a cigarette. Even though many women smoked, the idea of a woman smoking in public was still found offensive. Unless she saw Mrs. Moffat light up, she was just going to suffer in silence.

As Laura continued her tour, she discovered that she had been led into Mr. Moffat's private library. There she found Mr. Moffat and Nick enjoying a cigar and discussing business. The room had beautiful wood-trimmed walls, glass door bookshelves, and many velvet-covered, overstuffed chairs. Mrs. Moffat motioned for Laura to have a seat.

"So, young lady," Mr. Moffat began, as he turned his chair toward her and took a puff off his cigar. "My man Nick here says that you are his private secretary ... his little stenographer." Laura just sat and smiled. She peeked over at the typewriter sitting on a small table and prayed that nobody was going to ask her to use it. She'd read about them in her dime novels, but had never even touched one before.

As Nick sat and sang praises about Laura, he scratched a little at his neck, which made Laura laugh to herself. If only Mr. Moffat knew that the mark on Nick's throat was the result of her pushing him through a glass door just a week earlier.

As Nick and Laura said their thank you's and headed back to the carriage, Laura couldn't help but take a walk through Moffat's sunken garden. She felt like Alice in Wonderland. She loved that story and knowing that she had been named Alice because of the book just made it more magical.

As soon as they stepped into the carriage, Laura quickly grabbed a cigarette, lit it, and took a big drag. Sitting back, she started to relax. Remembering the money Mr. Moffat had slipped in her hand, she dug the small handkerchief out of her purse and opened it up. Inside was a $100 bill. She felt a little insulted. She had just risked her life to take $25,000 up to The Maid of Erin and all she got was $100 for her trouble. Shrugging her shoulders, she put the money back and took another long drag on her Sweet Caporal—ten for a dime.[56]

Back at the Rio Grande Hotel, Nick said his goodbyes to Laura. He needed to head back to Leadville, but wanted her to stay away until things had calmed down. She smiled as he gave her a quick kiss and walked out the door. She had already decided what she was going to do while she was in Denver ... she was going to get her daughter.

↦ 11 ↤

Roman gladiators and a head full of quail feet

1896–99 The next morning, Laura arrived at the Imperial Hotel, at 314 14th Street, to visit with Carrie Ward. She had been raising Lucille since she was a toddler, but now that Laura had found a town she liked, she was ready to move her.

Laura had always loved how sweet Carrie was with Lucille, and did feel sorry for her. Carrie Ward's husband had died just a few years before she started to take care of Lucille and the little girl was like the child she never had. But feelings aside, Lucille was still Laura's daughter.

Packing up Lucille's things, Laura said her goodbyes and boarded a train with Lucille that afternoon. She had already made plans to stay at the Denton Hotel in Salida and had a list of foster families to interview during the following week.

This train ride with Lucille was quite different from their first train ride four years ago. Instead of a screaming one year old, Laura was now sitting next to a five-year-old little girl who wanted to have a conversation … and an unexpected addition. Sitting in the cargo car was a three-year-old red Irish setter named Buster. Even though she didn't like the idea of bringing the dog, she had already removed her daughter from the only life she really knew. Not bringing the dog would just have been cruel.[57]

The next week was spent interviewing potential foster families and signing Lucille up for school. It was only the fall of 1896, and Lucille wouldn't be starting school until the next fall, but Laura wanted to get her paperwork done before she headed back to Leadville.

Left to right: Unidentified girl, Buster the dog, Lucille Evens (standing), and Mrs. Van Winkle, Salida, Colorado. Courtesy of Dick Leppard.

Seeing that Lucille was interested in helping to pick out her new foster family, Laura let her choose. She chose David and Sally Van Winkle. They had no children living with them and Lucille would have all their attention and be a good companion for Mrs. Van Winkle. Laura liked the family because, like her, their family was a little unorthodox. Sally Van Winkle was six years older than her husband, which caused some to call her a cradle robber. Laura liked Mrs. Van Winkle's tough spirit. She would need it when people started to ask questions about Lucille's real parents.[58]

With Lucille settled in, Laura could get to work finding new lays in Salida and learning the area. She stayed at the Denton Hotel and read the paper daily, waiting for news that the strike was over so she could return to Leadville. October turned to December with no end in sight.

On January 23, 1897, Laura did find a news story that was all the rage. An unusual death always got people talking, even if it was in West Virginia.

A woman named Elva Zona Heaster was found lying dead at the bottom of the stairs of her apartment building. She was found by a young delivery boy, with her body stretched out, her feet together and one hand on her stomach. The boy called for the police.

When the police arrived an hour later, the dead woman's husband had moved her body upstairs to their bed and had redressed her. He explained that it was for her funeral. He had put her in a high-necked dress with a stiff collar, put a scarf around her neck, and had placed a veil over her face. When the policeman tried to remove the scarf, the husband protested. The officer did see a bruise on her neck, but it was written off as caused by her fall. Her cause of death was listed as "The everlasting faint, due to female problems." She was never examined by a doctor.

On February 22, the victim's mother contacted the police and begged them to exhume her daughter's body. She stated that she had a dream the previous night that her daughter had her neck broken by her husband because she didn't cook meat for dinner.

Her body was exhumed and despite the protests of her husband, he was forced to be present. An autopsy confirmed a broken neck and a smashed windpipe with finger marks around her throat. Her husband was arrested.

The trial, referred to as the "Greenbrier Ghost Trial," found the husband guilty and he was sentenced to life in prison.[59]

Finally, on March 9 Laura got the news she had been waiting for. The strike in Leadville was finally over! After saying goodbye to Lucille and paying the foster parents their money up front for her care, Laura boarded the next train to Leadville.

Pulling into the Leadville station was like a breath of fresh air for Laura. The carriage driver loaded up her new trunk and helped her inside. To her surprise, Nick was sitting in the carriage waiting for her. They snuggled under the buffalo fur blankets together as he filled her in on everything that had happened since she had left. The strike had lasted eight months and twenty-one days and it cost the Colorado taxpayers $194,010.43 to fund the militia. In the end, the miners went back to work earning only $3 a day … the same as when the strike started.

The strike caused more problems than anyone realized. Some of the miners were back to work, but not all. Instead of mining ore, the miners were busy pumping water out of the mines and mucking out the piles of fine sand that had built up. It would take almost two years for all the mines to re-open.[60]

When Laura arrived at the boarding house she was swarmed with hugs from everyone. Nick, clearing his throat so he could command the attention of the room, pulled out a $10 bill, and with a smile, presented it to her. Laura stood back for a moment, as Nick waved the bill in front of her. A look of realization finally crossed over her face and with a smile, she grabbed at the money. "This is only half of the bet … that other tin soldier still owes me a drink!"

Within days, Laura was busy with parties and new lays. With the mines back open, she was stashing away more and more money toward her goal … her own parlor house. Laura didn't spend all her money like the other girls. If she wanted a new dress, she had a lay buy her one. If she was hungry, she had a lay buy her dinner or waited until the cook at the boarding house served the daily meals. She knew she wasn't getting any younger and she would need a way to support herself once she gave up this life, but she was going to have fun while it lasted.

Now that Laura was back, Jessie was pressuring her to get her portrait done. Laura was not too fond of having her picture taken, but seeing the smile on Jessie's face as she held her hands and pleaded with her, she changed her mind.

Within days, Jessie had not only secured an appointment for her and Laura to get their portraits done, but also a fellow inmate named Clara. Clara was new to the boarding house and had quickly joined in on any mischief that Laura could dish out.

When the day of the portraits arrived, the three women headed down Harrison Avenue and entered Brisbois Photography studio. The walls were covered in framed photos of men, women, families, and even people with their burros and dogs. The receptionist, Miss Rose Northrupp, a friendly young lady, showed them portraits of circus performers while they waited.

As Laura walked around, she spotted a photo of the Ice Palace. As she stood staring at it, trying hard to embed the photo to her memory, Miss Northruff walked up behind her and tapped her on the arm. "Ma'am, we do sell copies if you would like to purchase one." With a surprised smile and a quick yes, the receptionist found that she was selling not one, but three copies of the photo, along with the $1.50 fee for the portraits.

Mr. Brisbois was just finishing setting up his camera when they entered the studio. The room was very dark and the walls were covered in heavy velvet drapes. Along the walls Laura could see makeshift scenes

Portrait of Laura Evens taken in Leadville.
Courtesy of Dick Leppard.

Portrait of Jessie taken in Leadville.
Courtesy History Colorado, Fred Mazzula
Collection, #10049673.

Portrait of Clara taken in Leadville.
Courtesy History Colorado, Fred Mazzula
Collection #10049674.

set up to give the appearance of a mine shaft, an elegant living room, and even a flower-filled atrium.

"Good afternoon, ladies. Name's Alfred, and you must all be my one o'clock appointment." He smiled as he held out his hand. "Have you decided what type of scene you would like? We have many to choose from." Laura looked around and finally settled on her backdrop. She chose a simple grayish-toned wall hanging. She wanted her new suede riding jacket to be the center of attention.

Jessie chose the same backdrop, as did Clara, but Jessie added her locket she bought at the Ice Palace to the front of her blouse. The photos would be done within two weeks and the women happily left with their ticket stubs.[61]

Now that the mines were reopened, a lot of the investors and mine owners felt safe enough to check on their investments. One of those investors was Eben Smith. He had come down during the strike and had spent the entire weekend with Laura, but now he was coming down with his wife, daughter, and new son-in-law. Leaving the women at the Vendome Hotel, Mr. Smith brought his son-in-law to the boarding house to show him a good time.

As Laura and the other inmates entered the parlor, they were informed that Mr. Smith had "bought the key." This term was used when someone rented the entire boarding house for a private party. Many of Mr. Smith's friends were sitting on the overstuffed chairs, smoking their cigars while they told stories of the strike. Seeing that all the women had joined them, Mr. Smith decided to take charge.

"Now all you pretty things line up in a row," Mr. Smith slurred, as he took another sip of whiskey. "We are going to auction you off tonight." The inmates started to laugh as Mr. Smith got out of his chair and stumbled toward them. He handed his drink to a pretty, young blonde. "Hold this little lady ... but don't drink it," he added, with an awkward wink and a point with his right index finger.

He went down the line of women and his friends started to bid. When he got to Laura, he held his hand over her head and announced, "Now this lascivious bitch is only worth two dollars and fifty cents." Looking over to his son-in-law he added, "Is that the way you feel about it?"

Seeing that the young man wasn't too sure how to answer, Laura looked over at him and smiled. "What, are we going to go with this monkey?"

Before the boy could answer, Mr. Smith announced with a laugh, "Well, you're going to entertain him just like the rest of them! But watch out for this one, men, this hellion is liable to try to kill me!"

With all the women auctioned off, they all sat down for dinner, which included quail on toast. Seeing all the little quail legs lying on the plates gave Laura an idea. As the men ate, Laura motioned for the housemaid who was serving the food. "Hey, Rose," Laura whispered to the woman, who had to bend down to hear her. "Can you save all these quail feet for me please?" With a confused look and a shrug of her shoulders, she agreed.

As the night wore on, Mr. Smith stumbled more and more until he finally passed out on a purple velvet chair in the corner of the parlor. With the other men occupied, Laura made her move. Heading to the kitchen, Laura spied the plate of quail feet and carried it to the parlor. Setting the plate on a small table next to Mr. Smith, Laura started to tangle the feet into Mr. Smith's hair.

As Laura was finishing up, Clara walked into the room and tapped Laura on the arm. Turning around, she saw Clara holding out some thin pink and blue ribbons. "It's not done until you add the bows," Clara whispered with an evil smile. Working as a team, the two women added the bows and then placed his hat back on his head.

The next day Nick came by and had a story to share with the girls. It seems that Mr. Smith's wife was very upset and was threatening to kill him. As the girls laughed, Nick looked over at Laura with an accusing stare.

"He auctioned me off for only two dollars and fifty cents … Clara got two seventy-five!" Laura whined.

Nick started to laugh. "Well, at least he didn't have to get his head stitched back up this time."[62]

✦✦

As weeks turned into months, Laura stashed more and more money away. A working girl was worn out by the time she hit thirty, if not before, and the calendar was not being kind to Laura. She had no desire to become a seamstress when her time ran out.

In the spring of 1898, Laura gained the attention of a young judge named Charlie Cavender. He had a terrible reputation for being a drunk, and lived in the attic of a boarding house down 5th and Harrison Avenue. He was a young man with light-colored, childish eyes and a sweet baby face. To make himself appear older he had grown a beard and mustache, which just made him look desperate.

The snow was deep that spring, and Laura was returning to the boarding house after dropping her friends off at the Bingo hall. She was driving a sleigh led by her favorite horse, broken-tailed Charlie. When Mr. Cavender spotted Laura, he motioned for her to stop. "Hey Laura, I need a ride into Stringtown."

Laura looked down at him and said, "Well, Charlie. There are a lot of wagons down toward Stringtown and old Charlie here is scared of wagons and boxcars. He is libel to flip over the sleigh if he gets spooked."

Charlie appeared to be stumbling around a bit, and Laura was afraid that he would wander down the street and get run over.

"I have four pints of champagne for your trouble," Charlie offered, with a slur and an awkward smile. Laura thought a minute and motioned for him to get in. Every time she saw Charlie Cavender, he was stumbling-down drunk. She had spent a few nights in his rented room and he would always pass out before she could do her job with him. She didn't mind. She would slip her money out of his pocket, pay herself a tip, cover him up with a blanket, and head home.

Setting the box of champagne down with an awkward thump, Charlie climbed into the sleigh. Laura patted her horse and gave him a reassuring talk. "Now, let's go nice and slow and be my good boy."

As Laura headed toward Stringtown, which was just over a mile down the hill, she kept her eyes on old Charlie. The horse would jerk away from other sleighs and wagons each time they passed, and Laura realized this was a bad idea. With Charlie Cavender lying in the back of the sleigh, bottle in hand, Laura kept talking and reassuring her horse.

As they got close to Stringtown, Laura saw a wagon coming up on her left with a large box covering the back. The snow kicked up by the horses and the ice on the road caused the wagon to slide close to old Charlie. In a panic, Laura's horse started to jump up, so Laura let go of the reins and held on to the front of the sleigh. She had learned not to tether old Charlie to anything. After what seemed like an eternity, the sleigh finally hit some rocks and flipped over into a snowbank, which sent Laura and Charlie Cavender into the snow with a thump.

"Where's the horse?" asked a shaken Charlie Cavender, as he sat up and started to brush snow off his coat.

Laura sat up and looked around. "Oh, he will stop eventually. Let's look around for that champagne."

Finding the bottles, Laura sat down in the snow, opened one, and took a drink. After a couple of swigs from the bottle, Laura suddenly felt warm breath on her neck. Looking to her left, she saw her horse standing next to her. Patting him on the nose, she started to laugh. "You're such a bad horse," she teased.

To Laura's amusement, Charlie Cavender had an admirer ... the banker's wife, Mrs. Hunter. One day when Laura was in the bank making a deposit for Nick, the woman stormed up to her. Turning toward her, Laura was struck by the overwhelming smell of the woman's musk perfume. Jesus Christ, she thought, with a wrinkle of her nose, people must be able to smell her a block away!

Mrs. Hunter approached Laura. "Young lady, I wish to inform you that I want you to leave Mr. Cavender alone!" With a cross of her arms and a nasty look on her face, she stood in front of Laura waiting for her response.

Without missing a beat, Laura replied, "Well, you gray-haired bitch, go and tell him yourself! Don't tell me!" Seeing the shocked look on Mrs. Hunter's face, Laura added, "And musk is what the Niggers down south wear." With a satisfied smile, Laura turned and walked out of the bank.

Laura continued to spend time with Charlie. They would play bingo, cribbage, drink champagne, and eat turkey sandwiches. When Laura would visit his rented room, he enjoyed having her model his dressing gowns. Every man had something that turned his head—as long as he paid, she didn't mind.[63]

→←

As the months continued, winter finally turned to spring and Laura wanted to get outside and have some fun. Nick decided to take Laura to a new show and then out dancing.

Unfortunately, when Nick drank, he would get a little touchy with other women. When he was with Laura, he was to only be with Laura. He was her beau, and sometimes he needed to be reminded of that.

While Nick was spinning Laura around on the dance floor, one of the taxi dancers came up and started to talk with him. Laura understood that Nick was in charge of finding new girls for the boarding houses, so she gave him some space and went to get a drink ... on his tab of course.

1890s photo "The taxi dancer." Courtesy of Legends of America.

When she returned, she saw him dancing with the girl, so Laura found a chair and waited. As the songs played on and the first song turned into the third song, Laura decided that Nick needed to turn his attention back to her.

When the song ended, Laura was right there to prevent a fourth dance. She tapped Nick on the shoulder and motioned for him to step away and rejoin her. He smiled back at her and tried to wave her away as he turned back to the taxi dancer. Insulted, Laura grabbed his arm and turned him back toward her and insisted that they leave. The taxi dancer, seeing the look on Laura's face, quickly made her exit.

Nick started to mumble that he wasn't doing anything wrong, as Laura walked him toward the front door. Not yet receiving an apology, Laura started to shove Nick, finally getting him to the front door with its stained-glass panels. Giving Nick one more chance to save the evening and apologize, he again insisted that she was over-reacting. With a burst of anger, Laura punched Nick in the face, sending him through the glass door.

Trying to stop his fall, Nick's right hand went through the glass, followed quickly by his head and neck. Supporting himself with his right arm, which was now outside, Nick started to scream. Glass was sticking in his neck and arm, while the large shards, still attached to the door frame, were posed to strike if he tried to move. "Help Me!" cried Nick, as he struggled to hold himself away from the glass. "This evil bitch has me in a stockade!"

Laura stepped back as people ran to help him. They used a cane to break the rest of the glass free and then helped pull him back into the dance hall foyer. Sitting down, the glass shards were carefully removed from his neck and right hand, while the bystanders called for a doctor. As Nick held a towel to the gash in his hand, he looked up at Laura.

"So ... where is your little taxi dancer now?" Laura hissed. She kept his gaze a couple seconds longer, before opening up the front door, kicking the glass away, and heading home.[64]

Nick kept his distance from Laura for almost a week, but she didn't mind. She had heard that he had gotten a black eye from the door frame and wasn't leaving his cabin until it healed. She had kept herself so busy with lays that she was a little surprised when Mrs. Broroned handed her a note one afternoon. "Seems you have a package waiting for you down at the post office." With an excited smile, and seeing that it was a nice day, she walked the block down Harrison Avenue.

When she walked in, the express office clerk immediately recognized her, excused himself for a minute, and returned with a large box. Looking it over, Laura realized that it was a dress box from Daniels and Fisher in Denver.

"He bought me a dress!" Laura exclaimed, more to herself than to the clerk. In response, she heard an unfamiliar voice say, "Well, let's see the dress." When Laura turned, she found herself face to face with Winfield Stratton.

Taken aback for a minute, Laura set her dress box down and quickly approached him. With a huge smile, she shook his hand and said, "Mr. Stratton, I've wanted to meet you for so long. Thank you so much for everything you did for Cripple Creek during the fires."

"Well young lady, it's the least I could do. I spent a many shiny penny, but if it wasn't for Cripple Creek, I wouldn't have had those shiny pennies," he replied, with a proud smile. Not liking to be in the spotlight for too long, he quickly changed the subject. "Why don't you go into that back room and show me that dress? I'd like to see how you look in it."

The clerk allowed Laura to change inside a private office. When the clerk closed the door, Laura quickly opened the box. Pulling out the dress, she discovered that it was made of pink watered silk with big, pink, plush dots. It had a large Queen Anne collar and big puffy sleeves. It was so full of crinoline that she had to walk out the office door sideways as she held the train.

Walking out, she approached Mr. Stratton and spun around to show off her dress. "Well, if that's a society broad, how did she end up here?" Mr. Stratton responded, with an approving smile.

The clerk looked over at him and said, "Sir, don't you know her?"

Shaking his head, he responded, "Why no, I've never seen her before."

The clerk let out a quick laugh. "She is one of our Fifth Street girls."

Mr. Stratton was taken aback for a moment. "My, she looks like a high-society broad."

That evening at the boarding house, Laura was surprised to hear that she had a visitor. When she walked into the parlor she found Mr. Stratton waiting for her, holding a bottle of champagne. After having a glass, Mr. Stratton had an idea for a night on the town." I'd like to go slumming." With a laugh, Laura accepted.

Laura was excited to see Mr. Stratton's own personal carriage waiting for them. "Take us to State Street, good sir! We are going slumming!" instructed Mr. Stratton, as he poured whiskey into a small glass and took a sip. As they rode, Laura was finally able to get a good look at him. He was only in his late forties, but had the look of a much older man. His build was very thin, he had a head full of pure white hair and, just like that afternoon, still seemed intoxicated. Inside the carriage, Laura noticed many half full whiskey bottles. Why was such a rich man, a man who has everything, resorting to this?

As the carriage pulled down State Street, Laura educated him on the way the street worked. She explained how each dance hall had around fifty girls and that they had a morning shift and an evening shift. They just pile the girls inside like sardines. After riding around Leadville for a while, Mr. Stratton wanted to head back to his hotel, and invited Laura to join him. With a big smile, she accepted.

Laura was not surprised to see that Mr. Stratton was staying at the Vendome, off Harrison Avenue. She felt like a queen as she was helped out of the carriage by Mr. Stratton himself and quickly took his arm as they walked inside. The hotel was a four-story, 117-room wonder. It had steam heat, an elevator, a dining room that seated several hundred people, a barbershop, and a billiard room.

When they entered the elevator, the attendant was star struck by Mr. Stratton. As he nervously stuttered a greeting, the intoxicated Mr. Stratton asked if he, himself, could run the elevator. With a nervous nod of his head, the young man stepped toward the back of the elevator and instructed Mr. Stratton on how to handle the contraption. With the gate closed, it was put in motion. Unfortunately, Mr. Stratton didn't know how to stop it and the elevator crashed to a stop at the third floor. Slowly stepping forward, the young man asked if he could continue up to the fourth floor.

Inside his hotel room, Laura took a seat on the bed and started to remove her coat. Mr. Stratton walked up and, placing a hand on her shoulder, let her in on a little secret. "Young lady," he sighed, "I didn't bring you up here for relations. With my failing health, I'm unable to perform much like a man should." With a smile, Laura placed her coat over a nearby chair and did what she was brought up to his room to do ... listen.

As Mr. Stratton continued to drink, he told Laura about his life. Eager to learn anything she could from a man of such high standing, she sat and paid attention.

Winfield Scott Stratton was born in 1848 and spent his childhood changing the diapers of his eight sisters and learning construction from his father. But his father was a nagger. As a teenager, he had grabbed a rifle and took a shot at his father, which has haunted him his entire life.

As a young man, Stratton had married seventeen-year-old Zeurah Stewart. Until their wedding day, they had only exchanged a few kisses because she claimed to be pure. On their wedding night, she told Stratton that she was three months pregnant. She admitted that the father was a bartender at the Antlers Hotel in Colorado Springs, but that they could tell people that the baby was theirs. The next morning he bought her a train ticket, sent her to her parents, and filed for divorce. He had never trusted women since.

After earning his fortune through investments and mining ventures, he decided to give back to the communities that helped him get rich. He spent over a million dollars a year on improving both Cripple Creek and Colorado Springs. He bought homes for his mining employees, gave huge bonuses, donated land, built buildings, and even bought the Colorado Springs' streetcar system and spent $1.5 million making it one of the finest in the world. He built parks and bandstands ... but it wasn't

*Winfield S. Stratton.
Courtesy Denver
Public Library,
Western History
Collection, #Z-8875.*

enough. The more he bought, the more he tried to help ... the more people demanded more.

Every day, dozens of people sent him crank letters. As he walked down the street, people would beg for money. If he gave them money, or even spoke to them, these beggars would drag him into court for more. They would claim that he assaulted them or promised payments that he never delivered on.

"What are you going to do?" Laura asked with concern. "How will you spend your money without anyone getting their hands damp?"

With a pleased look on his face, he let her in on a secret. "Now this is between you and me ... because I like you." He paused for a moment to take another drink. "I've re-written my will. I'm leaving all my money to a new venture I'm working on. I've already bought the land." Mr. Stratton motioned for her to come closer, even though there was no one else in the room. He put his right index finger to his lips, reinforcing the fact that this was a secret. Laura played along, and leaned in close. "I'm building a home for orphans and widows. I'm calling it 'The My-ron Stratton Home,' after my father."

Laura smiled. "That's a wonderful idea, just wonderful! Your father would be so proud."

Being late, Laura spent the night in Mr. Stratton's room. The next morning, she was invited to spend the day with Mr. Stratton and get a private guided tour of one of his mines. Laura jumped at the chance. She hadn't been to the mines since the strike, and it would be nice to get a tour without riding on the back of a horse and getting shot at.

The morning was spent with a wonderful breakfast in the Vendome's dining room and then a tour of the mine. When he had his driver drop her back off at the boarding house, she realized that he hadn't paid her a dime. Shrugging her shoulders, she gave Mr. Stratton a quick kiss and waved goodbye as she walked into the boarding house. Up in her room, Laura threw her coat and bag on the bed and sank down into her chair. Looking over at her bag, she thought she saw something peeking out of it. Grabbing it, she looked inside and smiled. He hadn't forgotten about her after all.[65]

→←

As the months continued, Laura found herself thinking more and more about starting her own parlor house. She had learned so much from Nick and Mr. Stratton and was eager to put that knowledge to work. She had stuffed the linings of her trunks with cash, as well as her savings account. Now she just had to decide when to move back to Salida.

April 10, 1899, was a day that got everybody in Leadville talking. Horace Tabor, the former silver king, was dead. He had died down in Denver of appendicitis at the age of sixty-eight, after his wife "Baby Doe" refused to let doctors operate. Nobody in Leadville liked Baby Doe, so this just added to their distaste.

Tabor's silver mines had made him rich. He left his first wife, Augusta, for a divorced, young woman named Elizabeth Bonduel McCourt. Together they had two daughters, Elizabeth Bonduel Lily and Rosemary Silver Dollar Echo Honeymoon Tabor. The repeal of the Sherman Silver Purchase Act in 1893, along with Tabor's lavish spending habits, devastated his fortune and he was soon broke. He had been working as a postmaster in Denver until right before his death.[66]

The talk of Tabor's death started to wane as talk of the Ringling Brothers Circus was on everyone's lips. The show was set for May 27, but the performers showed up early in the week to set up the tents and advertise for the show. Watching the circus train arrive and elephants helping to set up the large circus tents kept everyone occupied.

On the day of the show, Harrison Avenue was lined with circus performers and peanut vendors. Laura, Jessie, and Clara planned on attending the matinee so they could be free for customers that evening when the mines had a shift change.

A new girl named Ivy asked if she could join them. Ivy had only been an inmate at the boarding house for about a month, but as of late, had been turning down lays. When she approached Laura, it was obvious that she was walking a little funny. Embarrassed at first, she finally admitted her secret.

1890s prostitute "Ivy." Courtesy of Legends of America.

"I'm sore down below," Ivy whispered. With that, Jessie piped up and offered to help her out. Going back up into Ivy's bedroom, the three women helped Ivy up onto her bed and Jessie lifted her skirt to take a peek. Shocked, the women saw the problem. Hearing the disgusted noises and whispers, Ivy begged the women to tell her what they saw. "You have a really bad abscess on your, ummm ... lady parts," admitted Jessie, as she squinted up her nose and gave a shiver.

The women considered calling the doctor, but with everyone getting ready for the circus, they were afraid the doctor wouldn't come until late. "Let's just put hot turpentine on it," suggested Clara. "It will break the abscess and let out the puss. Then she can just wear a monthly rag to handle the bleeding and we can all go to the circus."

With Clara staying upstairs to help Ivy remove her skirt and lay a towel beneath her, Laura and Jessie headed down to the kitchen and poured some turpentine into a pan and started up the stove. Not sure how quick it would cool, they heated it up to boiling before carefully carrying the hot pan upstairs. Grabbing a syringe that Laura found in the bathroom cabinet, she filled it full of the turpentine and handed the syringe to Jessie. When Jessie applied the hot liquid to the abscess, it quickly burned through and burst. Unfortunately for Ivy ... it also burned through to the skin underneath.

Mrs. Broroned could hear the scream from outside. She quickly ran into the house and upstairs to find a bloody mess. There was Ivy, with her pubic area covered in blood, while Laura, Jessie, and Clara were quickly trying to stop the bleeding. Setting on a side table, Mrs. Broroned could see a saucepan filled with a terrible smelling liquid and a glass syringe lying on the bed.

"I don't want to know! ... Just get her into the tub and run cold water over it! I'm calling the doctor!" Mrs. Broron yelled, as she ran back downstairs.

After being rushed to the hospital, Ivy spent the week on bed rest while Laura, Jessie, and Clara headed to the circus.

The circus was amazing. Strength acts, trapeze acts, aerial bars, contortionists, and high wire acts. There were trained pigeons, bulls, and even three elephants that were trained to play brass band instruments. During the finale, there were Shetland ponies being ridden by monkeys dressed as jockeys.

The day after the circus, the vendors were busy entertaining customers and had planned a chariot race down Harrison Avenue. The street vendors were selling a bucket of beer for $1 and after consuming a couple of buckets, Laura had an idea.

"I want to race a chariot down Harrison!" Laura announced, her voice full of determination.

Jessie just looked at her. "You're drunk ... shut up."

Laura turned back to her friend and with a sneer, said, "Just watch me." She looked around and found a young newsboy and offered him $1 if he would tell her where they kept the horses. Seeing the silver dollar, the newsboy led the women down the street to a set of chariots.

"How much will you charge me to drive? I don't care which team, black or white," Laura said, as she walked up to a young man dressed as a Roman gladiator. The man turned toward her, smiled a nervous smile, and then turned his attention back to his horses. Laura, not one to give up so easily, approached the man again. "Black or white, it doesn't matter, just up State Street and down Harrison."

The man turned around again and said, "Are you really wanting to drive a team? Do you have any experience?"

Jessie and Clara started to laugh. "She drives her pony into saloons, gets a drink, then backs the pony right back out. She can handle any horse," answered Jessie, before putting her arm around Laura's shoulder to show her support.

The man thought a minute and then said, "Well, all right. It will be five dollars, but I ride with you. You can even ring the gong if you get to the end. Do you other ladies want to ride?" he asked, while looking at Jessie and Clara as they started to pet the horses.

Jessie looked up and quickly shook her head no, but Clara thought a minute. "You're coming with us?" she asked, as an extra reassurance. Seeing the man respond with a nod, Clara reached into her bag, pulled out $5 and handed it to him.

The little Roman-style chariot weighed less than two hundred pounds and was brightly decorated and painted a shiny gold. There were no seats, so the drivers had to stand up, which was new for Laura. The man got Laura into the chariot first, accepted her $5, and then strapped in her feet. He then got Clara inside the chariot and strapped in her feet. Having both women place their hands on the front of the chariot, he then wrapped the last strap around their waists and secured it. Getting in behind them, he introduced them to the horses.

"It's always good to know the horses, so you can talk to them," the man explained. "The white team belongs to me and I've named them to fit their personalities. On your right in the front you have Zenobia and then Mermaid in the back. On your left you have Cyclone in the front and Harrison in the back. And I'm John Slater, but you can just call me John."

"He named his horse Mermaid?" whispered Clara, as she and Laura tried hard not to laugh.

Catching the joke, John replied with a stern expression, "She likes to swim ... shall we go?"

They slowly headed up State Street toward Harrison Avenue. Laura loved it. Here she was driving a Roman chariot, with a man dressed like a Roman gladiator, past all the parlor houses. All those girls hanging out the windows waiting for a lay, and here she was in a chariot.

As the chariot was about to turn onto Harrison, Laura wanted to see how fast they could go. She grabbed the reins and struck the two back horses to speed them up. "Come on Mermaid, swim faster! Come on girl! Come on Harrison!" The horses sped up and the chariot turned the corner on only one wheel as they entered Harrison Avenue. Seeing the gong up ahead, Laura raced toward it and reached up to strike it. With her hands free, John was able to grab the reins and slow down the team. The speed, combined with the noise from the gong, scared the pedestrian horses that were lining Harrison, which caused some of them to jump onto the sidewalk.

"Whoa, whoa!" yelled Clara, as John tried to stop the horses.

Laura leaned back toward John and said, "Turn up Ninth Street," she instructed, as she pointed to the right. Laura had made eye contact with several police officers that were patrolling the area, and knew she was going to get arrested. As John stopped the team, Laura asked John to untie Clara and let her go. Just as Clara disappeared into an alley, the police marshal and the mayor, Mr. Samuel D. Nicholson, came running up.

"You know I'm going to arrest you, Laura," the marshal told her, as he walked toward her.

Laura laughed and tried to lighten the mood just a touch. "What for? You want a little excitement, don't ya? Wasn't that a pretty sight?"

Mayor Nicholson stepped forward and asked, "Now what have you done, Laura?"

Laura looked up at him, and a little spark developed in her eyes. "I drove the team and I think they hurt me," she said with a whimper. She then started to rub her thigh and looked back up at him. Mayor Nicholson started to get a little nervous, and Laura could see it in his eyes. She replied with a smile, and hiked up her skirt to show him the scar on her thigh.

This scar wasn't from the chariot, or any horse for that matter, this scar was from a human bite. Back when Laura first started working in Leadville, Mayor Nicholson came to the parlor house and enjoyed Laura's company. To "mark his territory," he bit her hard on the thigh. So hard, in fact, that she had to have it cauterized ... and it left a small scar. Mayor Nicholson stepped back and turned toward the marshal. "Officer, please forgive her for she doesn't know what she did."

With a smile and a thank you, Laura excused herself and joined Clara, who was waiting for her in the alley. Together, they walked back to the boarding house.[67]

☞ 12 ☜

The insane asylum
and a dead president

As the months continued and winter was upon them, Laura found herself getting bored. She had money hidden in every pocket she could make in her trunks and her bank account was already in the five figures. There was nothing left to do ... but leave for Salida.

Laura sat down with Jessie and Clara and it was decided that they would leave in January—the start of the twentieth century.

Packing all their trunks and emptying their bank accounts, the girls boarded the train on January 26, 1900. Not one to miss a party, Laura packed one of her suitcases with champagne and the women were quite lit when they arrived in Salida that evening.

The women had made plans to stay at the Denton Hotel, off First Street. After watching all their trunks get packed into the wagon, and wanting to stretch their legs after the long train ride, they decided to walk. They each carried a bottle of champagne as they danced down the cold, snowy streets. Despite the inch of fresh snow on the ground and a temperature of 17 degrees, the women felt like it was spring. When they left Leadville that afternoon it had been 15 degrees below zero.

As the women danced, they continued to drink. When they were only a block away from the hotel, Laura slipped and fell into the gutter. Jessie and Clara laughed so loud that it attracted the attention of a nearby police officer.

"What's the matter? Are you hurt, miss?" the officer asked as he knelt down next to her.

Laura turned to him and gave him an awkward wink. "I'll be better if someone would help me up ... hey, shhhh ... wanna see something?"

Laura half whispered with a drunken slur, as she grabbed at her suitcase. Curious, the officer helped her reach it.

Opening it, Laura showed the officer five quarts of champagne. With a smile, the officer helped Laura up and asked where they were headed. "We are looking for a two-story saloon!" Jessie announced proudly, as she took a swig from her champagne bottle. After giving the women a concerned look, he offered to take them to their hotel.

Laura, Jessie, and Clara had all gotten rooms up on the fourth floor, which Laura referred to as "the roof." The hotel also had an old Hydro-Atmospheric water elevator. These worked with a water pump that supplied water pressure to a plunger encased inside a vertical cylinder. This allowed the platform to be raised and lowered. The contraption made Laura nervous, and she normally chose to take the stairs.[68]

The next morning, as Laura was unpacking her trunks and shaking out her dresses, she received a note that she had a guest in the lobby. Surprised, Laura headed downstairs and was greeted by Brady, an inmate from the boarding house in Leadville. She explained that she wanted to try out Salida and was also renting a room at the Denton. She had wanted to join them the day before, but had to tie up some loose ends first.

As the two women sat in the lobby and talked, Brady mentioned the possibility of heading to Honolulu or Seattle, Washington, and asked Laura to join her. Even though Laura had plenty of money, her friends didn't. Almost broke, her friends would need to earn some money first before taking on a new adventure.

Not wanting to travel out of state by herself, Brady decided to have a go of it in Salida. While meeting new lays, Brady quickly attracted the attention of a man named Johnny Burroughs. After spending the weekend with him, he offered her $500 to spend a week down in Pueblo. She quickly agreed and was off before Laura could talk her out of it.

As one week turned into two, Laura was concerned that Brady hadn't returned. She called and talked to the police chief in Salida. He reassured her that there were many parlor houses in Pueblo, and that her friend may have joined in with one of them. Laura thought it over and with a shrug of her shoulders, agreed with him.

As the weeks went by, Laura was so busy with her new lays that she had forgotten about Brady. She hardly even knew her and they had only seen each other during meals at the parlor house in Leadville.

Six weeks after Brady left for Pueblo, Laura got a note at the hotel from the Salida police. Worried that she was being asked to identify another body, she quickly grabbed up Jessie and headed down to the police station. Seeing the look on Laura's face, the police chief smiled as he waved his hand toward her. "Laura, Laura ... she's fine. They found her."

With a reassuring pat on her arm, the officer handed her a telegram with an address for a parlor house in Pueblo, run by a madam named Spuddy Murphy. "See, I told you she was just working at a new parlor house. The ladies of the red light are always moving around," he said with a calming tone. "She's fine."

A week went by before Laura decided to take the train to Pueblo to check on Brady. She wanted an excuse to check out Madam Murphy's parlor house to see if this madam was the same Spuddy she had known back in Leadville, and this was as good a time as any.

Laura arrived at 104 North Summit Street in Pueblo to see a party already in progress. Laura had decided the best way to check out a parlor house was on a Saturday night, and she was not disappointed. She walked right in the front door and found an old Negro professor playing the piano and singing. He had a beautiful tenor voice and Laura started to sing along. Unbeknownst to her, the madam was standing right behind her, arms crossed and not looking too happy. Getting a nod from the professor, Laura quickly turned and was face to face with Spuddy Murphy.

"Can I help you young lady?" the madam asked with a growl. Laura smiled and offered her hand, which was refused. Nervously clearing her throat, and trying hard to hide her disappointment in discovering the true identity of the madam, Laura asked about Brady, as she handed the woman the telegram.

With an annoyed huff, the madam quickly snatched the paper from Laura's hand and read the telegram, then turned it over, as though looking for a secret message. Shoving the telegram back toward Laura, she pointed at a red velvet couch in the parlor. Laura quickly took a seat and nervously held her hands in her lap as she looked around.

The parlor house was nicely decorated, but it had an air of coldness to it, which Laura was sure was ebbing out of the madam. As the house filled up, Laura noticed that nobody was dancing or singing along to the wonderful music. Finding herself going off into her own little world, she sat back and remembered all the fun she used to have with Spuddy.

How she made everyone laugh and how nobody could figure out half of what she was saying. As she watched the customers leave to go upstairs with different girls, Brady finally showed up in the parlor ... closely followed by Spuddy Murphy.

"We close at five in the morning," Brady announced, with a nervous tone as she refused eye contact. "Why don't we meet for lunch tomorrow ... say two o'clock?" Brady quickly moved her eyes toward the front door as though mentally begging Laura to leave.

"Yes, I'll come by tomorrow at two, Brady ... nice to meet you, Miss Murphy." Laura quickly stood up and politely extended her hand. Once again it was refused, but was answered with a quick jerk of the madam's head toward the front door. As Laura left, she told herself that this was no way to run a parlor house.

The next day Laura was finally able to spend some time with Brady, and her story of the previous seven weeks was not pleasant.

It seemed that Johnny Burroughs was not mentally stable, and the day after they arrived in Pueblo ... his family had him committed. He was sent to the Woodcroft Insane Asylum in Pueblo. Located at 1300 West Abriendo Avenue, the asylum was not situated in the safest area. Opened in 1896, the seventy-acre property had a self-sustaining farm and fruit orchard, like many other asylums, but the access road was found to be a danger not only to the patients, but the staff as well. The road crossed the train tracks and two patients and a nurse had already been killed by a train.

Unfortunately, Johnny's family was not very sane themselves. When they discovered that he had brought home a painted lady, the overly religious family locked her in a shed in their backyard in an attempt to cleanse her soul.

"They placed a Nigger to guard me and bring me food once a day," Brady explained. "I tried to reason with him, but he refused to let me out ... just handed me a Bible and told me to pray."

After many attempts to escape, Brady finally noticed some boys playing in the nearby yard. She took her diamond ring and used it to cut a small hole in the back window of the shed. When the boys got close, she dropped money out. When one of the boys picked up the coins, she begged him to call the police. Luckily, he did. "I asked the police to drop me off at the best whore house in town ... and that's how I ended up at Spuddy's."

Laura begged Brady to come back with her to Salida, but she just shook her head. She was sure that she could make money in Pueblo.[69] Within the hour, Laura was on a train back to Salida ... alone. When Laura arrived in Salida later that night, she had already decided ... she was ready to open a parlor house.

The next day Laura visited the local parlor houses and cribs around Salida. There were many parlor houses around town, but some were private homes located in residential districts. After an afternoon of carriage rides around town to check out all her options, Laura decided she liked the parlor houses and cribs on Front Street. It was only a block from the train depot and right off the main street, known as "F" Street. Meeting with the manager of the two-story cribs on Front Street, she discovered that there were three rooms available.

With a smile and a friendly handshake, Laura was introduced to Alma Osborn. After a tour of the simple cribs, which included a private kitchen and bathroom, Alma took Laura around the property and pointed toward the lot next door.

"And this empty lot right here is going to be my parlor house one day," announced Alma with a smile, as she pointed to a pile of dirt. Laura looked over at the large empty lot that stretched from the two-story cribs to the corner. "I'm either going to call it The Liberty Hotel or The Mascot, I'll decide after it's built."

"Are you going to paint the trim and doors yellow like the cribs?" asked Laura, as she took an unexpected tour of the empty lot.

Kicking a small rock, Alma thought a minute. "Yeah, I think that would look nice. Real homey like ... if I can just get the money together to buy the land."

Not wanting to sound too forward or appear as a threat, Laura carefully approached the topic of buying property on Front Street.

"Well, that's up to J.A. Phelan. He owns the entire block. He bought it a couple of years ago from A.G. Mulvany, and he even bought the cribs across the street." Laura looked over at a set of one-story brick cribs, as Alma's gaze also turned toward them. Laura liked how they looked. They didn't have the run-down feeling of the wooden cribs she saw in Cripple Creek and Leadville.[70]

"Have you ever seen the wooden cribs down State Street in Leadville?" Laura asked, as the two women entered Alma's rented room for

1894 "F" Street (main street) in Salida, Colorado. Courtesy Salida Regional Library.

a much-needed cup of hot coffee. Admitting that she hadn't, Laura filled her in as the women warmed up.

1900 prostitute "Alma Osborn." Courtesy of Legends of America.

"State Street, where the cribs are, is also called 'Stillborn Alley,'" Laura said. "When I spent a few days with Mr. Stratton, he wanted to go slumming and his driver drove us around. We saw little kids sitting outside the cribs, playing on the wooden sidewalks as their mom's worked. I've heard stories of dead babies and children left in the alleys by their drug-addicted mothers," Laura added, with a disgusted twitch of her nose and slight shiver.[71]

"Well, thank the Lord Jesus that doesn't happen here!" Alma said, as she stood up and made a clumsy sign of the cross over her chest. "The Bible thumpers would have us closed down in one quick swipe of the almighty sword and probably light a cross on our front steps!"

With a laugh, Laura quickly added, "My dad used to do that!"

As Laura pranced into Jessie's hotel room holding her arms up high as though she had just won the big game, she announced, "I found us cribs!" Jessie put down her embroidery and asked for all the details. Within minutes, both women were knocking on Clara's door to tell her the good news, but there was no answer. Concerned, they continued knocking, louder each time, until they attracted the attention of a maid cleaning a nearby room.

"She left," the maid answered, with a slight annoyance to her voice. "Knocking the door off its hinges won't make your friend come back." As Laura and Jesse stared at each other in disbelief, the maid got out her keys and opened the door.

As though entering a tomb, they quietly walked into the darkened room and discovered the closet and drawers empty. Lying on the bed was a note, held down with a small bar of soap.

My fellow Inmates,
I'm writing this to inform you of my decision to return to Leadville. I miss the parties and the millionaires, of which Salida has none.
Best regards,
Clara

As they held the note, the maid walked up behind them, and peeking over their shoulders, gave a huff. "Well, she wasn't as pretty as you girls anyway. Your hair is nicer." Turning back to look at the maid, both women started to laugh.

By the following afternoon, Laura and Jessie were busy cleaning up their new cribs and meeting the other inmates. Laura rented a room at 117 West Front Street and Jessie rented a room at 127 West Front Street, right next door.

The cribs were slightly odd, and were actually three buildings built up against each other. The original building was a small, brick, one story that held two cribs, one had two windows and the smaller crib only had one. The building was built in the mid 1800s and had survived the August 1892 fire that burned down most of Salida.

The second building was built right up against the first one, as though for good luck. It had two doors on the ground floor, each containing a window, while the second floor held four windows.

The third and last building, also built right up against the others, confused Laura and just made her shake her head. The first floor had one door and window on the left hand side ... but an odd tunnel on the right side, about eight to ten feet wide and eight feet high, that went straight through the building to the backyard. The second floor held four windows like the adjoining building. Alma explained that this "driving tunnel" was designed to allow lays to visit the inmates who rented rooms in the back.

After returning from a shopping trip the next afternoon, Laura and Jessie stopped outside the building and stared.

"Why? Why build a tunnel through a building? Can't the lays just

Driving tunnel through the two-story cribs in Salida. Courtesy History Colorado, Fred Mazzulla Collection, #1004968.

drive through the alley?" Laura asked, as she walked through the tunnel and out the other side. "I've never seen anything so stupid."[72]

The next few months flew by. Spring came and then summer. The talk around town had turned to politics and the upcoming Presidential election. Every lay would talk about nothing else. Colorado had voted back in 1893 to allow women the right to vote, and each lay would become an automatic promoter for his favorite candidate ... as soon as he was done enjoying the company of his rented lady.

Unfortunately, Republican William McKinley was re-elected. He beat out Democrat William Jennings Bryan on November 6, 1900. With Colorado being mainly a Democratic state, the inmates had to continue hearing about the outcome of the election for weeks. Everything then stayed pretty quiet on the political front, until the afternoon of September 6, 1901.

During a Pan-American Exposition in Buffalo, New York, a man named Leon Czolgosz shot the President. He proclaimed to be a Polish-American anarchist and follower of Emma Goldman. She was an advocate for "Propaganda of the Deed"—the use of violence to institute change.

Czolgosz shot the President twice at close range. One bullet deflected off a suit button, but the second bullet found its mark. It entered his stomach, passed through his kidney, and lodged in his back. Despite a frantic search, the bullet could not be found and gangrene soon spread. The President died at 2:15 a.m. on September 14. That afternoon, Vice President Theodore Roosevelt became the President of the United States.[73]

By Christmas all the political talk had calmed down, but a holiday-induced depression had set in. Christmas was the worst time for inmates. Despite attempts at decorating trees and exchanging gifts, it didn't replace the family that most of the inmates missed. To raise their spirits, one of the girls gave everyone a fancy drink to celebrate with on Christmas Eve ... paregoric and Coke.

Paregoric is a form of opium and when mixed with Coca-Cola it had quite a kick. Until 1903, Coca-Cola had nine milligrams of cocaine per glass.

Laura had never tried opium before. Paregoric was sold at the pharmacy, along with cocaine, heroin, morphine, and cannabis. As she drank it, she discovered that it didn't affect her head, it simply paralyzed her from the waist down. When she regained the ability to walk, she noticed how clear her head was. She was so calm and collected. By New Years, she was drinking it every day.[74]

✦✦

On February 22, 1902, Laura heard a knock on her door. Expecting a lay, she put on her Chinese-patterned silk komono and fixed her hair. She was surprised to discover a police officer standing on her doorstep holding a letter. Slightly embarrassed, the young officer handed her the envelope, tipped his hat, and quickly walked back down the street.

Back inside her crib, Laura opened the letter to read that Lucille's foster mother had just died. The letter explained that Mrs. Van Winkle had been suffering from cancer for almost two years, before dying the previous night in her home at 10:15 p.m. She was forty-nine. The letter was signed by Mr. Van Winkle. Getting dressed in her regular street clothes, Laura headed to the house.

When she arrived, Laura saw a very upset eleven-year-old Lucille being comforted by an older woman, as the house was filling up with mourners. Seeing Laura, Lucille walked over to her and gave her a hug. "My foster mom died. I don't think I can stay here anymore. Can I live with you now?" Laura walked Lucille over to a nearby couch and was quickly joined by Mr. Van Winkle.

Wiping a tear from his eye, Mr. Van Winkle explained what had happened to his wife. "She loved Lucille," Mr. Van Winkle added, as he pulled out a handkerchief and wiped his nose. "Some ladies from the church said they would watch her until you decide what to do."

Taking a minute to think, as Lucille stared up at her with a desperate expression, Laura informed Mr. Van Winkle that she would take Lucille home with her that afternoon. Gathering up her things, Laura promised to allow Lucille to attend the funeral before helping her inside the carriage.

Arriving at the cribs, Laura led Lucille inside and sat her down. With a loud sigh, Laura explained what it was that she did and why Lucille couldn't stay with her. As she talked, a couple of the other inmates invited themselves in and joined in on the conversation. Mentioning their own children, they discussed options for Lucille—stay in Salida or enter a boarding school.

Laura was worried about Lucille staying in Salida, and for good reason. As she got older, she might get teased or taken advantage of by the local boys. An all-girl boarding school sounded like a good option, but not Catholic—anything but Catholic.

When Laura had moved to St. Louis when she was thirteen, she was placed in a Catholic boarding school. Her family wasn't Catholic, but they felt it would give her a good education. They tried to make her Catholic. The priests told the girls to put a small pebble in their shoe, wrapped with a rubber band, to cause a little pain. The priests explained that when you first die, you enter purgatory. You need to suffer here on earth to free the souls in purgatory so they can enter the gates of heaven. She kept that pebble in her shoe for almost three months before she was allowed to remove it. She didn't want that for Lucille.

As the women discussed Laura's options, Hazel talked about her son and offered Laura a solution. She explained that she had become an inmate after her husband was arrested for robbing a bank in Pueblo. He was serving time in prison and she had no way to support herself and her little boy. "My husband buried the money up in the mountains and we will dig it back up after he is released," she added, with a proud smile.

Hazel described the boarding school in Boston she had sent her son to. Laura became increasingly intrigued, as Hazel added, "I'm heading up to Boston next week to visit him, I could take Lucille with me." With a smile, the plan was put into motion. Mr. Van Winkle agreed to watch Lucille until the train left the following week, and Laura could get back to work.[75]

✦✦

The months flew by. Spring, summer, and into fall. On September 15, 1902, talk around town caught her attention … Winfield Scott Stratton had died.

As a chronic alcoholic, Stratton had died of liver failure. He had fallen into a coma on September 13 and died 9:35 p.m. on September 14. He was only fifty-four.

Curious if Stratton had really changed his will like he had discussed during their time together, Laura read every story and listened to every rumor. As the weeks went on, she finally found what she was looking for … and she smiled.

Back when Laura had spent time with Winfield Stratton in Lead-ville, he had asked her to keep a secret. He said he could trust her. She thought it was just the ramblings of a drunken man, but she kept his secret. As Laura finished reading about his will, she was filled with pride. He had actually done it.

A week after Stratton died, his will was read. Nieces, nephews, and even the son of Zeurah Stewart were expecting a chunk of his enormous estate. Instead, they learned that his entire fortune—$6 million—had been set aside to build an institution to care for orphaned children and the elderly. He called it "The Myron Stratton Home," after his father.

Twelve women came forward and claimed to be Stratton's widows. The state of Colorado even had its hand out, claiming that the will's trustees were incompetent. But the trustees held strong and the home was built.[76]

As talk over Stratton's will continued and Laura basked in the secret she had kept, she started to notice that money was disappearing from her fur-covered trunk. The trunk had been a gift from Nick, back in Leadville, and was covered with the hide of a bear that he had killed. She had made many secret pockets between the wooden trunk and the hide … but she was discovering that a lot of money was missing. Worried, she asked Jessie to keep the trunk at her crib. Soon, Jessie discovered what was happening to the money.

Only days after agreeing to store the trunk, Laura came knocking on Jessie's door with a glazed look in her eyes. In her hand she held an empty bottle of paregoric and demanded the trunk. Jessie let her in and watched as Laura stuck her hand in a secret pocket, pulled out a couple of bills, and then staggered out the door.

By mid-afternoon, Laura was back to her old self and Jessie decided she needed to let Laura know the secret. Leading her back to the crib and closing the door, Laura was shocked to find that her addiction to paregoric had cost her so much. When she emptied out the trunk, she discovered that she had spent $7,000 in eighteen months. Disgusted, she never used opium again.[77]

⇥ 13 ⇤

A dead lieutenant
and the pot of soup

902–11   Eager to replace the $7,000 she had wasted on opium, Laura spent the next year focused on her dream of owning a parlor house. This time, she deposited her money into a savings account so she couldn't touch it … in case she had a relapse.

To commemorate her new sobriety, Laura decided it was time to add a more recent photo of herself and Jessie to her album. Leading Jessie's donkey Clarabelle from the stable, she had Jessie climb up and give her a pose. Unfortunately, Clarabelle didn't want her picture taken and refused to hold her head still. Coming to the rescue, Margaret came outside from her crib and offered to hold the animal's head still. With the one-story cribs in the background, Laura couldn't help but plead a little wish. Maybe one day she could own them.

Climbing off Clarabelle, Jessie led her over to Laura and took control of the camera. She decided to have Laura pose next to the new parlor house that was in such high demand. To keep the donkey's head still, Margaret stood just out of camera range and talked baby talk to it. Seeing the afternoon's entertainment unfolding outside, Alma came outside and placed her new white poodle in Laura's lap. As the poodle stared at her owner and Margaret talked to the donkey, Jessie finally got her picture.[78]

⇥⇤

As 1902 turned into 1904, talk returned once again to the Presidential race. This time around, Colorado was voting for a Republican … Theodore Roosevelt. By the November 8th election, Roosevelt had beat

Jessie on a donkey with Margaret holding the donkey's head still. Courtesy Salida Regional Library.

Laura Evens on a donkey in Salida. Courtesy Salida Regional Library.

out Democrat Alton B. Parker. On March 4, 1905, the country was interested, not only in the inauguration of the President, but what was on his finger.

The night before his inauguration, Roosevelt was given a special ring, which contained a locket of Abraham Lincoln's hair. Upon Lincoln's death, Dr. Charles C. Taft had cut a piece of Lincoln's hair as a memento. The attending doctor then sold the hair to John Hay on February 9, 1905, who had it embedded into a ring.

The excitement over the election continued when it was announced that President Roosevelt would be visiting Salida while traveling the country. His train stopped on May 8, and he gave a speech to the hundreds of eager listeners. He thanked the veterans of the Civil War and the railway workers, before mentioning how much he enjoyed Colorado.[79]

As talk continued concerning Roosevelt's unusual ring, news was released that the body of Abraham Lincoln was to be exhumed that September. In 1876, thieves had tried to steal the body of the President and hold it for ransom. Many people were convinced that the thieves had succeeded and that the vault was empty. To halt the rumors, President Lincoln's son, Robert, agreed to have the tomb opened to determine if it was empty. On September 26, 1905, the tomb was opened and twenty-three witnesses agreed that the body they saw was the body of the President. His body had not changed much since his funeral and Robert once again was able to see the face of his father.[80]

While talk was still focused on the deceased President, a surprising story hit the papers on October 5th. An invention called an "aeroplane" had just been flown. This was the inventors' third attempt, which resulted in the contraption staying airborne for thirty-nine minutes. The Wright brothers refused to fly it again until they had a firm contract to sell their invention.[81]

As everyone was busy with the news, Laura was busy with her own interests. J.A. Phelan's two-story parlor house, next door to the cribs, had been sold to Miriam Blondheim. Alma Osborn was livid. She managed all of Mr. Phelan's properties and was promised the chance to purchase the parlor house. In 1906, knowing that Alma Osborn had cash sitting in the bank, Miriam Blondheim sold the parlor house to Mrs. T. Ryan.[82]

Everyone was distracted from the parlor house feud two years later when the Wright brother's aeroplane contraption caused its first fatality on September 17, 1908. Orville Wright took Army Lieutenant Thomas

Selfridge on a test flight, but at one hundred feet up, something went terribly wrong. At that altitude, the propeller split and the flying machine crashed to the ground. Orville suffered a broken leg and four broken ribs, but Lieutenant Selfridge fractured his skull and died later that night.[83]

The gossip over the accident quickly quieted down as the 1908 Presidential election went into full swing. President Theodore Roosevelt had chosen not to run for a third term, and instead nominated his friend and Secretary of War, William Howard Taft. Colorado voted instead for the Democratic running mate, William J. Bryan. On November 3, William Taft became the thirty-first President of the United States.[84]

With the political news behind them, the parlor house war continued. An inmate at the house told Alma Osborn that Mrs. Ryan was behind in her mortgage payments to the bank and may soon be losing it. Whispers continued as Mildred Bommer was hired on as the madam and Mrs. Ryan was nowhere to be seen.

Finally, on September 17, 1909, Alma Osborn became the owner of the parlor house located at 129 Front Street. After Mrs. Ryan lost the parlor house to the bank, Alma Osborn proudly walked in and paid $4,500 for the building and lots 8 and 9, in cash. She also purchased lot 7, which included two, one-story cribs right next door. True to her word, she hired a local man to paint the doors and window frames yellow. The Liberty Hotel was now open for business.[85]

Only a month after helping her friend Alma celebrate buying the parlor house, Laura discovered that on October 17, 1909, Madam Jennie Rogers, the woman who had introduced her to the life of a soiled dove, had died from Brights Disease. She was sixty-five.

Brights Disease is a disease of the kidneys and was commonly found in diabetics. The symptoms are usually severe back pain, elevated blood pressure, vomiting, and fever. The only treatments were bloodletting, warm baths, diuretics, and laxatives.

When Laura told Jessie, she asked the question that Laura was thinking, too. "Do you think anyone has ever found the solid gold coffin? You know ... the one she buried her prized bull dog in?"[86]

In the spring of 1910, Laura realized that her dream of opening a parlor house in Salida was slipping through her fingers. She needed to find a new town with great prospects ... but where to go?

Not sure who else to ask, Laura headed down to the police station and surprised the officer at the front desk with her question.

"Ma'am," the officer asked, as he leaned closer to her and whispered, "you want me to tell you where a good place for working girls would be?" Seeing the serious nod of her head, the officer sat back in his chair to think. The confused look on his face attracted the police chief, who walked up and asked what the trouble was. After a quick whisper and a few finger pointings, the police chief pulled out a map and laid it on the table.

"Ma'am ... have you ever tried Central City?" the officer asked, as he pointed to the town on the map. "Big woman named Lou Bunch runs a little house up there, she seems to do okay." He quickly turned away just as Laura saw a red flush start to cover his face. "Some of my men have heard stories, that's all ... you know how people talk." With a nervous clearing of his throat, he tried hard to change the subject. "Lots of gold mines up there, ma'am, I think it's called the Glory Hole." Seeing that the chief was getting some awkward looks from his fellow officers, Laura gave him a quick handshake, a sly smile, and went off to send a telegram to Lou Bunch in Central City.

Louisa Bunch was born in 1857 and had been running a small parlor house in Central City since 1900. The only thing that made her stand out from other madams was her size, which was over three hundred pounds. She quickly responded to Laura's telegram and sent an offer that Laura couldn't refuse. She offered her the chance to not only rent her parlor house from her, but to be the madam.

Within days, Laura had gathered up a wonderful Negro piano player and five inmates who wanted a change of scenery. One hundred and thirty-eight miles later, the train pulled into Central City, and Laura had her first meeting with Lou Bunch.

"Laura! Laura Evens!" a woman's voice announced through the crowd, as the girls started to disembark the train. Looking toward the sound, Laura noticed a very large, short woman with graying hair walking slowly toward her. She appeared to be in her early sixties and stuffed into her clothes with amazing skill. Giving a friendly wave, Laura headed in her direction.

After many handshakes and hugs, the trunks were piled into the carriages and Laura got her first look at Central City.

Founded in 1859, the town looked like any other mining town, except this town was known as "the richest square mile on earth." The population had originally started out at 10,000 people, but by 1910, that had dropped to only 1,782. Laura was hoping that the nearby town of Black Hawk and the fact that Denver was only thirty-five miles away would give her the customers she needed to make a name for herself.

As the carriage pulled up to the wooden house on Pine Street, Laura quickly noticed something she wasn't expecting ... a large Catholic church. "Your red light district is right next to a church?" Laura asked with a gasp and a slight bit of shame.

Laughing, Lou Bunch pulled Laura to-

Laura's piano player with his lyre, Central City. Courtesy History Colorado, Fred Mazzulla Collection, #10049676.

wards her tight, as she pointed to the hill up above the church. "And up those wooden steps ... is the Saint Aloysius Academy," she added, as she jabbed Laura in the side. Seeing the shocked look on Laura's face, Jessie quickly walked over to her friend and together they both stood in an uncomfortable silence.

"This confirms it ... we are going to hell," Laura said.

Lou Bunch's house was a basic wooden structure with two front doors. The back of the house was built into the hill, which is where the coal would slide down. The house had bedrooms, a dining room, kitchen, bathroom, and front parlor. As the women walked into the house, Lou made the announcement that she had given the cook the night off. "I'm going to cook for you girls tonight, before I head back to Denver. The most delicious soup you've ever had." Shrugging her shoulders, Laura went about getting the house cleaned up and bedrooms assigned.

Soon the smell of food started to fill the rooms, as the girls began to unpack and the piano player was breaking the silence with his music.

Lou Bunch's house, third one up from the church, in Central City. Courtesy Denver Public Library, Western History Collection, #L-22.

Lou Bunch, Central City madam. Courtesy History Colorado, Fred Mazzulla Collection, #10038453.

Surprised, Laura saw Jessie quickly enter her bedroom and close the door behind her. "We have a problem."

Quickly sickened by the thought of what she had just heard, Laura followed Jessie into the kitchen to see the sight for herself. Hovering over the large pot of soup was a sweaty Lou Bunch ... with a mouth full of chewing tobacco. As they watched, Lou would turn and spit tobacco juice into a large pot on the floor. As she turned back toward the stove to stir the pot, small chunks of used tobacco were falling into the soup. Laura covered her mouth in shock. Jessie quickly leaned toward Laura and whispered, "I'm not eating that."

Dinner didn't go as planned. Not wanting to insult the woman who was renting her the parlor house, Laura and Jessie chose not to tell anyone about the soup. Jessie made the excuse that she was allergic to carrots, while Laura stated that bread helped ease her stomach after a long train ride. To assure that the bread was edible, Laura had personally walked to the nearby bakery and bought it herself.

After a round of after-dinner hugs, Laura handed Lou $60 for the monthly rent and thanked her again for the chance to run her own house. With a wave and a wish of good luck, Lou boarded the train back to Denver.

As the week began, Laura was pleased to see they had no shortage of customers. It was a relief when Sunday came and they could have a break. Deciding to check out the town, Laura and the inmates dressed in their best costumes and headed down to Lawrence Street. As they walked, they were so distracted by their own gossip that they came upon a sight they were hoping to avoid ... the faithful walking out of the church.

Saint Mary of the Assumption Catholic Church was built in 1892 of beautiful granite and red brick, with Gothic stained-glass windows. Laura had heard that inside was a thirty-one-foot high circular frescoed ceiling, but she doubted she would ever see it.

Trying to quickly pass the church, Laura couldn't help but notice the different people standing outside. She saw a woman who made the sign of the cross as she whispered a private prayer and others who covered the eyes of their children and shouted the words "Jezebel" and "whore" in a threatening manner. The men were the most entertaining, as they stood away from their wives and winked or gave a seductive smile as they elbowed each other, like school boys who had never seen a woman before.

After doing a bit of shopping around town, the women decided to stop by the Teller Hotel for a drink. The hotel was a four-story masterpiece built in 1872. As they sat at the bar, the bartender decided to share a popular story that happened years earlier, when President Ulysses S. Grant came for a visit.

The owner of this wonderful building, Henry Teller, invited his friend President Grant to visit his new hotel in 1873. To impress the President, the local mine owners decided to lay twenty-six solid silver ingots on the ground to make an elegant sidewalk to keep the President's shoes clean.

Instead of impressing him with the amazing riches found in the local mines, the President was insulted and chose to use the wooden sidewalk. At the time, Congress was debating on whether to back the dollar with gold or silver and the President was not about to show favoritism.

"When I worked in Leadville, the streets used to shine," Laura said, with a show of homesickness. "The mines would dump the sludge onto the streets to help keep the dirt from blowing around too much, and the silver dust would shine so brightly in the sun, it was like the streets were covered in diamonds. It was quite a sight to see."

After spending time at the bar, the women were soon quite lit and starting to get a little loud. The manager came up and offered to escort them through the back door. Eager to get a private tour of the hotel, the ladies followed the manager to the second floor and out a door that led right to the path behind their rented house. The women then danced down the path, past the now empty church, and back to their parlor house.

As the weeks continued, problems started to show themselves in the old house. The toilet, just off the kitchen, started to clog up and overflow. After many attempts to fix the faulty plumbing, the ladies admitted defeat and were forced to use the outhouse in the backyard. The open area under the house was a popular place for critters of all types to hide out. One night, a couple of the lays had to use a gun to break up a fight between a stray dog and a bear that were trying to decide who would have priority over the space.

When fall arrived, Laura realized that the wood burning stove, located in the parlor, wasn't enough to heat the house properly. She had to purchase small kerosene heaters for each room, which would get kicked over by the lays who had too much to drink while enjoying the girls' company. Laura also noticed a major problem with her bedroom that she wasn't expecting … it had a vengeful spirit.

Every night as Laura slept she would be awakened by the feeling that someone was watching her. Brushing it off, she continued to sleep in the room … until the night she woke up with the feeling of hands around her throat. Terrified, Laura took her mattress and started sleeping in the parlor next to the wood stove. If the spirit wanted the room, he could have it.

One Sunday afternoon while Laura was visiting with the bartender at the Teller Hotel, she brought up the spirit she felt was in her room. Waiting for the man to laugh, she was instead greeted by a serious look and an explanation.

Years earlier, when Lou Bunch had just opened her parlor house, a man fell in love with one of her girls. The girl did not return his affection and treated him like any other lay. One night he visited the parlor house and found her doing business with a local barber. Filled with jealousy, the man stormed into the room and strangled the barber.

Taking a quick drink of her beer, Laura looked at the bartender and smiled. "Well, that confirms it … I'm never sleeping in that room again."

After three months of doing business in Central City, Laura's clientele started to slow down. By six months, it had almost completely stopped. The mines were closing and she would soon be out of business. She contacted Lou Bunch, broke her lease, and prepared to return to Salida. Luckily, there were cribs available to rent for her and all her girls.

Before they left Central City, the girls had one more thing they wanted to do. The circus had come to Denver and the girls begged her to let them go. With a smile and a nod, she agreed, but confessed that she couldn't go with them. With so many people leaving Central City, she was afraid the parlor house would get robbed while they were gone.

The night the girls left, Laura was visited by four miners who had come into town for a meeting to discuss their futures, since the mines were shutting down. Eager for some company in the empty house, Laura offered to let them stay in the girl rooms, if they chose, so they didn't have to stay at the Teller Hotel. They happily accepted and Laura went about selling them beer at a dollar a bottle and playing cards. While they drank and gambled, one of the miners started to show interest in Laura.

"Sure is awful bad that you are in this business," a big, old German miner named Kristof Rasmussen exclaimed, as he took a swig of his beer.

Curious, Laura asked "Why so?"

With a quick smile and a sly wink, Rasmussen replied, "Well, if you weren't, I'd be mighty pleased to take you to the Knights of Pythias Ball, up in Black Hawk. I'm not anxious to go, but I would be if I could take you. Shame painted ladies aren't allowed."

"I'll bet you fifty dollars that I could sneak into your fancy ball and nobody would recognize me, " Laura replied, with a wicked look in her eye. As the other three men egged their friend on, Rasmussen agreed.

The masquerade ball was the following night, and being a woman, she would need a male escort in order to be allowed to attend the ball. After considering her prospects, Laura called up a friend of hers in Denver to ask a favor.

Laura loved to shop at a second-hand store in Denver, off Larimer Street, which was owned by an older Jewish couple. After explaining the nature of the bet, Laura asked the owner's wife, "Can I borrow your husband?" He was on the train within the hour.

Laura looked through her costumes for an outfit, not only for her, but for her friend's husband. She threw some silly colored clothes in a pile and quickly put together a clown outfit for him, but her outfit had to be perfect. It had to fool everybody, especially Rasmussen. Deciding that a shopping trip might be in order, Laura headed down the walking path behind the parlor house. Still deep in thought, she watched the school children walk from the Catholic church, up the long wooden steps to the school up on the hill. She kept her distance, not only out of respect for the nuns, but to avoid those hateful stares. As she waited … that's when it hit her … she should dress like a nun!

Running back to the parlor house, Laura pulled out a black fur-lined, satin opera cape, a roll of cheesecloth, and a white pillowcase. She found an old log chain that had a big tin cross hanging from it, and added a pair of white cotton gloves. Soon, her costume was complete.

When her evening's companion arrived at the train station, Laura quickly headed him up to the parlor house and got him ready. She dressed him in an old, red gown she had torn apart that had big black dots all over it. For a clown hat, she took one of her wool stockings and put it on his head. Realizing it needed something more, she tied a big knot on the end. Satisfied, Laura packed up both costumes, loaded them up into her carriage, and headed to Black Hawk.

When they arrived, they discovered that the only private place to dress was in the livery stable. Hiding in the back, away from prying eyes, they both quickly dressed. After giving her companion a good look over, Laura handed him his masquerade mask, put on her own, and headed into the ball.

Laura danced with her companion and had a great time. When it was time for the costume contest, he won first prize in the men's division. He loved swinging his head around so the knot on the end of the wool stocking would hit people. It was toward the end of the night when Laura decided to make her move.

While dancing the last dance, Laura pretended to slip on the floor and grabbed her ankle. Moaning in artificial pain, she attracted the attention of the host, Bill Williams. Bending down to check on her, Laura made a request. "Kind sir, I'm not asking for charity. Can I please see Mr. Rasmussen?" Mr. Williams stood up and asked around, until it was discovered that Mr. Rasmussen was busy dealing cards in the saloon. With her host helping her to her feet, she limped, with quiet a lot of theatrical flair, toward the saloon.

Seeing that Mr. Williams had left her side, she no longer had to put on her lame duck act and walked slowly into the saloon in search of her target. Spotting him dealing cards at a big table, she walked over and quietly stood by his side. Caught off guard, Rasmussen looked toward her. "Good evening sister, is it charity you're after?"

Disguising her voice, Laura said, "Not exactly ..." With that, she ripped off her masquerade mask and smiled at him." Pay me my fifty, you son of a bitch!"

Kristof Rasmussen let out a huge sigh and took a long puff of his cigar before pushing a hidden button under his gaming table. A man from the back came up to the table, asked his business, and with a nod, disappeared into the back room. Laura started to get a little nervous. It was against the law for painted ladies to attend proper social functions, and Rasmussen could easily get out of his bet by turning her in. Soon the man returned with an envelope, which Rasmussen slapped into her hand with an annoyed huff. She returned his look with a big smile as she opened the envelope to check its contents.

Satisfied, she turned back to her companion and motioned to him that they were leaving. Jumping up into her carriage, Laura quickly took off her costume and slipped her dress back over her head, as she gave the horses the signal to head back toward Central City. She wanted to get out of Black Hawk as quickly as possible.

The next morning, Laura packed her costume in a trunk and her companion headed back to his wife. Thinking that the night was over and forgotten, Laura concentrated on packing up Lou Bunch's parlor house and headed back to Salida. A month later, she discovered that she was mistaken.

Receiving a telegram, Laura was shocked to see a request for a photograph of her in the costume. It seems that her evening's companion had bragged about their adventure to everyone he knew back in Denver and it had attracted the attention of a visiting photographer. Intrigued, Laura boarded the train and headed out.

Arriving in Denver, she was greeted by her former dance partner and a young man from Ohio. As they headed up town to his photography studio, he explained that he was going to enter the photo in a contest. As Laura entered his studio, she saw amazing photography work and asked why he was out in Denver. Without missing a beat, he explained that he had been accused of taking advantage of a young girl and was lying low until things cooled down. Quickly changing the subject, Laura asked where she could get changed.

As she posed, photos were taken from the side, front, back, standing, and face shots. He was so determined to get the perfect picture, that Laura finally had to call for a break and sat in a nearby chair. "That's it! That's

Laura Evens dressed as a nun in Black Hawk. Courtesy Salida Regional Library.

the pose I want!" the man exclaimed, as he brought his camera closer to Laura. Holding her hands in the required prayer position, she tolerated more photos until the man was satisfied.

Months later, toward the beginning of 1911, the postman delivered a package to her crib. Inside she discovered a photo of her in her nun's costume and a letter explaining how the photo had won the photographer first prize. Turning the photo over, she discovered an uncomfortable description of herself written on the back: "An inebriate, a gambler, and proprietress of bawdy houses."

Laura sat back, a little stunned. "Why didn't he just tell them I was a murderer, too?" she said out loud, to nobody but herself. With a shrug of her shoulders she inserted the photo into a frame. "He would have won the grand prize if he just would have added murderer," she murmured, as she placed the photo on the side table with a satisfied smile.[87]

✧ 14 ✧

The fourth floor tower
and the blood-stained shirt

911–13 As Laura settled comfortably back into her life in Salida, her world turned upside down once again, only months into 1912. Jessie was leaving. Standing in Laura's doorway, Jessie quietly held out a letter from her father. It stated that her mother had died and that her father needed her to come home. Jessie had never hidden her painted lady status from her family and sent them money every month. It made her feel better about the shame she knew they must have felt. Laura and Jessie had known each other for seventeen years. Ever since that first meeting in the carriage, on the way to meet Jennie Rogers at the House of Mirrors, they had been inseparable.

In an attempt to ease the pain, Laura decided to treat Jessie to a grand send off. Gathering up three of Jessie's favorite inmates, they spent the rest of the afternoon and into the next day at a popular resort in the nearby town of Nathrop called "Mount Princeton."

Despite being a popular bathing spot for native Indian tribes of the area, the four-story hotel and resort wasn't built until 1879. The natural hot springs, which lined the river, were historically blocked off with rocks to make soaking pools, each being a different temperature. The resort entertained guests via a large dining room with fresh bouquets of flowers, live music, horseback riding, and of course swimming in either the indoor or outdoor pools. The natural soaking pools were located, down the steps, by the river.

Laura booked rooms for all the girls and then happily piled them into her new car. Well, new to her. The month before she had purchased a used 1908 Buick Model 10 and hadn't truly given it a test run. A Buick

Mount Princeton Hot Springs in Nathrop, Colorado. Courtesy Salida Regional Library.

Model 10 was a three-passenger touring car, but the top only covered the front seat, so it was best to only drive it on sunny days.

Piling five people into a three-passenger car made the twenty-mile trip exciting, as the women held on tight to each other and the sides of the car. Laura, wanting to give the car a true test run, got it up to its top speed of 60 mph as her passengers screamed for her to slow down. The women were quite a sight when they arrived at the resort, and quickly checked into their rooms to freshen up.

Unfortunately, the historic hotel was a little short on modern conveniences. Despite its size, there was only one bathroom on the first and second floors, but each guest room was equipped with a washstand and fresh towels. Heat was only available on the first floor, but there was a huge fireplace on the ground floor to warm up the guests after enjoying the pools.

After an afternoon of swimming, the women enjoyed the evening dancing and gossiping. As the night drew on, and the empty wine bottles started stacking up, the women decided that a private tour of the hotel was in order. It bothered Laura to no end when she discovered that the four-story hotel only rented rooms on the first and second floors.

She desperately wanted to visit the fourth floor tower that she saw from the road.

As the women clumsily shushed each other, they walked around the second floor until they discovered an unlocked door that led to the third floor. With the whispers of the intoxicated, they made their way up the stairs to find a surprise ... the third floor had never been finished. There were no rooms, no furniture, no rugs ... just a vast empty space. Curious, they headed up to the fourth floor and discovered the same. Happily, Laura found the tower she had seen from the road, and dancing around the fourth floor, claimed it as her own. Finding a pile of dusty blankets under an old tarp, the women spent the rest of the night in the tower, drunkenly claiming their love for each other and that their friendship would be eternal, until they slowly drifted off to sleep.[88]

The next few weeks in the cribs were hard on Laura. She was surrounded by friends, but with Jessie gone it felt empty. Looking for a distraction, she picked up the paper and found a story that had everyone talking. An ocean liner called the *Titanic* had hit an iceberg and sank.

The *Titanic* was touted as the "Safest ship ever built ... Unsinkable." The owners bragged that, "God himself couldn't sink this ship." The ocean liner, with 2,200 passengers and crew on board, struck an iceberg at 11:40 p.m. on April 14, 1912. By 2:20 a.m. on April 15, the ship slid under the frigid waters and took 1,522 people with it. A nearby ocean liner called the *Carpathia* rescued 705 survivors and brought them back to New York.[89]

The story and its numerous lawsuits and investigations that followed kept the newspapers and their readers quite entertained with plenty of gossip to go around. It wasn't until October 14 of the same year that the newspapers had a new top story ... the assassination attempt on former President Theodore Roosevelt.

In an attempt to receive the Republican nomination, Roosevelt was campaigning in Milwaukee, Wisconsin, when the shot was fired. At 8:00 p.m., Roosevelt had just entered his car when a flash from a colt revolver lit up the night. Roosevelt's personal stenographer quickly tackled the gunman, as the crowd demanded his immediate death. The former President reached inside his coat and felt a dime-sized bullet hole on the right side of his chest. He coughed three times into a handkerchief and not seeing any blood, determined that the bullet had not hit his lungs. He then told his driver, "Get me to that speech!"

As the ex-President climbed up to the podium, he announced his injuries. "Friends, I shall ask you to be as quiet as possible. I don't know whether you fully understand that I have been shot." He then unbuttoned his vest to reveal his blood-stained shirt. "The bullet is in me now, so that I cannot make a very long speech, but I will try my best. ... It takes more than that to kill a bull moose!"

The shooter, thirty-six-year-old John Schrank, managed to leave a bullet in the ex-President that could not be removed. Lodged against his fourth right rib, it was too close to his heart to risk surgery.

Unable to continue his campaigning, Roosevelt lost his nomination for the Republican Party candidacy. In a last minute attempt, Roosevelt formed the Progressive Party, also called "The Bull Moose Party." During the November 5th election, Roosevelt came in second with 27.4 percent of the vote, which allowed Woodrow Wilson to become the twenty-eighth President of the United States. Roosevelt would die on January 6, 1919, of suspected blood poisoning.[90]

A month after the shooting, on December 13, 1912, Laura received a knock at her crib. Wrapping herself up against the cold, she opened the door to discover a young couple smiling at her.

"I don't want to find Jesus today, if that's what your after," Laura announced, with a annoyed sigh. "You're both in the wrong section of town for any of that nonsense. Try the other side of the tracks, you might find some luck down there," Laura added, with a point of her finger.

The young woman started to laugh. "Mother, it's me ... Lucille ... your daughter?"

Laura hadn't seen Lucille since 1902, when she sent her off to Boston with Hazel to attend boarding school. She was only eleven years old then. Laura only knew that Lucille had graduated because the bills stopped coming in the mail. Yet here stood a younger version of herself, with a smile that showed no signs of hard feelings for the abandonment.

"Mother, can we come inside? It's a little cold out here," Lucille added with a false shiver, trying to break the shocked look that was causing Laura not to move.

As they all entered the warm crib, Lucille announced that she had a surprise for Laura, but that Laura had to sit down first. Quickly finding a chair, she obediently sat with a confused, but anxious look on her face. After exchanging a smile with the young man she was with, Lucille opened up her winter coat to reveal a small, fuzzy blue blanket. "You're a

Lucille Evens Leppard in her early twenties.
Courtesy of Dick Leppard.

William Edward Leppard in his late twenties.
Courtesy of Dick Leppard.

Alfred Dudley Leppard, Laura Evens'
grandson. Courtesy of Dick Leppard.

grandma," Lucille announced to Laura, with a nervous, uncertain smile. "Surprise."

Laura didn't know what to say. She quickly looked at the young man and then back to the blanket. Taking the baby from her daughter, Laura slowly unwrapped it. "His name is Alfred Dudley Leppard, Mother, he is almost ten days old now." As Laura ran her fingers across his cheek, she suddenly became worried.

"Is he a bastard?" she asked, as she nervously looked at her daughter and then back over at the young man. "Please tell me he isn't a bastard."

With a proud smile, Lucille held up her left hand to reveal a small diamond ring. "We were married in Pueblo on February third, so yes Mother … the baby is legitimate."[91]

As the shock wore off, the talking began. Lucille talked about boarding school and Laura mentioned a rumor that had been swirling around Salida—the closing of the red light district.

Talk around town was that the city was holding "anti-white slavery meetings," and the church types wanted to rid the town of the painted ladies once and for all.

"John Phelan has even offered me the chance to buy this entire building and the one-story building next to it for five thousand dollars. He wants to be rid of it in case the vote goes through," Laura said. "I figure I can always rent them out as apartments, if need be. There is even a third building with rooms in the back and a nice sized yard. I need to be able to support myself and renting to the railroad types is as good as any."

On January 13, 1913, Laura took John Phelan up on his offer and handed him $5,000 cash. She figured the money wasn't doing anybody any good rotting in the bank. The sale included the three buildings and a large lot with room to expand. She could finally be a madam in her own parlor house, as short lived as that title might be.

As talk around town continued, so did the offers to buy up more of Front Street. On February 7 … less than a month after purchasing the cribs … Laura sat in a banker's office and paid cash for not only the coveted Liberty Hotel parlor house, but for the one-story cribs across the street from it. In a desperate bid to escape a sinking ship, Alma Osborn sold the Liberty Hotel to Laura for $9,000 cash and John Phelan sold Laura the one-story cribs across the street for $6,000, which included riverfront property. A girl in the front and a view in the back.

Now the proud owner of most of a city block, Laura couldn't help but smile. She could finally get off her back for a change and let someone else service the men. At almost forty-two years of age, Laura was past her prime and it was time to sit back and enjoy being the madam for however long it lasted.[92]

As the months dragged on, so did the talks and meetings regarding the closing of the red light district. Finally, in May 1913, the red light district was officially shut down. Laura sat and held her breath.

Within a month, the city announced that they would re-open the red light district. With heads held low, the city officials admitted a fatal flaw. Blinded by the morality issues, the city forgot one crucial element … the red light district's fines and fees were what funded the entire city government's budget.

Law officers levied regular "fines" on the parlor houses, cribs, and the individual working girl. Any gambling house that wanted to stay open was also "fined." Criminal fines for things such as drunkenness, deadbeats, fights, and petty theft were also collected, but put into a different account. When the red light district was shut down, the city took a long, hard look at the fines being collected. Prostitution fines often brought in over $100 a month, where petty fines brought in only around $15.

During a town meeting, it was decided to simply segregate the women. "The first boundary line has already been drawn. It encircles the residential district. No woman of the half-world will be allowed to cross that line. The people are entitled to protection against her. As soon as we have been able to protect the residential section against the encroachment of these unfortunates, then we will turn our attention to the hotel districts."[93]

Confidant that her buildings were still going to be pleasure palaces and not apartments for railway workers, Laura could now concentrate on making her new jewel, the Liberty Hotel, her own version of the House of Mirrors.

As you entered the parlor house, you were faced with a staircase that led up to the second floor and the existing girls' rooms—three rooms on each side of the hall with a shared bathroom at the end. Each of the girls' rooms was equipped with a sink, a large walk-in closet, and its own heater or wood stove.

On the main floor and to the right was a large ballroom, which Laura felt was simply wasted space. Over the years, Laura had learned that men didn't come to the parlor houses to dance. Instead, she had three small rooms built in the area. The front two were girls' rooms, the first containing the coveted window, and the third room was a viewing room with a large glass window. From here, men could sit in overstuffed velvet chairs and watch other men have sex.

She had a large bar built against the back wall and a gaming table on the left side of the room. She scattered large overstuffed, velvet ottomans around the room and pushed large, velvet couches against the walls. In recreating the image of the House of Mirrors, Laura hung large mirrors on the walls and crystal chandeliers on the ceiling to help the room to glow. Tiffany-style floor lamps with hanging crystal fringe helped to complete the look.

To add a touch of comfort for men new to a parlor house, Laura bought two macaw parrots and a collection of canaries and had their cages scattered around the first floor. Where a shy customer might not feel comfortable talking to one of the girls, they always felt comfortable talking to a parrot, since the bird normally started the conversation. To

A second floor girl's room in the Liberty Hotel after Laura bought the parlor house. Courtesy of Dick Leppard.

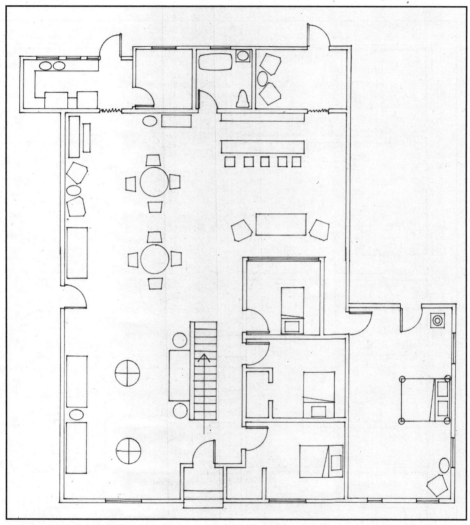

Floor plan of the first floor of the Liberty Hotel. Laura's bedroom is the addition on the right.
Author's personal collection.

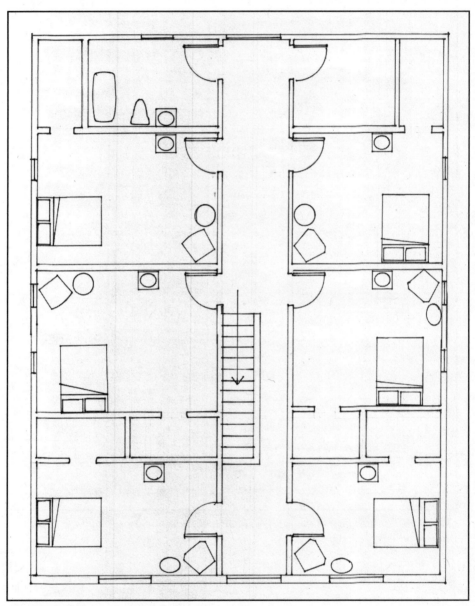

Floor plan of the second floor of the Liberty Hotel. Author's personal collection.

increase the comfort level, she had a plate of bird treats placed on a nearby table.[94]

Word of Laura's newly decorated parlor house not only attracted customers, but new girls from all over Colorado. She had every room filled and on weekends hired a local band to play alongside her piano player. Unfortunately, October 24, 1913, became quite an eye opener for her … her first suicide.

She went by the name "Diamond Dick Valentine." She was only forty-two when she died, but she had already lived a long, unfortunate life that she decided to end.

Dick had worked in Salida before and had rented a crib on Front Street. She came with a maid and seven trunks. Her success attracted more than just customers. Soiled doves were very easy prey to scam artists when it came to natures of the heart. Having a boyfriend who might

Diamond Dick Valentine.
Courtesy of Dick Leppard.

steal them away from their chosen lifestyle was accepted with open arms and sometimes an open wallet.

After giving much of her earnings to a young suitor and purchasing him a house that was to one day be theirs, she discovered that he was not only married, but had children.

Picking herself back up, she decided to move to Denver and make mortgage payments on a parlor house. Since lessons of the heart are learned the hard way, she again fell for another lover, whom she discovered she couldn't trust. One night, while sneaking around to learn more about his ways, she tripped and fell down a flight of stairs, breaking her back. During her two-year hospital stay, she not only lost her parlor house, but everything she owned. Entrusting her beautiful wardrobe to a friend for safekeeping, she discovered upon her release from the hospital that it had been lost in a house fire. She had nothing left.

Distraught, she returned to Salida and asked to rent one of the cribs across from the Liberty Hotel. Laura was concerned, as Dick was unable to stoop or even reach down to the floor due to her back. Not wanting to turn her down completely, Laura offered her a job as a housekeeper or as a manager for one of her buildings, but she refused. Dick informed Laura that people called her "the wax image," and she wanted to prove to herself that she could still work. Reluctantly, Laura rented her a crib.

Within weeks, Dick attracted the attention of a customer from Wyoming and after a wild night of partying, returned to her crib very lit. Her curtains remained closed the following day, but that didn't attract much attention. A crib girl worked for herself and simply rented the room. At 9:00 p.m. that night, a young man handed Laura a note, smiled, and left.

Laura,
By the time you receive this I will be beyond medical aid.
Don't try to send for a doctor, because I won't allow him to attend me.
With no regrets,
Au Revoir

"Holy Christ!" Laura screamed, as she quickly rushed to call Doctor Parker. "She bought chloride of mercury tablets, I'm sure of it! That's what they all use!" she informed him, while pleading for him to hurry.

Hanging up the phone, Laura grabbed her passkey and headed outside to find the street blocked with people—bad news traveled fast. Entering the crib, she found Dick sitting in a chair with phlegm pouring out of her mouth in long, thick strands.

"Dick … what have you done?" Laura asked, as she grabbed a towel in an attempt to clean her up.

"I'm tired of living. What do I have to live for? I have no friends. I haven't anybody and I'm tired," Dick replied, as she allowed Laura to wipe her mouth.

Doctor Parker arrived and pushed past the curious to find Laura sitting next to Dick with a concerned look. He announced that he would have to put her in his car and asked Laura to help him. With her pride showing, Dick stood up and demanded that she walk out unaided. Wiping her mouth once more, she grabbed a second towel and tried to control the strong flow of phlegm as she entered the car. The crowd stepped back as she tried to hold her head high, but they knew.

Laura visited Dick the next day at the hospital. Faye Weston, another of the crib girls, was by her bedside and it was obvious to Laura that their bond was very strong. Faye left the room and Laura saw from Dick's pale appearance that the suicide attempt would work.

Seeing that they were alone, Dick asked for a piece of paper and a pen. Despite struggling to write, she managed to scribble down a series of numbers before motioning for Laura to come closer. "This is my bank account number. Please pay my doctor bill with it. I don't want to be in anyone's debt." With a smile and a nod, Laura took the paper and motioned for Faye to re-enter the room. It wouldn't be long.

Not wanting to get distracted with other things, Laura headed straight down to the bank to withdraw Dick's money. She would need enough to cover not only the doctor bills and her hospital stay, but her funeral, which was in the very near future. Any remaining money she would send to Dick's family, if she could find them.

Her bank account held only $50. Laura sighed as she closed the bank account and walked out with the money.

Laura was deep in thought when she walked into the parlor house. She tried so hard to keep everyone happy, tried hard to talk to each of her girls and now this happened. As she took off her coat, Hazel came running up to her and said, "Miss Laura … we can't find Nora."

Laura grabbed her passkey and headed across the street to the cribs.

Not finding her there, Laura and Hazel ran around the block of buildings ... and that's when Laura found her. Screaming for Hazel, she gently tapped Nora on the shoulder, and despite the phlegm pouring out of her mouth, she managed to talk. "He doesn't love me," Nora slowly gurgled.

Images of Laura's old friend Nora Kirk lying on the metal table of the Denver mortuary flooded Laura's memory as she called out Nora's name and screamed for Hazel to help her.

When Hazel arrived, she saw Nora lying between the two coal boxes in the backyard. The commotion drew the attention of Laura's housekeeper who ran outside, still in the process of wiping her hands on her apron. "Get me some raw eggs and milk!" Laura instructed her, as she tried to sit Nora up. Hazel quickly ran inside and called the doctor. Once at the hospital, Nora was placed in the room right next to Dick's.

Dick lived for almost six days. The doctor said she had taken twenty tablets of dichloride of mercury, which was nearly thirty grams. She never would reveal her real name or any family. No matter. There wasn't any money left to send to them anyway. As Laura planned a simple funeral, *The Denver Post* newspaper printed a story of how Laura Evens was such a villainous landlady that this poor girl had to commit suicide just to get out of her clutches. Laura was on the next train to Denver.

Laura found the building and the reporter. She cornered him in the hallway. "You go to work and write lies about me? Don't you dare walk down the street in Salida! I will tear your head off wherever I see you!" Laura screamed, as the reporter squeezed past her and ran out of the building.

When Laura returned to Salida, she was surprised and a little hopeful when she saw that Nora was still alive. Despite the girl's desire to live, the doctor could only keep her alive for two more weeks. She was only thirty-five.

The Denver Post never ran a story about Nora's death.[95]

Nora. Courtesy of Dick Leppard.

Virda (left) and Hazel (right). Courtesy History Colorado, Fred Mazzulla Collection, #10049679.

❧ 15 ❧

A $20 gold piece and bottles of bootleg booze

1913–16   After the suicides, nobody wanted to rent either of the empty cribs across the street. Laura kept the shades drawn and watched as people would sneak over and try to peek in the windows, expecting to see the spirits of the dead. Luckily, a new girl coming from out of town hadn't heard the stories.

Her name was Lillian Powers. She called Laura in mid-November, 1913, and related an interesting story. She was renting a crib in Cripple Creek from a familiar soiled dove … Leo the Lion. Laura and Jessie had met Leo during a bad cold snap when they went slumming down Poverty Gulch on their way to their internship for Jennie Rogers in Leadville. That was over seventeen years ago.

Lillian sounded a little desperate on the phone as she related her story. It seemed that Leo saw her favorite customer leaving Lillian's crib and went banging on her door. Lillian opened her door to find a gun in her face and a very angry Leo.

"You double-crossing bitch! Get out of that crib, get out of Cripple Creek or you're dead!" screamed Leo, as she jabbed the shotgun into Lillian's shoulder. Running past Leo, Lillian ran to the pharmacy and picked up the phone." Please, please patch me through to Miss Laura Evens in Salida."

Despite never seeing the girl in person to gauge her earning potential, Laura agreed. She needed to rent those cribs. Even if the girl didn't stay long, at least it might break the curse that now held itself over those rooms.

Lillian arrived two days later on the train. Being her first visit to

Salida, she was surprised to see Mexicans. "Oh my, isn't this terrible," she mumbled under her breath, as she grabbed at her bag just a little bit tighter. The taxi driver loaded up Lillian's trunk, as he asked her where she was going.

"Miss Laura's house," she answered, as she got into the backseat, carefully pulling her dress inside.

"Which one, Miss?" the driver asked, as he pulled away from the train station.

"There's more than one?" she said, slightly confused, but very impressed.

As the driver pulled onto Front Street, Lillian got her first look at Salida's red light district. She could hear piano music playing and all types of hooting and hollering pouring out of the buildings, as girls stood in doorways and hung out of windows. "Miss Laura lives in the two-story building at the end," the driver announced, as he pulled the taxi up to the curb.

A nervous feeling suddenly fell over Lillian as she exited the taxi. She knew she looked terrible. She hadn't sponged herself off, she had no makeup on, she hadn't slept, and her hair was up in a messy bun. She clumsily pushed the loose strands of hair out of her face as she walked up the front steps and rang the bell. Waiting, she tried to straighten out her dress the best she could and held her shoulders back in an attempt to hide her obvious exhaustion.

The door was opened by a thin, young girl who looked her over with an extremely sour expression on her face. Before Lillian could speak, the girl called back into the house. "Miss Laura, there is a crib girl here to see you." Lillian felt a stab of shame at the description. A parlor house girl was a classy, beautiful woman, where a crib girl was known to be a used up, sad version of a soiled dove.

"What does she look like?" Laura called back, as she headed toward the door.

Giving Lillian a second look over, she replied, "Not much. Dirty and old." With a look of defeat, Lillian was suddenly worried that Miss Laura might not give her a crib like she had promised over the phone. What if she wasn't good enough? Where would she go?

As Laura stepped up to the front door, Lillian was taken aback. She had been expecting a big stout woman, all dolled up, with a beautifully styled dress and diamond earrings. Instead, the woman who stood in front of her looked like a housekeeper. She was a tiny, five-foot, six-inch tall woman, wearing a floor-length house dress, an old fashioned apron tied around her waist, and her long hair was braided in two strands—one hung in the front, while the other hung down her back. On her head she wore a little old cap of some kind, which tilted at a weird angle. Shaking off her shock, she quickly regained her composure.

"Are you Miss Laura Evens?" Lillian asked, trying hard to hide her disappointment in the woman who stood before her.

"Oh yeah, that's me. Or, what's left of me. Do you want to come in?"

Lillian Powers, standing to the far left in a black dress with white hat. Courtesy History Colorado, Fred Mazzulla Collection, #10049684.

Laura said, as she moved off to the side of the doorway.

"Oh … no thank you. Ummm, I'm the one who called about the room," Lillian added, with a touch of uncertainty.

"Oh, yes!" Laura answered with a touch of relief. "I've got it. It's right across the street … are you sure you don't want to come in?" she offered, with a touch more enthusiasm.

"No, thank you. I really would like to pay you the back rent for the days that I engaged about the place. I didn't get here until now because I had laundry out," Lillian replied, as she pushed a loose hair from her face. After the nasty greeting she got from the young girl who answered the door, the last thing she wanted to do was to step inside and show herself off to the others.

Seeing that the new girl had no desire to come inside, Laura shrugged her shoulders and reached over to a box to retrieve the key. While walking Lillian over to the crib across the street, Laura explained how the crib girls were simply thought of as an extension of the main parlor house.

"You can come over to make change, join in on the nightly parties and pick up lays whenever you like," Laura added, as she reached the doorway.

"I see you have Mexicans here," Lillian pointed out, as Laura unlocked the door to the crib that had been occupied by Nora. "They were all chased out of Cripple Creek years ago. The mine owners cut their wages because they couldn't talk," Lillian added, in a failed attempt to start a conversation.

As they entered the crib, Lillian was surprised to see the kitchen floor covered in broken coal. "I'll send my handyman over tomorrow to clean that up. He's an old Negro who wears a straw hat and is always singing. You can't miss him," Laura said, with a friendly smile as she handed Lillian the key. Lillian looked the crib over, made the bed with her own clean sheets, and fell asleep.

Lillain Power's bedroom in the one-story cribs. Courtesy of Dick Leppard.

The next morning Lillian woke up to a knock on her door. Peeking through the curtain, she saw a Negro man wearing a straw hat. He gave a quick wave and smiled, as she signaled for him to wait until she unlocked the door. The rest of the day was spent cleaning, scrubbing the walls, putting up her favorite curtains, and hanging her pictures. Feeling ready to introduce herself to her new town, Lillian washed up, applied her makeup, and dolled herself up. In no time she had attracted her first customer, but he handed her a $20 gold piece. Too nervous to open up her trunk in front of the lay, she excused herself to go make change.

"Can you change this for me please?" Lillian asked Laura, as she stood on the front steps of the parlor house holding up the gold piece.

Laura looked the girl over with a confused expression. "Well, yes ... but who are you?"

Lillian straightened herself up and tried to remove the puzzled look from her face. "I came here yesterday ... I'm renting the crib across the street," she said, as she turned around and pointed to the building and then back at herself, "I'm Lillian Powers."

Laura took a step back. "Well, by George, I didn't know it was you ... you look so different! Perhaps I need to move you into the big house here!" Lillian smiled and gave a quiet sigh of relief. She was reassured now that she fit in with Laura's girls.[96]

><

Entering 1914, Laura had high hopes for her new parlor house, but July introduced Laura to a whole new threat ... the local businessmen.

At the parlor house, Laura had hired a young seventeen-year-old girl named Annabelle as a housekeeper and cook. She was the bastard daughter of one of the Negro girls from Mary Humphrey's place down the block. Nigger Mary, as she called herself, owned the second half of the two-story cribs ... the one with the strange tunnel ... and housed the Negro girls. Annabelle was a half-breed, as her assumed father was white, and her mother wanted her kept a virgin and out of the business. But as a beautiful, mixed girl, she attracted the attention of the clientele.

Annie, as the jealous parlor house girls called her, had beautiful cocoa-colored skin, long, wavy auburn hair, and piercing green eyes. Some of the parlor house girls would throw food on the floor or ring their call bells at all hours, just to make her life miserable. They felt that Laura treated her like a prize pony, dressing her in high-necked, black and white maid costumes styled after the popular French uniforms. As the girl served drinks, Laura watched the men follow her with their eyes. Unable to find the girl alternative employment, Laura kept a watchful eye ... but it did her no good.

On July 24, Laura was called over to the two-story cribs to break up a fight between two of her soiled doves. Seeing an opportunity, one of Salida's city councilmen grabbed Annie and dragged her into a side bedroom and raped her, and so did the other prominent business owners who were there. With four soiled doves servicing customers upstairs, there were only three soiled doves downstairs that were able to stop it, but they just smiled and encouraged the men.

Laura Evens in the backyard of her parlor house in Salida. Courtesy of Dick Leppard.

When Laura returned, she was heartbroken. Lying on the bed was Annie, bleeding profusely from the combination of the rape and her lost virginity. Standing off to the side, the city councilman and the businessmen were zipping their pants and smoking cigars. Laura knew that the trick to keeping her business was keeping the men in charge happy ... but not this time. Laura quickly grabbed a broom and chased not only the culprits out of her parlor house, but also the three soiled doves. "None of you are ever welcome back! Not to my house! Not to any of my cribs! ... Ever!"

Laura was so upset that she was shaking. The screaming had alerted the four girls from upstairs, who were shocked to see Laura standing in the front doorway holding a broken broom handle. Lizzie Darling slowly approached Laura and closed the front door. Facing Laura, she asked her what was wrong as she slowly slid the broom handle out of her hands. With a very faint, almost breathless whisper, Laura said, "Annabelle's in the front bedroom … she's in the front bedroom."

With a quick jerk of her arm, Lizzie Darling motioned for Maggie, Susie, and May to go check the front bedroom. Seeing that Laura wasn't moving from her spot near the front door, Lizzie Darling grabbed a chair and slowly sat Laura down, before checking on Annabelle. The doctor was called and Doctor Parker was almost as worried for Laura as he was for Annabelle.

1900s prostitute "Lizzie Darling." Courtesy of Legends of America.

1900s prostitute "Maggie." Courtesy of Legends of America.

After a restless night's sleep, Laura was awakened by a knocking on her front door. Hearing the cook answer it, she slowly got up and put on her robe. Gracie soon knocked on Laura's bedroom door, and delivered a shock she didn't need. The red light district was being closed down ... again.

Calling all her crib girls and what was left of her parlor house girls, Laura instructed them to all dress in their best costumes. She personally walked over to Nigger Mary's and asked her to join them, and after hearing the story of what happened to Annabelle, they all jumped at the chance. With a parade of red light girls walking to city hall, it didn't take long to attract the attention of the townsfolk.

Walking through the front doors, the soiled doves filled the building to overflowing as Laura stated her case. As the morning continued, and stories told, the city decided that no charges would be filed against the culprits, but Front Street would remain open. A story of the temporary closing of the red light district did make the paper the following day, but the charges against the businessmen were not mentioned. It was a common belief that a soiled dove, or anyone working in a house of such, could not be raped.[97]

Laura was able to quickly replace the parlor house girls she had thrown out and had offered Lillian a chance to get a coveted front room, if she liked. With a smile, Lillian refused. She preferred her own hours and the quiet that only a crib could provide.

In an attempt to create a feeling of family, Laura decided that she wanted a picture of her parlor house girls. Since the girls always had Sunday off, Laura decided that their weekly drive would be the perfect time. Pulling over after their picnic near the town of Turret, Laura announced her idea. With seven girls piled into a three-seater car, Laura had to do some arranging. She had the three girls in the back stand, while she tried to arrange the four girls in the front seat. Lillian, not wanting to have her photo taken, kept hiding behind Hazel. As she took the photo, Laura told herself that she really needed a bigger car.[98]

Four days later, on July 28, 1914, the newspaper started printing stories of a war in Europe. The Archduke of Austria, Franz Ferdinand, and his wife, Sophie, had been assassinated on June 28—their wedding anniversary. They were shot while riding in an open car by nineteen-year-old Gavrilo Princip, a Serbian nationalist. On July 28, Austro-Hungarians declared war on Serbia. Russia supported Serbia. Germany

Laura's car, photo taken on trip to Turret, Colorado. Courtesy of Dick Leppard.

then invaded Belgium and headed for France. In turn, Britain declared war on Germany. Meanwhile, the United States was staying neutral.[99]

As the months passed, the stories of the war filled the paper. On May 7, 1915, a familiar name graced the front page ... the White Star line. As the owners of the now legendary *Titanic*, they had now lost another ocean liner, the RMS *Lucitania*.

As a war casualty, the ship was sunk by a German U-boat. Since the war broke out, ocean voyages had become extremely dangerous. All ships headed to Great Britain were instructed to look out for U-boats and to travel at full speed in a zigzag pattern. Unfortunately, Captain William Thomas had slowed the ship down due to a fog bank and was traveling in a straight line. This was his 202nd trip across the Atlantic.

At 1:40 p.m., just fourteen miles off the coast of southern Ireland, a German U-boat launched a torpedo and sank the ship in only eighteen minutes. Unlike her sister ship the *Titanic*, the *Lusitania* had enough lifeboats, but due to the severe list of the ship and the rate of speed in which it sank, most were not deployed. Where the *Titanic* lost 1,522 lives, the *Lusitania* lost 1,198. Of the dead, 128 were Americans, angering the United States, which was trying hard to stay neutral.[100]

As everyone was caught up in the war, another foe was lurking around the corner and threatening the peace of the United States. The government was talking about making alcohol illegal. In an attempt to get America focused on something else, the film industry released a movie that took people's minds off the news, for just a little while. *Inspiration* hit the theaters on November 18, 1915, and made box office history. Being the first non-pornographic movie to show a fully nude woman, the censors were afraid to ban the movie, fearing they would also have to ban Renaissance art as well.

The movie, starring Audrey Munson, tells the story of a young sculptor who searches for the perfect model to inspire his work. Finding a poverty-stricken young girl, he spends the movie trying to find her by visiting every famous statue in Manhattan.[101]

Despite all the praying that went on during the following weeks, Prohibition went into effect in Colorado at midnight on December 31, 1915. *The Denver Post* ran the headline on January 1, 1916, which read: "Denver drinks health of New Year in lemonade as joy liquid vanishes."

Prohibition was the result of the Temperance Movement, which blamed alcohol for many of society's problems, especially crime and murder. Members of the movement hoped that it would stop husbands from spending all the family income on alcohol and prevent workplace accidents caused by workers who drank during their lunch hours.

Despite the ability to obtain a prescription for "medicinal alcohol," Prohibition started a new business venture ... bootleg booze. And unlike alcohol bought at the local saloon, this popular drink could kill you.

Referred to as "sugar moon" or "Leadville moon," the new hootch was cooked up using the Colorado sugar beet. The Leadville version was rumored to be made with black powder and old miners' overalls. If the distillation and filtration was done improperly, traces of methanol and lead could leach into the liquor from the still. The result was abdominal pain, anemia, renal failure, hypertension, blindness, and death. The blindness was caused by the methanol reacting with the optic nerve in the eyes.

Laura needed liquor or she was out of business. Men came to the cribs and parlor house to enjoy a cigar, a drink or two, and the company of a young girl. Alcohol, also referred to as "liquid courage," helped make all that happen. Luckily, the local bootleggers understood that, and made it so.

With no intention of following the law, local stores would order their hootch, which was delivered in five-gallon tin boxes with the regular grocery delivery. Taking the boxes into a back room, the liquor was separated into pints and placed inside small paper sacks. When an order was made, an underage delivery boy would wrap a newspaper around the sack, deliver the package, and receive a nice tip for his trouble and to keep his mouth shut.

To assure that Laura and her crib girls had enough hootch to sell to customers, Laura would meet the bootleggers at the base of Monarch Pass. Using her handyman's truck, she would pick up her load in the early morning and even made some deliveries for them to the local stores.[102]

As everyone fell into the rhythm of Prohibition, the talk of the war in Europe was still a daily reminder in the newspapers. The Presidential race was quickly approaching and current President Woodrow Wilson was running on the slogan "Keep us out of the war." Winning the people over once again, Wilson was re-elected on November 7, 1916, and became the thirty-third President of the United States, beating out Republican Charles E. Hughes.

Despite all the campaign promises, people wondered if we could really stay out of the war.[103]

Billie, one of the Salida parlor house girls in 1916. Courtesy History Colorado, Fred Mazzulla Collection, #10049662.

✦ 16 ✦

The boxer's wife and
a bottle of Lysol

1916–19 November 29, 1916, was quite a day in Salida. Jack Dempsey, also known as the "Manassa Mauler," the famous boxer from Manassa, Colorado, had booked a fight in the local gym. Laura had already given her girls the night off and was very eager to sit in her front row seat.

Born William Harrison on June 24, 1895, and raised a devout Mormon, Jack was taught to fight by his older brother, Bernie. Chewing pine tar and soaking his face in brine to toughen his skin, he was hard to beat.

The night of the fight, Laura got all dolled up—white silk suit and a large hat with beautiful, white mephisto plumes. She was quite a sight and wanted to make sure that the town knew she was there and so were her girls.

The fight was promoted by Max Zeller, who led Laura and her girls to their seats, which were nailed to the wooden floor. "Keeps them from falling over if someone goes over the ropes," Max announced with a smirk, as he shook the chairs to show off their stability.

To start off the show, Jack Dempsey's opponent, "Baby-faced Hector," entered the ring. Dancing around, he looked way too pretty to be fighting Jack, or anyone else for that matter. Overhearing the ladies sitting behind her, Laura soon learned why Hector wasn't meant for this match.

"I heard he covers his entire body in cold cream every night and even powders himself," the lady whispered, as she pointed up to the fighter. Laura relayed the rumor to Lillian, who quietly laughed while

173

Jack Dempsey publicity photo. Courtesy of Dick Leppard.

spreading the story among the other girls. Laura's money was on Jack.

Jack Dempsey entered the ring to a loud round of applause. He gave a slight wave, but not too much. He wanted to keep his appearance as intimidating as possible. He would have time to smile later.

Taking a quick jog around the ring, he sized up his opponent. "Jeez, ain't that a cute powder puff?" Jack mocked, as he continued his dance. Heading over to the promoter, Jack asked, "So, what's the receipts for the house?"

Max looked down at his books, then back up at Jack. "Four hundred."

Jack looked back over at Hector, gave him a quick nod, then replied, "I'll give him four rounds."

As the fight began, Hector started his shadow boxing and dancing around the ring. The ladies, who had been talking about Hector earlier, began to yell to him and even profess their love for their favorite fighter. Jack cracked a sly smile as he started to stalk his prey around the ring.

"Well, Powder Puff," Dempsey said in a cold, threatening manner, "I guess I'll have to put you in your lady friend's lap."

The fight went into the fourth round, as Jack promised. As he made his final move, Hector went flying through the ropes, but missed his mark. Instead of landing in his admirer's lap, Hector landed straight into Laura's. The chairs held strong to the floor as the fighter landed on her, before quickly sliding onto the floor. The blood pouring out of his nose splashed onto her new, white silk suit, as she quickly jumped up to avoid any more injury to her outfit, but it was too late. With a loud sigh and a disgusted shake of her hands, Laura walked over to collect her winnings.

Seeing Jack, she gave him a smile as he leaned over the ropes and apologized. He was too handsome to stay mad at.

"You're welcome to come over to my house with your boys. I'll promise you a good time," Laura offered, as she gestured toward her girls.

"No thank you, ma'am. I'm a married man now. Got my wife Maxine right over there," he said, as he pointed toward the back of the room. Laura glanced over to see a homely woman with dyed red hair.

"Hope you don't take offense, but she looks a bit older than you," Laura said, as she leaned closer to keep the statement private.

Jack just laughed. "Yes, ma'am. She is fifteen years older than me. Might be older, if she's lying."[104]

Jack's men showed up at the parlor house about an hour after the fight and were happy to see that Laura didn't follow the law when it came to alcohol. She had ordered a barrel of beer just for the occasion, and charged them each $1 a glass. The beer attracted other cus-

Dollie, one of Laura's Salida parlor house girls. Courtesy History Colorado, Fred Mazzulla Collection, #10049672.

tomers from the fight and one of them showed up in a brand new 1916 Dodge touring car. As the car was admired, the owner explained how he had acquired it.

Henry was engaged to a rich, older woman up in Leadville who had bought him this car as an early wedding present. She knew he was down in Salida for the fight, but not that he was spending her money on pleasures of the flesh. After a couple of beers and a roll in the hay, the man decided to take the party to the nearby town of Poncha Springs and have a dip in the hot springs.

Loaded up in the car and bundled up in blankets to ward off the November cold, the group of seven headed up to Poncha. The hot springs was a popular bathing spot and was open all hours. It included hand-plastered rock pools, cabins, sleeping rooms, baths, and nude bathing from 9:00 p.m. to 6:00 a.m. The temperature could get up to around

168 degrees, but the winter weather was guaranteed to keep them cool. By 5:00 a.m. … Laura's parlor house was a hospital.

Showing off in his new car, and three sheets to the wind, Henry missed the crossing, flipped the car down an embankment, and narrowly missed a ditch. Rolling over twice, it ejected most of the passengers and landed on its top. Luckily, the accident was seen by a rancher, who piled the victims into the back of his hay wagon and hauled them back to Salida.

As the rancher helped the victims into the parlor house, Laura called for the doctor. One young man was out cold and they couldn't get him to wake up. Laura had him laid out on the sofa and the maid filled a hot water bottle and placed it on his head. Within minutes of his arrival, Doctor Curfman announced his first diagnosis.

As Mildred was helped up the stairs, she winced in pain. "There is something cracking in me," she cried, as she held her back. The doctor finished getting her upstairs and looked her over.

"Can you move around?" he asked, as he felt her back. Laura took the girl's hands and walked her a couple steps and helped her dance a little. She fainted dead away. With a sad shake of his head, the doctor looked over at Laura and said, "Her pelvis is broken. I have to wrap her up. It will be about a month before this knits."

With Laura's help, he moved her to a back bedroom and removed her clothes. Looking her over more thoroughly, he discovered that it was worse than he thought.

"My God! Did the car fall on top of this poor girl? Her chest is smashed in!" he announced with a start, as he continued to examine her. "She has at least three crushed ribs." After wrapping her injuries the best he could, he turned to Laura with a solemn expression. "She can't be moved."

As Laura covered Mildred and tried to make her comfortable, the doctor examined Liz Fisher and discovered that she had a bad cut over her eye and a nasty gash on her head. Both would need to be stitched. Finding Mabel still downstairs, the doctor examined her and found, to his added displeasure, that her arm was broken.

As he was already downstairs, the doctor decided to check on the men. He was so consumed by worry over the still unconscious young man on the sofa that the scream from upstairs made him jump. Assuming it was Mildred, he got ready to run back up, but stopped short. Two

Mildred. Courtesy of Dick Leppard.

"Liz Fisher." Courtesy of Legends of America.

Mabel. Courtesy of Dick Leppard.

Vivian. Courtesy of Dick Leppard.

boys were running down the stairs, holding their eyes, with two soiled doves close behind.

"You damn son-of-a-bitch!" screamed Vivian, as she continued to smack the boy hard over the head with a shoe. "How dare you try to steal from me!"

The doctor looked over at Laura and said, "Wow, what a house."

Turning back to his male patients, he was pleased to see that his unconscious patient was starting to wake up. Laura had her maid bring her a rag and a basin of hot water. She carefully washed his face and head, which revealed a long, nasty gash that needed to be stitched. Digging around in his medical bag, Doctor Curf-

Henry's car after the accident. Courtesy Salida Regional Library.

man pulled out a pair of scissors and handed them to Laura.

"I need you to cut his hair around the gash so I can stitch it up," he instructed, as he carefully moved the hair away from the injury. Hearing the first cut, the boy started to fidget. "You better not be leaving me threadbare!" the boy threatened. Turning to face Laura, he cried out in pain and grabbed his chest. Doctor Curfman laid him back down and removed his shirt with an irritated sigh. Looking back at Laura he announced what she already knew—his ribs were also broken.

The young driver, Henry, was the last to be looked at. He had stood around, off to the side, with his hand wrapped with a towel. Hiding like a child who was scared of getting the switch, Doctor Curfman discovered that Henry's hand was gashed open. With a sigh, and an irritated roll of his eyes, the doctor gave Henry a ride to the hospital.

Hours later, after everyone had fallen in to a drug-induced sleep, Laura called her mechanic to have the car towed back to the parlor house. Being such an expensive car, she was afraid it would disappear if she waited too long. On the phone with Wilbur Stoddard, she gave him the location, which was based on the best guess of the rancher who had discovered the wreck. She just had to hope he was right.

Within three hours, Laura had the car sitting right outside the parlor house. As she walked around the car, she noticed that it had held up pretty well, just two broken fenders and both headlights smashed. Walking into the parlor house, Wilbur went to talk to the car's young owner about payment. As he stammered about his wealthy fiancée and how he didn't have the $300 it would take to fix the car, the mechanic just looked over at Laura and lowered his head in annoyance. It seemed that Henry's rich lady friend had heard about the accident and was refusing to pay for the damages. As a friendly gesture, and to get the car off the street, Wilbur agreed to store the car in his garage. Henry was on the next train back to Leadville.

Weeks later, and with no sign of Henry, Laura got a bit of interesting news. It seemed that the mechanic had gotten his nose damp and had accidentally burned down his garage. The car was gone. And with no insurance, it was a total loss. Like the hospital bill Henry skipped out on, nobody got paid.[105]

As Laura's injured girls recovered in their rooms, the year quickly changed to 1917, and the war in Europe was getting more interesting. Despite the story that the United States was staying neutral in the war, the newspapers said differently. In January 1917, a telegram from German Foreign Minister Arthur Zimmerman to the German Minister in Mexico was discovered. It offered U.S. territory to Mexico in return for joining the German cause. On April 6, 1917, the United States declared war on Germany and its allies.

As the country stayed glued to the daily reports of the war, Laura was experiencing a shock of her own. Answering a knock at her front door on May 30, she was face to face with Jack Dempsey's wife, Maxine. And she wanted a job.

Intrigued, Laura invited her inside. Maxine strutted into the parlor house and smiled at the men playing cards at the back table, before sitting down on the overstuffed sofa. Motioning to the maid to bring coffee, Laura took a seat next to Maxine and they started to talk. And it seemed that the stories Laura had heard about Maxine were true.

Jack had met Maxine while she worked the red light district in Salt Lake City, Utah, called Commercial Street. After only a short time together, they were married on October 16, 1916, by a justice of the peace. Jack wanted to turn a whore into a housewife, but it didn't work. He traveled and she solicited customers. Just weeks earlier, they had separated. She informed Laura that she was traveling around, looking for a place to settle down, and needed a job. Seeing a quick buck, Laura gave her a key to a crib across the street. Despite being thirty-seven years old and a little long in the tooth to be selling her wares, Laura knew that she could attract customers just on her name alone. The chance to lay with Jack Dempsey's wife would surely attract business.

Maxine didn't stay long. It being the beginning of summer, the warm weather only encouraged Maxine to show off her wares. Despite explaining the rules of the house, Maxine insisted on parading up and down the street in a see-through crêpe dress. When Laura would try to catch her, she would quickly run into the parlor house, strip off her dress, and solicit customers. She was also a drunkard, which was not the type of girl Laura wanted in her house.

On her last night, Laura was alerted to a small crowd standing outside Maxine's crib window. Each crib came with a private door and a large picture window. Where the other girls would simply hang out of the doorway to attract a customer, Maxine was obviously trying a new approach.

As Laura walked closer to the crowd of men, she could see that Maxine was putting on a private show for them, which included rubbing her naked body against the window and licking the glass. Disgusted, Laura reached into her apron, pulled out her passkey and unlocked the door. She quickly closed the curtain, to loud protests from the viewing audience, and threw a nearby robe at Maxine.

"I run a first class sporting house! Can't you get that through your head? ... And put some goddamn underpants on! Men should pay to see a woman's blind eye," Laura explained with an annoyed huff. "I don't mind if you want to solicit trade, but this isn't a nudist colony!"

Shocked, Maxine tried to apologize, but it came across all wrong. By the morning, she was gone and her key was on the dresser. But Laura hadn't heard the last from her.

A week later Laura received a visit from a farmer. She was tickled to see that he had driven his horse and hay wagon up to her front steps.

Coming outside for a closer look at the big, old-fashioned tire rims, she asked his business.

"Laura," he started, with an upset tone to his voice. "My son has brought one of your girls back up to the ranch and she is drunk all the time."

Laura gave him a serious look and asked if she was an old redheaded gal. Hearing that she was, she gave an understanding nod. "Have you got a ditch down below? You could throw her in the ditch. She is no good for herself or anybody else, anyway." With a laugh, the farmer agreed.[106]

A month later, Lillian and Laura decided a movie was in order. One of Laura's favorite actresses, Theda Bara, was in a new picture called *Cleopatra,* and Laura was dying to see it. As she was getting ready, her maid brought her a beautiful purple silk suit to wear. With a confused look, Laura stared at the outfit and turning it over, questioned where it came from.

"I couldn't get the blood stains out of your white silk suit from the boxing match, so I dyed it purple," she replied, hoping she did the right thing. Laura's smile caused the maid to relax.

She quickly changed into the suit and pranced around her room. "It's the same shade of purple as the high school's colors," she said with a laugh. Suddenly getting a sparkle in her eyes, Laura put a strand of white pearls around her neck. Pleased with her choice, she turned back to the maid. "There," she smiled. "Now I have team spirit. I'm purple and white."

※

As the year faded into the next, Colorado was faced with a new threat … the Spanish influenza. The name came from a terrible flu that had killed millions of people in Spain, starting in May 1918. September of the same year, the flu hit American shores. It was believed to have arrived through a Boston port during a shipment of machinery and supplies for the war.

The flu was first discovered in Colorado in October 1918, when military recruits reporting for duty at the University of Colorado started to show symptoms. By late October, the flu was spreading throughout the entire state. The death rate among miners was found to be very high due to their weakened lungs, and people from higher elevations fared no better. Salida, with an elevation of 7,083 feet, had the entire town under quarantine.

By October 11, 1918, Salida had banned all public gatherings and closed the schools, churches, theaters, and even the post office lobby. A quarantine was issued by Salida Mayor C.F. Johnson. No one was allowed to enter or leave the town. Guards were posted at the train depot and anyone trying to violate the quarantine was arrested.

The flu itself was very deadly and quick to kill. The first signs were extreme fatigue, fever, and headache. Soon after, the victim would turn blue and cough with such force that some tore their abdominal muscles. As they started to die, foamy blood would pour out of their mouths and noses. Some would even bleed out of their ears. Many victims died within hours of showing their first symptoms.

Not understanding the severity, children created a rhyme that they would sing while they played:

> I had a little bird
> Its name was Enza
> I opened the window
> And in-flu-enza.

Despite the mandatory closing of Laura's parlor house, the cribs remained open. As "privately rented apartments," the town wasn't able to prevent the girls from selling their wares, and they had no shortage of customers.

With the town running out of nurses, Doctor Curfman came knocking on Laura's door. Since the parlor house girls were out of work, most of them agreed to help out, but none as much as Jessie.

Jessie was a beautiful, petite, large-busted married woman who wanted to work the red light district after her husband was sent off to war. Laura didn't know if her husband, Earl Keller, was aware of her job, but she understood that Jessie needed money. Her husband's check that was sent to her was only $15 a month. She had been renting crib #6 since he was sent overseas. She hadn't been married very long, as she had only married him in an attempt to keep him from being drafted.

Jessie's breasts baffled Laura, as they hung very low when she undressed. Laura once even asked her why she didn't have "those things" cut off.

Since the sick had overwhelmed the hospitals, many were treated in their own homes by nurses. Being short on help, Jessie was sent to tend to an unlikely family—Reverend Oakley's. As the head of the committee to close down the red light district, Laura found it comical that his family was being treated by a soiled dove. Unbeknownst to the family, when Jessie went home at night, she was also taking in customers.

Laura herself was also treating a friend in one of the downstairs bedrooms, a bootlegger named Brady. Having no family, and the hospitals being overrun with the sick, Laura insisted that he stay with her. As Brady lay resting in bed, Laura borrowed his truck and collected all his whiskey. Storing it in her basement, she was able to continue making money while the flu ran its course. Luckily, Laura's decision to wipe down her entire parlor house with Lysol every day saved her life and the life of Brady. Laura never got sick.[107]

As everyone was battling their own war against the flu, the war in Europe had ended. Germany surrendered on November 11, 1918, and with that, the remaining nations put down their weapons. The Treaty of Versailles was signed by every country involved except the United States, which didn't agree to its terms. Among other things, they felt it favored the British.

One night, as Laura was delivering booze, concealed in a newspaper, she noticed the night marshal, Mr. Jim Blunkoff. Hesitant to approach him for fear of getting arrested, she kept her distance until she noticed that he was dragging a body down the alley. Tucking the whiskey behind an old tire, Laura approached him. Seeing Laura, he stood up straighter and talked to her with an exhausted tone.

"Oh, hi Laura, whew … I've never been so tired in my life. Dragging these bodies out in a laundry basket is not easy work," the man said, as he wiped his forehead. Allowing her eyes to get accustomed to the darkness, she suddenly realized that there must have been around fifteen bodies lying in the alley. Seeing her shocked look, he let out a sigh. "Yeah, they're not even embalming them. Just laying them outside in the cold air. Guess they won't rot so fast."

With a childish smirk, Mr. Blunkoff addressed a topic Laura was hoping to avoid. "You know, I could really go for some whiskey. Shame about Prohibition … yeah, shame I don't know anyone who might have something to help me get through this night."

With a nervous rub of her neck, Laura looked toward the hidden bottle before looking back at the marshal.

"Jim, would you like a drink?" she asked, with a slight hesitation.

The man's face lit up as Laura retrieved a bottle and handed it to him. "Oh God! Thank you! Thank you!" With a smile, Laura headed back to her hidden stash to retrieve a second bottle. She still had a delivery to make.[108]

The quarantine stayed in effect until March 10, 1919. In total, eighty people died from the flu in Salida. In the United States, the total loss was almost fifty thousand.

When the flu had passed, Reverend Oakley was sorry to see Jessie go. Desperate to keep her around, he offered her a job as a companion to his wife and children. With a smile, Jessie refused. "I'm sorry Reverend, but with the flu gone it's time for me to head back to Miss Laura's."

Despite many attempts to sway her and "save her soul," Jessie returned to the cribs. In an interesting turn of events, Reverand Oakley never again mentioned closing the red light district.[109]

✦ 17 ✦

The Chihuahua puppy
and a bottle of happy dust

919–33   With the war and the quarantine both over, Laura could get back to business. Her parlor house was back in full swing and with all the returning servicemen, it had plenty of customers. What she wasn't expecting was to fall in love.

His name was Dudley Gardner O'Daniels, and he was sixteen years younger than Laura, but she didn't care. He was handsome, had a great smile ... but was a chronic alcoholic. As he sat with Laura and talked about his short enlistment, he pulled out his discharge papers. "Discharged. Chronic alcoholism with acute cerebral symptoms existing before enlistment, June 17, 1918."

Laura didn't care. He made her feel young again. She loved the way he would only look at her and how they would talk into the wee hours of the morning—he shared his love of swimming, which is where he got his nickname "Speedy," and that he was on the Salida baseball team.

Laura never missed a game. She would dress in her best costumes and cheer on her man. After the game, they would go back to the parlor house for a few drinks, then out dancing. He made her feel young again, and she hadn't realized how much she missed that.[110]

After a great game, watched by Laura and four of her girls, she decided to celebrate the win by taking a picture. With her new 1910 five-passenger Buick Model 17 parked in the empty field near the ballpark, she piled her girls inside. She wished she could afford a 1919 Buick ... maybe one day.

With her girls sitting down, Laura convinced five of Speedy's teammates to pose with him. Speedy stood in the front, between the headlights, while his friends stood around the car. The team captain quickly jumped into the driver's seat and grabbed the wheel. As Laura was trying to take the picture, a neighborhood boy walked up to the car. Refusing to leave, Lizzie Darling, seated in the front seat, started yelling at the boy. The boy then started an argument that soon attracted attention. Not wanting to miss her picture, Laura snapped the photo. Seconds later, the boy was chased off by Speedy. It seemed that swimming wasn't the only thing he was fast at.[111]

Speedy O'Daniels, standing between the headlights. Courtesy History Colorado, Fred Mazzulla Collection, #10049680.

As the newness of their relationship started to wear off, Laura began to pay closer attention to his addiction. He was drinking a lot of her booze, and she needed to make sure he was paying for it. She was getting too old to be taken advantage of.

After a long talk about his drinking, Speedy decided to play with Laura a bit. He would start to drink, but then hang the cash out of his pants pockets and make her chase him. "See woman, I've got money for ya," he would tease, as he ran around the parlor. But the games stopped when Laura was woken up one night by the sounds of someone opening up her secret stash box.

Laura had a Wurlitzer piano. Years ago, with the desire for a secret hiding spot, she had a locked drawer installed in the back. Opened only with a key, Laura entrusted very few people with its whereabouts. Now, as she lay in bed, she could hear the key turning. Thinking it was her Negro janitor, Laura tiptoed out of her room and into the parlor.

Grabbing a nearby baseball bat that Speedy had given her for such a purpose, she approached the figure and smacked him as hard as she could. Hearing the thump of a body hit the wood floor, she quickly turned on a floor lamp. She wasn't surprised—lying on the floor was Speedy. Kicking him in the side, she sat herself down on a nearby ottoman and held her head.

Laura needed to keep her distance from Speedy. He wasn't any good for her, and she knew it. When he would show up at the house, she would have the girls turn him away. But being an alcoholic, and with a stash of booze in her house, she knew he wouldn't stay away long.

Almost two weeks later, during a lively party, Speedy was able to enter the house unnoticed. Walking up to Laura, he held his head down as he handed her an envelope. Irritated, but curious, she opened it. Inside was money ... not a lot, but some. He told Laura how he had done some repair work at the electric light plant and that the money was his entire paycheck.

Laura didn't know what to say. Seeing her hesitation, he took her hand and led her to a quiet corner to talk. Sitting down on the sofa, he gave her a hug and told her how sorry he was. Laura knew he meant it— Speedy hated to work. Against her better judgment, she started to cry.

As the years passed, and 1919 turned to 1921, Laura had learned to accept Speedy's faults. She decided that men pay for lays with her girls and she paid for a relationship with Speedy by supplying him with whiskey. It was a sad way to have a relationship, but she enjoyed his company too much to end it.[112]

On March 5, 1921, Laura walked out of the kitchen to see her daughter Lucille and her grandson talking to her parrots. Surprised, she wiped her hands on her apron, and gave Alfred a quick hug.

"We have a surprise for you, Grandma!" Alfred announced, with his hands behind his back. As Laura played along, she heard a noise that sounded like a kitten. Thinking her grandson had gotten her a new cat, she started to walk around calling, "Here kitty, kitty. Where's the kitty? Is he behind Alfred's back? Is he inside Alfred's shirt?"

Audrey Lucille Leppard, Laura Evens' granddaughter. Courtesy of Dick Leppard.

As Laura started to tickle her grandson and stick her hands up his shirt in search of her new pet, Alfred started to laugh. "Grandma, that's the baby."

Stunned, Laura quickly looked over at her daughter. With her head down, as though ashamed of making another child, Lucille walked up to Laura and handed her the baby.

"Why don't you ever tell me about the children until after you have them?" Laura asked, with a slightly irritated tone. Hearing the word baby attracted all the girls and they came streaming out of their rooms to have a turn holding her. Audrey Lucille Leppard was born February 19, 1921.[113]

As the months rolled by, Speedy's drinking continued to get worse. He was spending his nights gambling and his days sleeping. On August 1st, Speedy was invited up to Glenwood Springs to spend time with his old baseball teammates. Laura was happy to send him with spending money and for him to finally do something besides hang out in her parlor ... but she wasn't expecting the phone call she got on August 2. Speedy was dead.

Despite being a great swimmer, the alcohol was just too much and he drowned. He had been playing around, going up and down in the water and then he just didn't come up again. Despite a lifeguard being on duty, they didn't get him out in time.

Laura was in shock. She knew Speedy was no good for her, she knew he was spending her money, but she loved him. After having his body returned to Salida, Laura found herself in a daze of funeral arrangements and visits from those closest to him. Hoping for help from his family, she unfortunately found herself stuck with his final expenses.[114]

Looking for a distraction, Laura picked up the newspaper and started to read a story about the President wanting equal rights for Negros. Turning to her housekeeper, she read her part of the story.

"It says here that the President feels that African Americans should have full equality in employment, education, and political life. He said in a speech, down in Alabama, that the black man should be allowed to vote if he is fit and the white man should be prohibited to vote if he is unfit."

As Frieda dried her hands, Laura handed her the paper. "That type of talk is going to get President Harding killed," Frieda responded in her deep German accent.

"You mean President Wilson," Laura corrected her, "the President is Wilson."

With a smile, Frieda turned the paper around and pointed her finger to the headline. "Seems like someone has not been paying attention."

"When in God's name did this happen?" Laura asked, as she grabbed for the paper. Scanning the story, Laura sat back. "Well, you're right ... we do have a new President."

After the November 2, 1920, election, Republican Warren Gamaliel Harding was now the twenty-ninth President. Despite not ending Prohibition, like she would have wanted, she did find him entertaining. Rumor had it that he had been caught drinking alcohol in the White House, despite Prohibition, and that he had fathered a child with a woman thirty-one years younger than him. As the years passed, the scandals continued until his death in 1923.

While in California, after a first-ever Presidential visit to Alaska, President Harding became ill. He complained of cramps, indigestion, a fever, and shortness of breath. His doctor felt it was food poisoning, but other doctors felt differently. A few days later, on August 2, 1923, despite showing signs of improvement, the President suddenly shuttered and died suddenly. The official cause of death was a heart attack, but rumors surfaced that he had been poisoned. On August 3, Vice President Calvin Coolidge became the thirtieth President of the United States.[115]

>❖<

Knowing that no time was the right time, Lillian Powers needed to talk to Laura. She had saved up all her money from the last nine years and was ready to own her own parlor house. She had found a nice house in the town of Florence, over an hour away, and was ready to start the next chapter of her life. To soften the blow, Lillian had bought Laura a gift that she hoped would make it less painful.

Sitting Laura down, Lillian explained her plans and then excused herself to retrieve the present, a brown and black Chihuahua puppy. Laura was ecstatic! As she cuddled the small dog, she announced his new name ... Mister Pimp Powers, after Lillian. Eager for a change of scenery, Laura drove down to Florence and helped Lillian set up her new parlor house ... and brought the dog along.[116]

Laura's dog, Mister Pimp Powers, a gift from Lillian Powers. Courtesy of Dick Leppard.

As the years passed, Laura was having a harder time paying the bills. Prohibition had really hit her hard, and the money spent on buying her illegal hootch wasn't comparing with how much people were willing to pay for it. She needed the booze to bring in customers, but she was losing money fast. With no other option, Laura decided to sell the two-story cribs next door.

Margaret Weber, a crib girl, had been hinting at wanting to run her own house and was interested in Laura's two-story cribs. She had rented a crib from Laura for years and had a good head on her shoulders. She was a tall girl of Cherokee Indian decent, with brown hair and long bangs that hung down to her eyes. She always parked her prized car, a Hudson, in the back to avoid anyone from messing with it.[117]

As the details of the sale were being worked out, Laura noticed a newspaper story, on September 20, 1925, that attracted her attention. The youngest daughter of Horace and Baby Doe Tabor had been found dead.

Rosemary Silver Dollar Echo Honeymoon Tabor had been found dead in Chicago at the age of thirty-five. She was a burlesque dancer who did small acting parts under the name Ruth Norman and loved to date dangerous men. She was found scalded to death in her apartment, with an empty kettle lying on the floor next to her. Neighbors, who were interviewed by police, mentioned how she enjoyed drinking and partaking in the "Happy Dust."

Her father Horace had died years before and her mother refused to accept that the dead woman was her daughter. Rosemary had sent her mother letters saying how she had become a nun, and Baby Doe believed her. Her body was never claimed.[118]

On October 7, 1925, Margaret Weber became the owner of the two-story cribs for $5,000, which was the same amount Laura had paid for them in 1913. She had made improvements, but she felt it was fair market value. Not having the cash up front, Margaret agreed to pay Laura $200 a month.

Needing more money to get by, Laura got a $2,000 loan on the remainder of her properties, which included the parlor house, on December 7, 1925. With that, she walked right over and signed for a brand new 1926 Pierce Arrow touring car. The car wouldn't be out for a couple of weeks, but she wanted to get it ordered.

Laura's 1926 Pierce Arrow and her driver. Courtesy of Salida Regional Library.

It was a beautiful car—a maroon, seven-passenger marvel with a white convertible top. Plenty of room for all of her girls and her new driver, Manny Durant, a railway worker who enjoyed the attention of driving the soiled doves around. At almost $7,000, she would be making payments on the car for quite a while.[119]

>‹

As 1925 turned into 1928, talk of the upcoming Presidential election had people in a tizzy. Expecting current President Calvin Coolidge to run, people were surprised to find that he had refused. In a speech he delivered to explain his decision, he stated, "If I take another term, I will be in the White House till 1933. Ten years in Washington is longer than any other man has had it. Too long!"

Instead, Herbert Clark Hoover was nominated by the Republican Party to run against Democrat Al Smith. In a landslide, Hoover got forty states while Smith only received eight. On November 6, 1928, Herbert Hoover became the thirty-first President of the United States.[120]

Laura Evens holding a pet duck while feeding her other pet ducks in the backyard of her parlor house in Salida. Courtesy of Dick Leppard.

As everything calmed down, and the country was getting comfortable with its new President, October 1929 turned the country on its head.

On October 27, 1929, the stock market crashed. Called "Black Thursday" by some, it soon turned into what became the Great Depression. When the stock market fell, brokers called in their loans, which couldn't be paid. The banks, in turn, began to fail as depositors withdrew all their money in droves, referred to as a "bank run."

By October 1930, 774 banks had failed and by April 1933, seven billion dollars in deposits had been frozen inside of failed banks. By the end of 1930, almost nine thousand banks had failed. Unfortunately as with any crisis, comes thieves and snakes.[121]

His name was Charles O'Leary. He was a tall, well-dressed man with dark hair and blue eyes ... and he was married. Working as a traveling salesman, he lived in Denver with his wife and children, when he wasn't looking for an easy mark.

Laura had met him at a hotel in Denver during one of her shopping trips for the house. As a salesman, he was set up in the "sample room" near the lobby. Always looking for anything new to add to her parlor, Laura found herself talking up a storm with Charles. Later, at dinner, he told her all the things a woman wants to hear. Swooned once again, Laura traveled to Denver many times to visit the man she referred to as her boyfriend. At fifty-nine, Laura was thrilled to have a man in her life once again. The fact that he was married didn't bother her—it just assured her that he wouldn't want anything too serious.

1900s prostitute "Eva." Courtesy of Legends of America.

After almost a year of visits, Charles convinced Laura to travel with him to California. He had gotten wind of a card game and, knowing that Laura was an ace at cards, begged her to join him. Understanding that he was going to expect relations during the trip, and past that time of her life when she cared about such things, she brought along Eva. Laura felt pressured to lay with Charles when she visited him in Denver, but with Eva along, he was sure to leave her alone.

Getting to California was quite an eye opener. Convincing her to gamble with her own money, she lost thousands due to the game being fixed. Later, as he drove her out to a deserted campground, he tried to convince her to invest her money in a combined business venture. When she awoke the next morning, she discovered both Charles and her fox fur coat missing. In a rage, she and Eva packed up their things and left him behind.

The drive back to Colorado was tough on Laura. Lucky to have Eva to drive, Laura laid in the back seat. Taking Laura to the closest hospital, the doctors felt she just had the flu. By the time they arrived back in Salida, she was in bad shape. Eva and Fern spent the nights checking to see if Laura was still breathing. Doctor visit after doctor visit was no help. Laura spent thousands on doctor bills. Some thought it was her appendix; others x-rayed her and gave her bottles of pills; she was put on special diets and told to rest.

Months later, and still weak, some lays had brought ducks over to cook the girls for dinner. As Laura sat in her bedroom, the smell

Laverne "Fern" Pedro (left) and Laura Evens (right). Courtesy History Colorado, Fred Mazzulla Collection, #10039977.

of roasted duck filled the house. Against doctors' orders, Laura came out of her room, grabbed an entire roasted duck, ran back to her room and locked the door. Eating the entire duck was heaven, but soon the pain started. Scared, Fern and one of the lays placed her in the back of the car and drove her to the hospital in Pueblo … two hours away.

Finally, with her pain so severe, they were able to diagnose her correctly. She was suffering from an intestinal stricture, also known as stenosis, which was an obstruction of the bowel. The symptoms were the same that Laura had been experiencing all along—abdominal pain, cramping, bloating, nausea, constipation, and vomiting. Surgery was performed that day and the restricted segment of her intestine was removed. After spending thousands of dollars on doctors, the surgery cost her only $40.12.[122]

⇒⇐

The upcoming November 8, 1932, Presidential election was very important to Laura. President Hoover was running against Democrat Franklin Delano Roosevelt, and not doing very well. Roosevelt repeatedly blamed Hoover for the Depression, the worsening economy, and the 20 percent unemployment rate. Roosevelt was also promising to end Prohibition. That alone made him Laura's favorite candidate. With forty-two states in his pocket compared to Hoover's six, Roosevelt became the thirty-second President of the United States.

Keeping his promise, on March 22, 1933, Americans saw the first sale of 3.2 percent beer and wine. It was felt that 3.2 percent beer couldn't get anyone intoxicated, so it was the first to be allowed. In Colorado, 3.2 percent beer was made legal at 12:01 a.m. on Friday April 7, 1933. Crowds gathered as the first case of legal beer rolled out of the Coors Brewery in Golden, Colorado. Prohibition was fully ratified on December 5, 1933.[123]

Despite alcohol being legal once again, it didn't fix the Depression. Many families were struggling to heat their homes and put food on the table. The abandoned mining town of Turret, miles up into the mountains outside Salida, found a new life as the empty cabins filled up with families who couldn't afford rent. Laura helped when she could, but knew that many people wouldn't want to know that the help came from her. Since the grocery stores took orders, and groceries were delivered, Laura had hundreds of food baskets delivered to families. The sound of coal filling coal bins early in the morning filled the air, as Laura had her cook make pancakes for the neighborhood children before they went to school each morning.

One man hit by the Depression held Laura's heart. He worked for the railroad and his son was one of the many grocery delivery boys in town. Telling Laura of his dad's injury just tore at her heart. The man had been a switchman for the railroad and worked long and hard to support his family. One icy winter night his hand got caught in a gearbox and was mangled. Unable to work, and doctor bills piling up, the little boy was the only income the family had.

Soon, the man was offered a job—with an odd twist. He was to sell newspapers from inside a warm store for an unusually high salary. The job gave the man time for his hand to heal and for him to re-learn how to use what was left of it. When the boy would deliver Laura's groceries, he always had an extra hug for her.

The lack of jobs also brought out the despair in men who could no longer support their families. Embarrassed over the handouts, men would turn on their wives and assault them. One night, a young paperboy came to Laura's door holding a baby. The boy was bruised and the baby was screaming. Quickly bringing them into the house, Laura listened as the boy told her how his dad had beaten up his mom. As the boy started to cry, he told Laura that his dad had hit him when he tried to protect his mom.

Accompanied by her handyman, in case the woman's husband tried to get violent with her, Laura went to the house and offered the woman a safe place to sleep. In order to keep the woman comfortable, Laura re-arranged the bedrooms and gave the woman and her children the back bedroom downstairs.

After word got out, Laura was forced to free up her three bedrooms downstairs to fill the need, and moved her girls across the street to the cribs. The violence against the women turned her stomach and they had nowhere else to go.

To allow the neighborhood kids to earn extra money, Laura would let them wash her car for a quarter. The car got washed so many times a day she was afraid it would melt.

Laura's girls having fun in the Salida parlor house backyard. Margaret Galanes is helping one of her fellow inmates attempt a back flip. Courtesy History Colorado, Fred Mazzulla Collection, #10049664.

Laura learned an inside secret about the local butcher shops that stopped her from ever eating rabbit stew again. To help the local men with money, the butcher shops would buy skinned rabbits from them. But when no rabbits could be found, the men killed stray cats. A skinned cat, with its head and tail removed, looks just like a rabbit.[124]

Despite the Depression, life went on for most. In 1933, the Elks lodge was holding its annual Elks convention, and this year it was being held in Leadville. Seeing an opportunity to make some extra cash and spend some time in Leadville, Laura packed up her girls and headed up.

Every year in July, the Benevolent and Protective Order of the Elks held their annual convention in a different city. A representative from each of the fifteen hundred orders would attend the convention and the week-long meetings. Despite not being allowed to attend the meetings, the girls were welcome at the parties held later, which gave Laura time to show her girls around her old stomping grounds.

Laura loved being back in Leadville. At sixty-two years of age, Laura wanted to have the kind of fun she experienced when she was younger. Finding a horse and buggy, Laura begged the owner to allow her to drive it up and down Harrison Avenue with her girls. Intrigued by her story, but having no memory of that time, the horse's owner hooked up the carriage and handed over the reins.

The wind in her hair and the familiar clomping sounds of the horse's hoofs brought back so many memories for Laura. She drove the carriage past the first parlor house she worked in with Jessie and the Vendome Hotel where she had spent time with Mr. Stratton. She told her girls stories of the mining strike, the murder of the fire chief and of the Ice Palace. As she felt the years fade away, Laura pulled the carriage over and did something the girls were not expecting … she climbed onto the back of the horse. The rest of the trip was spent with Laura doing her guided tour on horseback, while the girls sat back and enjoyed the ride.

The party after the Elks' meeting was just what Laura hoped it would be. Her girls quickly found lays and were easily making money from the out-of-town visitors, as they sneaked into back rooms and coat closets. As the night progressed, Laura noticed that glasses of champagne were being assembled on a back table. Curious, she asked one of the men what they were for. "Oh that? Yeah, see we have a tradition were at eleven o'clock we have a toast to our absent members, then we sing 'Auld Lang Syne,'" the man informed her, as he finished placing the glasses on the table.

Just as promised, the room was quieted by the exalted ruler, who held up his glass and commanded the attention of the room. As the room got silent, he began his speech. "You have all heard the tolling of eleven strokes. This is to remind us ..." As Laura was listening to the speech about the missing members, it made her think of the one member who wasn't getting a drink ... the elk. As the men continued with their toast, Laura snuck behind the exalted ruler's chair and hoisted herself up onto the head of the elk, located right above it.

As she began to pour champagne into the mouth of the mounted elk head, she heard the members start to sing "Auld Lang Syne." Singing along to the song, the men quickly noticed her and insisted that she get down. Laura just laughed and said, "He isn't drinking any from the front end, guess I'll have to try from the back," as she turned around and started to pour the champagne down the neck of the mount, where it attached to the wall.

It was quite a sight. The girls could hear "Should old acquaintance be forgot and never brought to mind? Should old acquaintance be forgot ..." on one side of the hall and the sounds of men trying to convince Laura to climb down from their elk without getting her shoes on the exalted ruler's chair on the other side of the hall. As men took photos, the girls watched as Laura was helped down to a round of applause, followed quickly by her being shown the door. Acting like she had just won a prize, Laura blew kisses and waved at the men as she was led outside. She came to Leadville to have a good time ... and she did.[125]

☆ 18 ☆

The historic President and the alien encounter

934–49 The arrival of 1934 didn't bring much change concerning the Depression that seemed to consume the country. As the months continued, and with so many people out of work, Laura had gotten used to people coming to her door asking for a job. But she was surprised to see the Methodist pastor knocking on her door one afternoon. Assuming it was another attempt to "save her soul," she politely invited him inside and offered him some coffee.

Countless religious groups had knocked on her door over the years trying to convert her to this or that form of Christianity, only to turn around and ask for tithes for their church. With a smile, she would pay them a little something and show them the door. But she soon discovered that this pastor wanted more than tithes … he needed a new roof.

On June 8, 1934, the Salida Methodist Church caught on fire. The church, built in 1908, caught fire around 2:45 p.m. and suffered a lot of damage. Unfortunately, the church only had $4,000 in insurance and that wasn't enough. As the pastor spoke, Laura shocked him with an offer.

"Would it help if I just paid for the whole damn thing?" she asked, as she sat back and sipped her coffee. "Might just save my retched soul, pastor, you never know," she added with a sly smile. Shocked, the pastor almost spilled his coffee. He had the money that afternoon.[126]

As the Depression continued, the one high note for Salida was their high school football team. Undefeated in 1933 and 1934, they were on track to continue their winning streak. Proud of his team, and wanting to keep up team morale for the 1935 season, Coach White knocked on doors to solicit money for new uniforms. Despite knowing it could start tongues wagging, Coach White held his head high and walked down Front Street to knock on Laura's door.

Coach White loved his team. To encourage attendance at the games, he got the entire town to close their stores so everyone could attend. Laura laughed as she saw him enter her parlor. Giving him a curious, accusing look, she asked him his business. As some of Laura's girls approached him, he nervously held out a catalog of football uniforms. With a laugh, Laura invited him to sit down and show her the catalog.

"I like the satin ones," Laura commented, as she flipped through the pages.

"Purple and white satin uniforms would look beautiful on the field," Coach White agreed, but showed her that the price was more than the other uniforms. Looking over their shoulders, Laura's girls were putting in their two cents worth and making Mr. White just a tad bit uncomfortable.

"If you let the boys wear satin, I'll pay for the whole bunch," Laura informed him. "I've known most of these boys since they were little. Hell, they delivered my groceries. Some still do," Laura added. With a firm handshake, the deal was made. The team went on to be undefeated through 1935, and looked great doing it.[127]

❖

Every day the newspapers printed story after story of hardship. Eager to read something different, Laura was surprised to find that Baby Doe Tabor was dead ... and she had died a terrible death.

On March 7, 1935, at the age of eighty-one, Baby Doe had been found frozen to her cabin floor. The doctors listed her death as a heart attack in an attempt to ease the minds of the people of Leadville, who did nothing to prevent it. In her advanced age, Baby Doe—Elizabeth Bonduel McCourt Tabor—was living in a small tool shed next to her deceased husband's beloved Matchless Mine. With hardly any heat and walls covered in insulation to keep out the bitter cold, the beloved wife of Horace Tabor—known as "The Bonanza King of Leadville"— froze to death.

In life, she lived her final years in squalor and seemingly forgotten by the people of Colorado, but in death there was a renewed interest in her life. Seventeen iron trunks, which were stored in Denver, were opened to reveal riches that would have allowed her to die an honorable death. Four more trunks, stored at the St. Vincent's Hospital in

Baby Doe Tabor. From Silver Queen: The Fabulous Story of Baby Doe Tabor, *Bancroft Booklets, 1955.*

Baby Doe at her cabin at the Matchless Mine in 1933, one of the last pictures taken of her. From Silver Queen: The Fabulous Story of Baby Doe Tabor, *Bancroft Booklets, 1955.*

Leadville, were opened to reveal wonderful bolts of fabrics, tea sets, and jewelry. In death, people flocked to the auctions to purchase a piece of her history, that in life they had no interest in.[128]

With the Depression continuing, the upcoming Presidential race filled the newspapers. Democrat and current President Franklin D. Roosevelt was campaigning against Republican Alf Landon. During his presidency, Roosevelt had enacted new policies such as Social Security and unemployment benefits, which were very popular with most Americans. The November 3, 1936, election was one for the record books.

Roosevelt went on to win the greatest electoral landslide since the beginning of the two-party system, which was started in 1820. He carried every state except Maine and Vermont. He won 523 electoral votes, which was 98.49 percent.[129]

➤✦

In early 1939, with the economy looking a bit more stable, Laura decided it was time to get a new car. Her 1926 Pierce Arrow touring car was getting a little out dated, and at thirteen years old, she wanted something new. One of her good friends owned Argus Motors, which had just gotten a new shipment of cars in.

Walking around the car lot, she finally decided on a 1939 Nash Ambassador for $1,200 cash. With a handshake, Laura promised to return within the hour with the money. Expecting a bank check or cash, her friend Richard was surprised when Laura brought back a moneybag. Dumping it out slowly, she revealed that it held silver dollars instead.

The shocked look on the man's face told Laura that he was looking for an explanation. "That's how I earn it and that's how I spend it," she answered. Pulling up a nearby chair, Laura sat back with a smile as the employees watched their boss count twelve hundred silver dollars.[130]

As the year continued, the talk of war increased. A war between the Empire of Japan and the Republic of China had been in the newspapers since its start in 1937, but now there were whispers of Germany threatening to invade Europe once again. Everyone was on edge. On September 1, 1939, the newspapers revealed the inevitable—Germany had invaded Poland. In turn, France and the United Kingdom declared war on Germany. The United States announced they were staying neutral ... again.

As the war in Europe continued, the United States got prepared. On September 16, 1940, the first peacetime draft was announced, and

Frieda, Laura's housekeeper (left), and Laura Evens (right) next to Laura's 1939 Nash Ambassador. Courtesy History Colorado, Fred Mazzulla Collection, #10039978.

by October 16, the draft of sixteen million men began. The Presidential election on November 5, 1940, was also unexpected—President Roosevelt had decided to run for a third term. If elected, he would be the only President to ever win a third term ... and he did just that.

Running against Republican Wendell Willkie, Roosevelt received 449 electoral votes to his opponent's 82. It wasn't the landslide he experienced during his last run for office, but it was all he needed.[131]

Franklin D. Roosevelt ran on the promise to not get the country involved in a foreign war. He tried his hardest to keep his promise, but on December 7, 1941, Japan attacked the United States naval base at Pearl Harbor, Hawaii.

Laura had her hands full just dealing with a lot of problems at home. Her daughter Lucille had gotten divorced and moved from Salt Lake City, Utah, back to Salida with her daughter Audrey. Weeks later, Audrey ran away to Chicago and Lucille moved to Denver. When things seemed to have calmed down, Laura learned that Lucille had left nasty flyers all over Salida.

On October 28, 1940, Lucille had placed flyers on the doorsteps of most of the houses in town. In it, she made charges against a bank official, a lawyer, an undertaker, a widowed hotel employee, and Laura. Leaving it unsigned, it was soon discovered who delivered the flyers. Despite placing them around town between 1:00 and 3:00 a.m., the vehicle used had Nevada license plates. She later admitted the act.

In a letter sent to a Salida businessman, she explained why she wrote it. She talked about how she was the daughter of Laura Evens and that she was angry because Salida society wouldn't accept her. She also expressed her contempt for her mother, saying that she was a neglected child. "Even a rattlesnake will take care of their young," she wrote.[132]

Victoria, one of Laura's prettier girls. Courtesy of Dick Leppard.

Audrey finally did return to Denver to live with Lucille. Laura was hoping it would calm Lucille down now that her daughter was back. Her son Alfred had chosen to stay in Salt Lake City with his father after the divorce. Everything seemed fine until Laura received a frantic phone call from Lucille on April 30, 1941 … Audrey was dead.

The twenty-year-old granddaughter of Laura Evens had died of appendicitis. Despite being in pain, Lucille didn't take her to the hospital in time, and her appendix had burst. After helping Lucille with the funeral, Lucille moved back to Salt Lake City.[133]

As the war continued, the stories just keep getting worse. After Japan bombed Pearl Harbor on December 7, 1941, the United States declared war on Japan on December 8. In turn, Germany and Italy declared war on the United States on December 11, and Hungary and Romania declared war on the United States on December 12. The United States declared war right back. We were now deeply involved in World War II.

A ban on new cars was enacted on January 1, 1942, to save on steel. And, as an added twist, Thailand declared war on both the United States and Britain on January 25. American forces started to arrive in Europe on January 26.[134]

As the years dragged on, the newspapers ran daily stories of the devastation. The only good news came on December 4, 1943, which announced that the Depression had finally ended, but it was due to the war-related jobs.

During the November 7, 1944, Presidential election, President Roosevelt did something completely unheard of ... he ran for a fourth term. His opponent was Republican Thomas E. Dewey, who only managed to receive 99 electoral votes to Roosevelt's 432. The newly re-elected President, unfortunately, wouldn't live to see the end of the war.

On April 12, 1945, President Roosevelt was enjoying a relaxing day at his home in Warm Springs, Georgia. He was joined in the living room by his mistress, Lucy Mercer, and artist, Elizabeth Shoumatoff, who was painting his portrait. Around 1:00 p.m., the President suddenly complained of a terrible pain in the back of his head and collapsed unconscious.

A doctor was immediately called, who recognized the symptoms of a massive cerebral hemorrhage and gave the President a quick shot of adrenaline into his heart. It was no use. President Roosevelt was pronounced dead at 3:30 p.m. He was sixty-three.

At 5:30 p.m., back in Washington, First Lady Eleanor Roosevelt and her daughter, Anna, both dressed in all black, spoke to Vice President Harry S. Truman, who hadn't yet heard of the President's death. When told, he asked the First Lady if there was anything he could do for her. She replied, "Is there anything we can do for you? For you are the one in trouble now."

Luckily for the new President, the war was almost over. On May 8, Germany surrendered and after the bombings of Japan, they surrendered on August 14.[135]

The years following the war were spent in readjustment. Wives were used to working outside the home and had enjoyed the freedom, while husbands had to get used to being home from the war. A little over two years later, Americans were faced with a new threat ... aliens.

On June 25, 1947, a pilot named Kenneth Arnold reported seeing several objects while flying near Mount Rainier in Washington State. He described the motion of the objects as "flying like geese and moving like a saucer skipped across the water," which introduced Americans to the new term "flying saucers." The age of UFOs was born.[136]

Laura Evens sitting on the stairs celebrating the end of World War II. Courtesy of Dick Leppard.

On July 8, newspapers reported that a crashed spaceship had been found in Roswell, New Mexico. Stories of alien bodies and the government hiding the crashed ship filled the papers.[137]

With the story still fresh in people's minds, a spacecraft once again covered the headlines on June 11, 1948. This time, the government wasn't hiding it. Instead, the story of Albert the monkey was all the rage. Albert, a Rhesus monkey, was launched into space and made it to a height of thirty-nine miles, but the excitement soon ended when it was discovered that he had suffocated before the rocket was even launched.[138]

November 2, 1948, saw the Presidential election take a new turn, with three candidates. President Harry Truman was running, but was faced with two competitors: Republican Thomas E. Dewey and "Dixiecrat" Strom Thurmond. Despite the all the media attention, Harry Truman remained the President of the United States.[139]

In Salida, on July 7, 1949, Laura was once again faced with the death of someone close to her. Margaret Weber, the woman she had sold her two-story cribs to, had died. She was only fifty-eight. Curious how a seemingly healthy woman could die so young, Laura anxiously waited for the autopsy results, which shocked even the mortician.

Margaret suffered from a condition called "pica," which is where someone eats non-food items, and her autopsy revealed that for her … it was wooden matchsticks. Joe Stewart, of Stewart Mortuary, informed Laura that Margaret's insides looked like a porcupine was living inside her. It was obvious that she not only sucked the sulfur and glass powder off the matchsticks, but had been swallowing them whole. When he opened her up, hundreds of wooden matchsticks were poking out from the inside of her stomach, intestines, and lower bowels.

Joe Stewart informed Laura that Margaret's condition may have been caused by "celiac disease." A disease of the small intestine, it caused the body to be hypersensitive to gluten, which caused difficulty in digesting food. He had heard that sulfur helped with the pain. Cleaning out Margaret's bank account, Laura found herself planning another funeral. Unfortunately, this was not the last death she would be faced with.

Even with Margaret's passing, her cribs were still being rented. One of the tenants was a seventeen-year-old girl named Gloria Martinez. Gloria had been "worldly" since the age of thirteen, when a man named Marcus Martinez was found enjoying her company. Threatened with prison due to her young age, he agreed to marry her. He had moved them to the nearby town of Texas Creek, but he got a job in Salida at the bakery. His shift started at 4:00 a.m. and he would bring his young wife to Salida while he worked.

Bored and restless, Gloria rented an upstairs crib from Margaret and serviced men while her husband worked. When he discovered the betrayal, it became deadly.

On August 3, 1949, less than a month after Margaret's death, the Salida police department got an unusual visitor—Marcus Martinez. Walking into the police station, he approached the first officer he saw and announced, "I just killed my wife." Contacting Stewart Mortuary, who also drove the ambulance, the Stewarts found themselves faced with a horrific sight. Gloria wasn't dead … but she was trying to be.

Climbing the narrow stairs of the two-story cribs, they entered a large room with a wood stove. Looking around, they discovered Gloria on the bed. It appeared that her husband had attempted to kill her by beating her with an iron. As they approached her, they could only stare in disbelief as she violently thrashed around. Her whole body was cut up and blood was everywhere, as her husband mainly focused on her head. Grabbing the hospital cot, they attempted to strap her down. With the strength of a horse, her dying body fought their every attempt, until they finally got her secured. They then had the task of taking what appeared to be a living dead woman to the hospital.

Carrying the cot straight into the emergency room, they were greeted by Chief Surgeon Rex Fuller, who pulled away the bloody sheet in an attempt to examine her. Taking one look, he quickly ran to the nearby bathroom and vomited. "I wished I had time to do that," Joe Stewart exclaimed, as he placed the bloodied body on the table.

Returning, after washing his face with cold water, Doctor Fuller looked up at Joe and said, "She's not going to make it."

Nodding his head, Joe responded, "Yeah Rex, I know. But what do we do now?" Pumping her body full of morphine, they stood back and waited. Within thirty minutes, Joe was taking her body to the mortuary.

The newspaper ran the story, which included her husband's confession. He had stated that he had heard rumors down at the Victorian Tavern that his wife was up in the cribs. Finding the room, he opened the door and discovered his naked young wife sitting on a bed. When he insisted that she leave with him, she informed him that her lover, a Mexican named Boostez, was on his way. That's when he attacked her. With nobody willing to claim her body, she was buried—in a shipping case due to her large girth—in the potter's field.

With Margaret gone, and the crime scene in the upstairs crib still closed off, nobody was willing to run the building. Fortunately, Laura was able to convince Rosie, a heavyset former soiled dove, to become the landlord until Margaret's family could be found, or the building could be sold.

By October, the red light district saw yet another casualty ... Nigger Mary. Mary Humphrey had been a working girl since the 1890s. She had worked all over Colorado until she settled in Salida, around the same time as Laura. Mary ran a "Coon dive," with colored and mulatto girls. She charged less than Laura's house, but it wasn't based on color, it was based on size and age.

Mary owned half of the building that contained the two-story cribs, and could be seen sitting on the front steps soliciting customers. With her dress pulled up to show her lack of panties, she would call out to

Rosie. Courtesy History Colorado, Fred Mazzulla Collection, #10049667.

Laura Evens (left) and Mary Humphrey (right), the self proclaimed "Nigger Mary." Courtesy of Dick Leppard.

the passing men, "Hey Sugar! Nigger Mary is two hundred pounds of black, quivering passion."

She loved to tell people the story of her best day. It was back when she was much younger, on the 4th of July, when she made $125.50 … at 50 cents a pop. She would have made an even $126, but one of the half dollars was a slug, with no eagle on the front. Mary had fallen onto hard times as she got older, and Laura had hired her as a housekeeper to help her pay her bills. But for the last three months, Mary's adult nephew had moved in with her and nobody had really seen much of her … until October 20, 1949.

Worried about her friend, Laura knocked on her door, but there was no answer. Concerned, she called the police, and what they found was disturbing. Mary was lying on the floor, next to the wood-burning stove, and appeared to be dead. Lying on the bed was her nephew. The crib smelled strongly of urine, whiskey, and vomit. Seeing the nephew roll over and sigh, the officers turned their attention toward Mary. Covering their mouths with their jackets in an attempt to block the smell of death, they carefully turned her body over and discovered large bruises, burns … and a pulse. The officers quickly contacted Joe Stewart.

Carrying the cot up the same staircase they had used to retrieve Gloria just months earlier, Joe Stewart and his assistant were greeted by such a horrific smell that it made their eyes water. As they approached Mary, they could see from her wounds that she appeared to have been assaulted. Curious as to who the culprit might be, Joe took a peek at the hands of the man lying passed out on the bed. Sure enough, Joe noticed bruising around the knuckle areas. Disgusted, he gave the man a violent shove as he turned back to Mary.

Lying on her back, as the officers had left her, Joe started to examine her. The whites of her eyes had a dark orange tint, which indicated jaundice, and looking at the piles of empty liquor bottles, he wasn't surprised. As he looked at her exposed skin, he noticed scars, bruises, and open wounds that appeared to be burns. With her proximity to the wood-burning stove, it wasn't hard to realize where those came from. As he touched the burns, he noticed white pus oozing out. Wiping a burn with a nearby shirt, he was taken aback by the appearance of maggots. He quickly summoned his assistant to help him get her to the hospital.

Joe Stewart got quite a surprise when he arrived at the hospital … they refused to take her. They said she was too far gone and they couldn't help her. They insisted, instead, that he just take her to the mortuary and just wait for her to stop breathing. Calling around, he finally found a nursing home that would take her.

Disgusted that she was refused at the hospital, the nursing home staff quickly assisted Mr. Stewart in getting her into a room to be examined. Beneath her soiled clothing they discovered that she was covered in bed-sores that had become gangrene. The infected areas of her skin appeared to be deep craters where the skin had turned a putrid black and green color. She was carefully cleaned up and her sores treated with ointment. Sores this bad would normally require surgery, but they wouldn't consider it unless she regained consciousness ... which she didn't.

The self-proclaimed "Nigger Mary" was pronounced dead six days later, on October 26, 1949. She was seventy-five. With no family to claim her, she was buried in a pine box in the potter's field. No charges were ever filed against her nephew.[140]

Dolly Howlett was one of Laura's girls that ran off and married a Salida farmhand. She was quiet around people after her marriage, always afraid she would be judged. She was known as a great cook, which shows in the later photo of her. Her husband said that prostitutes make great wives. Courtesy of Dick Leppard.

✦ 19 ✦

Noisy parrots and the water mill

1949–53 With everyone safely tucked into their graves, Laura could finally focus on the end of her own world ... Salida was closing her down.

After almost fifty years in Salida, the men in charge came to her parlor house on December 4, 1949, and told her it was over. They actually seemed sorry. She was only fifty-four days shy of her fiftieth anniversary.

At almost seventy-nine years old, she was going to have to start over. Her girls left, but some didn't go far—they either rented the cribs next door or rooms above the businesses on F Street and still worked their trade. Laura's parlor house and the one-story cribs were empty.

Walking around her parlor house, she only had the company of her birds. Her precious little dog Mr. Pimp Powers had died in 1943 at the age of thirteen, while he sat on his fancy little chair during a late-night card game. She didn't have the energy for another dog.[141]

Laura still owed $2,400 on her parlor house from an old loan she had taken out years ago. She had been making payments, but had taken out new loans in order to help people during the Depression. Now she was afraid she would lose her house.

Eager to start over, she put ads in the paper in an attempt to rent out her rooms, but found that people were shying away. They acted like something nasty would rub off the walls or the doorsills. Finally, a railway worker brought her a conductor who needed a place to stay. Despite being able to rent him one of the cribs across the street, she invited him to stay upstairs in the parlor house. She even framed the first dollar he gave her for rent.[142]

Laura pointing to a "no girls" sign on the front door of her parlor house. Courtesy Salida Regional Library.

Laura's empty parlor house. Her bedroom is the one story, small addition on the right side. Courtesy History Colorado, Fred Mazzulla Collection, #10049681.

Ever since reading about Baby Doe's tragic death, she was afraid to be alone. Always the strong one, Laura kept her aches and pains to herself. As she stared at her bottle of digitalis, she realized that she needed to share her secret with someone ... she had congestive heart failure. Luckily for her, good deeds don't go unrewarded.[143]

Within days of her closing, Laura heard a knock on her door. Standing in the doorway was Glen Ayers, a man she had known for almost forty years. He started out delivering her groceries when he was ten years old, after his daddy left, and he had stayed in touch over the years. He had never felt awkward bringing his wife and young daughters to visit, and now he was bringing his granddaughters over to meet her. "I figured you could use the company," he said with a smile.

The little girls were fascinated with her house and all the pretty things. They ran their fingers through the beaded lampshades and listened to them tinkle, then petted her animal skins that hung from her bedroom walls. They marveled at all the large mirrors covering the walls and played with her grand piano while Glen and Laura talked.

Seeing that the girls were interested in her birds, Laura got up and opened the parrots' cage. She had two red and green macaws that happily hoisted themselves up to the perch above their cage. "Are those the same birds from when I was little?" Glen asked, as Laura got out the crackers and handed them to the girls.

"Yeah," she replied with a sigh. "Damn things just won't die. They live like seventy-five years!" Happily seeing the crackers, the parrots began to screech and squawk. "Shut up you son of a bitch!" Laura screamed over the noise. Glen just laughed.[144]

As the months went by, Laura noticed a pattern in the newspaper. The city had managed to chase the remaining soiled doves out of town, but now they had a new problem ... sexual assaults were on the rise. Laura had been one of the last parlor house's left in Colorado, and it seems that her closing was not being handled very well.

It took until April 24, 1950, before Laura was able to rent out another room. She refused to rent rooms to any of the people who had spited her or any of their friends ... and she had an amazing memory.

By June 30, Laura had rented out all her rooms and even the cribs across the street. She now felt comfortable and the house didn't feel empty anymore. She was able once again to play cards into the wee hours of the morning. She wasn't used to retiring until 4:00 or 5:00 a.m., and with most of her renters working for the railroad, there was always someone up to talk to or play Pan.

On July 7, 1950, as she answered her door, Laura was surprised to find the police chief standing in her doorway. Asking if he could come in, Laura curiously stepped aside while he entered her parlor and removed his hat. "Laura," he started out with a loud sigh, "we have a big problem we need your help with." Relieved that he wasn't there to inform her of another death, she happily motioned for him to sit at her poker table.

With a look of desperation, the police chief stated his business. "As you know, there have been a lot of rapes in the last couple of months," he said, with a concerned look. "And we think it would be best if you re-opened."

Laura sat back in shock. The town had been trying to close down the red light district for years and now that they had, they regretted it. Sitting deep in thought for a moment, Laura glanced over as a railway worker, tired from a long day, came over and gave her a quick kiss on the cheek before heading into the kitchen.

"I'm happy with my renters," she answered, with a smile. "All my girls are gone now, and I wouldn't even know how to find most of them anyway." As she looked at the police chief, she felt a spark of her old self reemerge. "Everyone has to live by the decisions they make, and you made a bad decision." Leaning closer to him, she added, "Just keep this in mind … you all wanted this."[145]

As the year continued, Laura found herself with an unexpected renter … her daughter Lucille. She had moved back to Salida with her new husband and needed a place to live. As Laura looked the man over, she wondered if this was Lucille's third or fourth husband. Shrugging her shoulders, she handed the key to an empty crib over to her daughter.[146]

⟶⟵

As 1950 turned into 1951, Lillian Powers decided to come up from Florence to spend time with Laura. She had been worried about her health, and Laura wasn't a spring chicken anymore. As the women joked about their ailments, Laura informed her of one of hers. "I had a kidney infection awhile back. Doctor Smith gave me pills that made me pee blue," she joked. "When he came by to see how I was, I told him … Well, it's not good for much of anything else, so just turn it into an ink well!"

As the women joked, Lillian felt the time was right to approach

Laura with a touchy subject. "I went by the bank when I got into town, and they said you still owed twenty-four hundred dollars on that old loan," Lillian said, as she pulled a small moneybag out of her purse. Before Laura could say anything, Lillian pulled out twenty-four, one hundred dollar bills. Desperate to erase the despondent look from Laura's face, Lillian playfully started to throw the money at her. As Laura began to laugh, Lillian added, "Just be glad I didn't get silver dollars like we used to!"

Loading up into Lillian's car, the women drove to the bank to pay off the loan. As they walked toward the doors, Lillian reminded Laura of the pig incident. Years ago, a customer had given Laura two baby pigs. She found them adorable and made leashes for them so she could take them for walks. One day she had walked to the bank and then accidentally left them in the lobby. A frantic bank employee wasn't sure how to return them, so she called the police.

"Well, that wasn't as bad as the time the cow fell into the cellar!" Laura added, as the two women sat in the bank's lobby waiting to be seen. "I had to hire a man to use a crane to hoist her out of there! It cost me more than the cow was worth!" Laura added, with a huff.

"Yes, and as he was trying to hook up the cow, your turkeys kept attacking him!" Lillian added with a laugh.

"Remember all the kittens?" Laura asked, as she sat back in the lobby chair. "They were everywhere! I even had a litter right in the middle of my brand new bedspread!"

As the women reminisced, they were caught off-guard by the manager, who had been enjoying their stories. With a smile and a wave of an envelope full of money, Laura walked into his office and paid off her final loan.[147]

In late 1951, as winter was setting in, Laura had need for more rooms. Not wanting to turn away anyone in need, Laura sold her car and used the money to convert her garage into sleeping rooms. After spending $700, she had room for four more renters, which brought in $40 a month, at $10 a head.[148]

Luckily, Glen and his family had kept their promise and stopped by almost every day. Laura loved the company and looked forward to their visits. One day, as the girls were playing in her bedroom, she surprised them by letting out her canaries. She placed little dishes of water around the room and they sat and watched the little birds take baths. As the birds flew around, the two girls played with Laura's extensive doll collection and ran their fingers around the teeth and glass eyes of the taxidermied animal skins hanging above her bed.

"Why do you have so many dead animals in your bedroom, Miss Laura?" Mary Ann asked, as she knelt on Laura's bed and petted the animal's fur.

"Well, when I was younger, I went to an Elks Lodge convention and they had a Navajo Indian man selling the skins. By the end of the convention, I had bought a couple and I looked quite the sight carrying those skins to the elevator!" Laura laughed, as she pointed out a bear and a mountain lion skin hanging near her four-poster bed. "Later, men just brought them to me. That's how I got all these dolls, too," she added with a smile.[149]

✦

As 1951 turned into 1952, it seemed Laura's luck was running out. While walking across the street to check on one of her cribs, she fell. Only two months shy of her eighty-first birthday, Laura found herself lying in the street, unable to sit herself back up. Curious, she tried her left arm. With effort, she sat herself up and ran her left hand up and down her right arm, looking for the break. Hearing a car stop and a door open, she turned her head … and passed out.

Laura woke up to the sound of a man and her daughter Lucille talking. As she slowly sat up in the hospital bed, she got a sharp pain in her right arm and let out a yell. Returning to her bedside, the man informed her that her arm was broken and that it needed time to heal.

"Why does my head hurt so goddamn bad?" she asked, as she touched her head to find a gauze bandage. As Lucille explained what happened, the doctor took out his penlight, looked into her eyes, and asked Laura her name.

"Doctor Smith, I've known you long enough … do you know who you are?" she asked with an annoyed huff.

With a laugh, he continued his questions. "Do you know what day it is?"

Laura thought a minute "Well, rents due today … so it's April six, nineteen fifty-two. Do I get a treat? A lolly perhaps?" she added, with a sarcastic tone.

Doctor Smith put away his penlight, and looked over at Lucille. "She's fine."

Lucille took Laura home the next day and helped her up the stairs. Sitting in her favorite leather chair, Laura let out a sigh, as Lucille went to brew coffee. She knew her days were numbered.

Two days later, Laura was jolted awake by a pounding headache. As she sat herself up in bed, blood started to drip from her nose. Hearing a renter in the parlor, Laura tapped on her bedroom wall with her cane. He quickly came in and found Laura in such a state that he ran to call the doctor. Returning with a dishrag, he sat with her.

"Well, well," Doctor Smith announced, as he walked into Laura's bedroom. "How is my favorite patient?" Laura turned to look at him, which caused him to jump just a little. "Looks like you took an interesting turn, young lady," he added, as he placed his bag on the table.

"Jesus Christ, what few brains I got left are coming out my nose!" Laura announced, as she wiped at her face and held out the blood-stained rag.

After examining her, he placed his stethoscope back around his neck. "Seems you may have had a blood clot in that head of yours that burst during the night. Gave you a nice little black eye in the process, too," he added, with an affectionate pat on Laura's leg. "Just looks like you need to rest. I'll go get Lucille and see if she will sit with you."

Each night as Laura recovered, Glen Ayers and his wife, Svea, would stop by and bring Laura her dinner. It gave Lucille a break from cooking for her mother, which she did during the day. When Glen's little granddaughters came along one night, they asked a question that Laura wasn't sure how to answer.

"Miss Laura, why do you have a funny lamp of a naked lady upstairs?" Mary Ann asked, as she and her sister came down from playing. Not sure which lamp she was describing, she asked where the lamp was. "It's on a little table at the top of the stairs, right up against the window facing the street. The lady stands like this," she added, as both little girls stood near Laura and held their hands above their heads. Laura knew which lamp this was, and it used to have a red silk scarf covering it.

The term "red light district" was invented after railway workers would take their red train lanterns with them when they visited a crib or a parlor house. While they were inside enjoying a soiled dove's company, they would hang their lantern outside in case anyone needed to find them. Later, a red light meant the parlor house or crib was open for business.

When Laura bought her parlor house, it didn't come with a red light. One of Laura's girls felt it needed one and took it upon herself to supply the lamp. Placing it on a small table, between two velvet benches, the lamp would be covered with a red scarf every evening.

Looking over at Glen, Laura saw him trying hard not to laugh. "So, what are you going to tell them?" Glen teased, as the little girls waited for an answer.

Giving him a nasty look, and playfully smacking him on the leg, Laura turned back to the girls. "The lamp is a statue of a Greek goddess, girls. I just thought it was pretty," Laura answered with a straight face … as Glen and his wife started to laugh. After giving their grandparents an odd look, the girls ran back upstairs to play.

By June, Laura was getting her cast soaked off. Doctor Smith returned to the house and placed Laura's arm into a bowl of vinegar. As it softened up, he took a little saw and finished the job. She was so happy to be free of that cast—she hated asking people to roll cigarettes for her. Now she could do it herself, and correctly.[150]

As the year continued, the 1952 Presidential race was in full swing. Current President Harry Truman had decided not to run and was replaced by Democrat Adlai Stevenson. During the November 4, 1952, vote, Republican Dwight David Eisenhower won 442 electoral votes and 39 states to win the Presidency. "I like IKE" was the popular slogan, with President Eisenhower becoming the oldest elected President, at the age of sixty-two, since 1856—President James Buchanan had been sixty-six.[151]

As 1953 began, Laura just wasn't feeling right. She was tired all the time and just wanted to sleep. When Glen discovered her in bed in the early evening, he knew something was wrong. Feeling her head, she felt hot. As his wife went to make Laura some tea, Glen sat her up in bed. While placing pillows behind her back, she started to cough. Frantically grabbing at tissues, green mucus started to come up. As Svea came back in the room, Glen shook his head—Laura needed a doctor.

"We need to stop meeting like this Laura," joked Doctor Smith, as he walked into the bedroom and put down his bag. Checking her over, he diagnosed her with pneumonia. "Now I know you hate swallowing pills, and Glen can crush them up for you, but you have to take them. It's penicillin," Doctor Smith informed her, as he gave an understanding glance over at Glen.

With a serious look, Doctor Smith sat on the side of Laura's bed. "Now Laura ... I want you to understand, that with your heart problem ... we might not be able to cure this."

Laura looked up at him and then over at Glen and Svea. "Well, I can't live forever, Doctor ... Doctor ... ya know, I've never known your first name," Laura commented, as she took a drink of the tea.

"It's Howard," Doctor Smith said, with a childish smile.

Laura looked over at him and thought a minute. "Hummm, don't think I ever fucked a Howard ... nope, can't say that I have. Might of, they don't always give you their names," she added with a sly smile, as they all started to laugh.

As the months continued, Laura wasn't getting much better. The coughing and fever had stopped, but she was just so tired. When Glen came over, she asked him to bring his granddaughters the next time he came. She wanted to finish things. The girls came over the next night. Not realizing what was happening, they followed Laura into her bedroom and climbed up onto her bed. "Now, I know how much you girls enjoy my dolls, so I want you to each pick one to take home," Laura announced, as she sat in a nearby chair.

Anne Patterson, one of Laura's girls, admiring the dolls on Laura's bed. Courtesy History Colorado, Fred Mazzulla Collection, #10039973.

As the girls carefully looked over each doll, Laura turned to Glen and Svea. "Mary Ann isn't the right name for that child. She is just such a beautiful little girl," Laura whispered, as the girls started to pet the animal skins. "It's a shame really. You should have made your daughter name her Princess Pat. Yes ... I like that better," Laura said with a smile.

Walking over to Laura, Mary Ann held up the Mae West doll, whose leg had fallen off years before. "Miss Laura, I like this doll, but her leg is missing," she announced.

"Oh Honey, it's in that top drawer over there," Laura instructed. "I always figured that she doesn't really need it. She isn't going to walk anywhere anyway," she added with a smile. With the dolls chosen, and the missing leg recovered, Laura received hugs from both girls before they left.

The next morning, April 3, 1953, Laura sat up suddenly with a sharp pain in her chest. Reaching for the phone on her nightstand, she called the operator. Struggling to breathe, she was only able to whisper Doctor Smith's name before she broke out in a coughing fit. Calling Doctor Smith, the operator relayed the strange message in hopes that he knew who it was. Unfortunately, he did.

Joe Stewart, who drove the ambulance as well as ran the mortuary, quickly showed up at Laura's. Joe and his assistant carefully helped Laura dress into her dressing gown before helping her walk to the ambulance. He knew she would want to leave the house on her own two feet. In his mind, this woman was a queen and deserved to be treated like one.

Doctor Smith was waiting at the hospital when they arrived. It didn't look good. The pneumonia had made her heart failure worse, and her body couldn't fight it. She died at 8:30 the next morning. She was only two months away from her eighty-second birthday.

Despite all the things she had done for Salida, which included a new roof on the Methodist church, none of the churches would conduct her funeral. When asked why, the response was always the same, "We don't want to be known as the church that conducted Laura Evens' funeral." Disgusted, Joe Stewart made sure she received the funeral she deserved.

Held at 2:00 p.m. on April 8, 1953, Laura had a beautiful ceremony. Soloist Mrs. H. E. Scull sang and organist Mrs. T. J. Preecs played "The End Of A Perfect Day" and "Beyond The Sunset," as Laura laid in her satin-lined, velvet-covered coffin.

Laura Evens' funeral service. Courtesy History Colorado, Fred Mazzulla Collection, #10039993.

Laura's funeral conducted by Joe Stewart, with her former girls standing off to the right. Courtesy History Colorado, Fred Mazzulla Collection, #10039992.

Laura laid to rest in her coffin. Laura's daughter Lucille is fourth from the left, holding her hat. Fred Mazzulla, who conducted years of interviews with Laura, poses third from the left with his hat in his hand. Courtesy History Colorado, Fred Mazzulla Collection, #10039991.

Twenty families purchased flowers and plants, which were set around her coffin. To make sure her easel spray was the largest the town had ever seen, twenty-seven people donated money toward the spray, which was made of white Easter lilies and pink carnations—her favorite flowers.

Buried at Fairview cemetery in Salida, Laura was surrounded by the people who loved her the most—her girls, her daughter Lucille, her friends, and the many railway workers who rented her rooms. Her tombstone lists an incorrect birth date, but it does show the correct spelling of her last name. Despite the fact that she signed her papers "Evans," her former husband, John Cooper, spelled his last name "Evens."

As a final tribute to Laura, Joe Stewart described her occupation on her death certificate with pride and respect: "A resident of Salida for many years. Operator of the Laura Evans institution of free will and unrestricted morals club for many years."[152]

⊁⊰

Out of admiration for the woman I have grown to love and respect, I would like to end her biography with the words to her favorite song.

Listen to the Water Mill
    Listen to the water-mill all the live long day
    To the creaking of the wheel as it wears the hours away
    Languidly the water glides tireless on the still
    Never coming back to that water-mill
    And a proverb haunts my mind as the spell is cast
    That the mill will never grind with the water that has past

Chorus:
    And this proverb haunts my mind as the spell is o'er me cast
    That the mill will never grind with the water that has past

    Oh, the wasted hours of life that have floated by
    Oh, the good we might have done, that's lost without a sigh
    Love that we might once have had, only for a word
    Thoughts conceived but never penned, perishing unheard
    Take the lesson to yourself, take it, hold it fast
    That the mill will never grind with the water that has past

Chorus

Take the lesson to yourself, honest heart and true
Golden years are passing by, and youth is passing too
Try to make the most of life, lose no honest way
All that we can call our own lies in this to-day
Power, intellect and strength may not, cannot last
For the mill will never grind with the water that has past

Chorus

>‹

Rest in peace Laura Evens. I hope I have made you proud.

Endnotes

The sweet taste of candy and the white fur coat

1. Fred Mazzulla interview with Laura Evens, May 4,1951, Tape #4, second cassette, side 2, p. 2.
2. Ibid., April 27, 1952, Tape #7, side one, pp. 16–20.
3. Ibid., April 27, 1952, Tape #7, track #1, p. 8.
4. Jan Mackell, *Brothels, Bordellos and Bad Girls: Prostitution in Colorado 1860–1930* (University of New Mexico Press, 2004), pp. 63–64.
5. Fred Mazzulla interview with Laura Evens, Reel #9, p. 127.
6. City directory, Denver, Colorado.
7. Ibid.
8. United States Federal Census, 1900.
9. Missouri History Museum, Library and Research Center, St. Louis, MO:
   Final Will and Testament, Elizabeth Leeds (Laura Evens' mother-in-law)
   Final Will and Testament, Ellis Leeds (Laura Evens' father-in-law)
   Family tree, John Cooper Evens, Sr. and Elizabeth Leeds-Evens
   John Cooper Evens, Jr., United States Federal Census, 1870–1900
   Alice Chapel Reed, United States Federal Census, 1880 (Laura Evens' birth name)
   Hugh M. Reed and Martha A. Ray family tree (Laura Evens' parents)
   Hugh M. Reed Civil War record (Laura Evens' father)
   Fred Mazzulla interview with Laura Evens, Tape #5, p. 4.
   Personal interview with Dick Leppard (great-grandson of Laura Evens)
10. Fred Mazzulla interview with Fern Pedro, January 20, 1954, Reel #10, p. 4.
11. Fred Mazzulla interview with Laura Evens, Reel #9, p. 156.
12. Fred Mazzulla interview with Fern Pedro, January 20, 1954, Reel #10, pp. 4–5.

A mirrored ceiling and the crystal chandelier

13. Kay Reynolds Blair, *Ladies of the Lamplight* (Western Reflections Publishing Company, 2000), pp. 79–82; Linda R. Wommack, *Our Ladies of the Tenderloin—Colorado's Legends in Lace* (Caxton Press, 2005), pp. 48–50, 54–57.

Fuzzy burros and the bottle of Listerine

14. Colorado railroad map, Colorado Railroad Museum, Golden, CO.
15. Linda R. Wommack, *Our Ladies of the Tenderloin—Colorado's Legends in Lace* (Caxton Press, 2005), pp. 55–57.
16. Fred Mazzulla interview with Laura Evens, May 4, 1951, Tape #4, second cassette, side 2, page 2.

17. Fred Mazzulla interview with Laura Evens, May 4, 1951, Tape #4, second cassette, side 2 , page 2; Leland Feitz, *Cripple Creek's Red Light District* (Little London Press, 1967), pp. 14–17.

18. Leland Feitz, *Cripple Creek's Red Light District* (Little London Press, 1967), pp. 18–28; Caroline Bancroft, *Six Racy Madams of Colorado* (Bancroft Booklets, 1965), pp. 5–8.

The salmon in the sandpit

19. Fred Mazzulla interview with Laura Evens, May 4, 1951, Tape #4, p. 2A.
20. Ibid., Reel #7, p. 31.
21. Photo, (page 48), Courtesy Dick Leppard.
22. Ibid.
23. Fred Mazzulla interview with Laura Evens, Reel #7, pp. 53–55.

Arse bandits and dickey dazzlers

24. Jan Mackell, *Brothels, Bordellos and Bad Girls: Prostitution in Colorado 1860–1930* (University of New Mexico Press, 2004), pp. 2–3.
25. Andrea Tone, *Devices and Desires: A History of Contraceptives in America* (Hill and Wang, 2001), pp. 1–9, 14, 18–19.
26. Michael Butler, *Upstairs Girls: Prostitution in the American West* (Farcountry Press, 2005), pp. 71–77.
27. Jan Mackell, *Brothels, Bordellos and Bad Girls: Prostitution in Colorado 1860–1930* (University of New Mexico Press, 2004), pp. 45.
28. Fred Mazzulla interview with Leverne "Fern" Pedro, Reel #10; author interview with Ted Argus, 2009; Michael Butler, *Upstairs Girls: Prostitution in the American West* (Farcountry Press, 2005), pp. 71–77.

The pony ride

29. The History of Kodak 1878–1929, www.kodak.com.
30. Photo, History Colorado, Fred Mazzulla Collection, Denver, CO.
31. Personal interview with Norma Friend, 2009.

Chocolate teapots and an ancient forest

32. Personal interview with Norma Friend, 2009.
33. Tom Sherlock, *The Origin of Saint Vincent Hospital, Leadville, Colorado,* http://coloradohealthcarehistory.com.
34. Fred Mazzulla interview with Laura Evens, May 4, 1951, Tape # 4, p. 7.
35. Rene L. Coquoz, *King Pleasure Reigned in 1896: The Story of the Fabulous Leadville Ice Palace* (Johnson Publishing Company, 1969), pp. 11–14.
36. Fred Mazzulla interview with Laura Evens, Reel #7, pp. 63–64.
37. Rene L. Coquoz, *King Pleasure Reigned in 1896: The Story of the Fabulous Leadville Ice Palace* (Johnson Publishing Company, 1969), pp. 15–17.
38. Fred Mazzulla interview with Laura Evens, Reel #7, pp. 64–65.
39. Rene L.Coquoz, *King Pleasure Reigned in 1896: The Story of the Fabulous Leadville Ice Palace* (Johnson Publishing Company, 1969), pp. 20–24.
40. Fred Mazzulla interview with Laura Evens, Reel #7, pp. 65–67.

41. Rene L. Coquoz, *King Pleasure Reigned in 1896: The Story of the Fabulous Leadville Ice Palace* (Johnson Publishing Company, 1969), pp. 25–26.

Canaries and diamond garter buckles

42. Fred Mazzulla interview with Laura Evens, Reel #7, p. 15.

43. Marshall Sprague, *The King of Cripple Creek* (Friends of the Pikes Peak Library District, original print date 1953, reprinted 1994), pp. 54–58.

44. Fred Mazzulla interview with Laura Evens, March 29, 1952, Tape #1, pp. 1–4.

45. Ibid., Reel #7, p. 30.

46. Jan Mackell, *Brothels, Bordellos and Bad Girls* (University of New Mexico Press, 2004), pp. 64–66.

A toothy grin and the gray jumpsuit

47. Fred Mazzulla interview with Laura Evens, May 4, 1951, Tape #4, second cassette, side 2, p. 7.

48. Edward Blair, *Leadville: Colorado's Magic City* (Fred Pruett Books, 1980).

49. Fred Mazzulla interview with Laura Evens, May 4, 1951, Tape #4, p. 5.

50. Edward Blair, *Leadville: Colorado's Magic City* (Fred Pruett Books, 1980).

51. Marshall Conant Graff, *A History of Leadville, Colorado* (Nabu Press, 2010), pp. 116–117.

52. Fred Mazzulla interview with Laura Evens, May 4, 1951, Tape #4, p. 5; Edward Blair, *Leadville: Colorado's Magic City* (Fred Pruett Books, 1980).

53. Fred Mazzulla interview with Laura Evens, Reel #7, Track #1 of second reel, pp. 34–37.

$25,000 and a shot between the ears

54. Fred Mazzulla interview with Laura Evens, "The Bustle," complete transcript, page 126A; Fred Mazzulla interview with Laura Evens, Reel #7, pp. 74–79; Fred Mazzulla interview with Laura Evens, Reel #9, pp. 124–126.

55. Fred Mazzulla interview with Laura Evens, Reel #7, p. 80.

56. Fred Mazzulla interview with Laura Evens, Reel #9, pp. 128–133; Fred Mazzulla interview with Laura Evens, Reel #7, p. 81; Fred Mazzulla interview with Laura Evens, May 4, 1951, Tape #4, second cassette, side 2, p. 4.

Roman gladiators and a head full of quail feet

57. Photo courtesy Dick Leppard.

58. United States Federal Census, Lucille Evens, 1900 (Laura Evens' daughter); United States Federal Census, David VanWinkle, 1900 (Lucille Evens' foster parent).

59. *Baltimore American* (newspaper), March 9, 1897; July 5, 1897.

60. Edward Blair, *Leadville: Colorado's Magic City* (Fred Pruett Books, 1980).

61. Photo of Laura Evens courtesy of Dick Leppard; Photo of Jessie courtesy History Colorado, Fred Mazzulla Collection, Photo of Clara courtesy History Colorado, Fred Mazzulla Collection; Thomas Jacob Noel, *Colorado Revisited: The History Behind the Images 1870–2000* (Westcliffe Publishers, 2001).

62. Fred Mazzulla interview with Laura Evens, May 4, 1951, Tape #4, pp. 7, 9–10; Fred Mazzulla interview with Laura Evens, Reel #7, Track #1 of second reel, pp. 34–38.

63. Fred Mazzulla interview with Laura Evens, May 4, 1951, Tape #4, pp. 9–10.

64. Ibid., Reel #7, Track #2, pp. 62–63.

65. Marshall Sprague, *The King of Cripple Creek* (Friends of the Pikes Peak Library District, original print date 1953, reprinted 1994), pp. 84–94; Fred Mazzulla interview with Laura Evens, May 4, 1951, Tape #4, pp. 1–2, 3, 2A.

66. Judy Nolte Temple, *Baby Doe Tabor: The Mad Woman in the Cabin* (University of Oklahoma Press, 2009).

67. Ringling Brothers Route Book, 1899; Fred Mazzulla interview with Laura Evens, May 4, 1951, Tape #4, pp. 7–8; Fred Mazzulla interview with Laura Evens, Reel,#7, Track #1 of second reel, pp. 57–62; Fred Mazzulla interview with Laura Evens, Reel #10—additional inserts, pp. 7, 55A, 56A: Fred Mazzulla interview with Laura Evens—complete transcript, Chariot Race.

The insane asylum and a dead president

68. Fred Mazzulla interview with Laura Evens, Reel #7, Track #1 of second reel, pp. 39–41.

69. Nell Mitchell, "Colorado State Hospital Annex: A white Elephant?" (CMHIP Historian); Fred Mazzulla interview with Laura Evens, Reel #7, pp. 41–43, 45.

70. Real Estate Conveyances pertaining to lots 5–12, Block 5; Salida Mail City Directories, Salida, CO.

71. Fred Mazzulla interview with Laura Evens, May 4, 1951, Tape #4, p. 2.

72. Colorado Cultural Resource Survey—Architectural Inventory: Form #5CF406.113 "The Plaza Apartments"; Form #5CF406.122 "The Laura Evens House."

73. *New York Times* (newspaper), September 7, 1901; *Buffalo Enquirer* (newspaper), September 14, 1901; *Buffalo Commercial* (newspaper), October 29, 1901; William DeGregorio, *The Complete Book of Presidents* (Gramercy, 1997).

74. Fred Mazzulla interview with Laura Evens, Reel #9, pp. 115–117.

75. Personal interview with Dick Leppard (Laura Evens great-grandson, 2009); *Salida Mail* (newspaper), February 25, 1902.

76. Marshall Sprague, *The King of Cripple Creek* (Friends of the Pikes Peak Library District, original print date 1953, reprinted 1994), pp. 92–95.

77. Fred Mazzulla interview with Laura Evens, March 12, 1948, Transcript #1, p. 3; Fred Mazzulla interview with Laura Evens, Reel #7, Track #1 of second reel, p. 37; Fred Mazzulla interview with Laura Evens, Reel #9, pp. 115–117.

A dead lieutenant and a pot of soup

78. Photos from the Salida Regional Library.

79. Theodore Roosevelt, *The Autobiography of Theodore Roosevelt* (The Macmillan Company, New York, 1913).

80. Eastern National Park and Monuments Association, 1982; *Life Magazine*, original story printed February 15, 1963.

81. Walt Burton and Owen Findsen, *The Wright Brothers Legacy: Orville and Wilbur Wright and their Aeroplane in Pictures* (Harry N. Abrams, 2003).

82. Real Estate Conveyances pertaining to lots 6–12, Block 5, Salida, CO.

83. Walt Burton and Owen Findsen, *The Wright Brothers Legacy: Orville and Wilbur Wright and their Aeroplane in Pictures* (Harry N. Abrams, 2003).

84. William DeGregorio, *The Complete Book of Presidents* (Gramercy, 1997).

85. Real Estate Conveyances pertaining to lots 5–12, Block 5, Salida, CO.

86. Fred Mazzulla interview with Laura Evens, Reel #9, p. 105; Linda R. Wommack, *Our Ladies of the Tenderloin: Colorado's Legends in Lace* (Caxton Press, 2005), pp. 64–65.

87. Saint Mary of the Assumption Central City, Roman Catholic Churches, Waymarking.com; "Central City Colorado: A Brief History" (Gilpin County Museum); Fred Mazzulla interview with Laura Evens, Reel #9, pp. 68–70, 73–75, 77; Fred Mazzulla interview with Laura Evens Tape #1, side 2, p. 57A; Fred Mazzulla Interview with Laura Evens, Reel #9, pp. 134–144.

The fourth floor tower and the blood-stained shirt

88. Cynthia J. Pasquale, *100 Years in the Heart of the Rockies* (Arkansas Valley Publishing Co., 1980); Kim Swift, *Heart of the Rockies: A History of the Salida Area* (Johnson Printing, 1980), p. 65; Personal interview with Norma Friend, 2009.

89. *Evening Bulletin* (newspaper), April 19,1912 (Philadelphia, PA).

90. Theodore Roosevelt, *The Autobiography of Theodore Roosevelt* (The Macmillan Company, New York, 1913).

91. Personal interview with Dick Leppard (Laura Evens' great-grandson, 2009); State of Colorado Certificate of Birth—Alfred Dudley Leppard, File #21375 (Laura Evens' grandson).

92. Real Estate Conveyances pertaining to lots 5–12, Block 5, Salida, CO.

93. Cynthia Pasquale, *100 Years in the Heart of the Rockies* (Arkansas Valley Publishing Co., 1980).

94. Personal tour of Laura Evens' Parlor House, 2010; Personal interview with T.J. Gardunio 2010; "Orville Wright, Cat House Tales," *Colorado Central Magazine* No. 116, Local History, October 2003.

95. Fred Mazzulla interview with Laura Evens, Reel #8, pp. 31–40; *Salida Mail* (newspaper), October 24, 1913 and October 31, 1913.

A $20 gold piece and bottles of bootleg booze

96. Fred Mazzulla interview with Laura Evens, Reel #6, pp. 1–2; Fred Mazzulla interview with Lillian Powers, Reel #11, side 2, pp. 64–65, 69–73; Fred Mazzulla interview with Lillian Powers, Reel #2, pp. 69–72.

97. Personal interview with Norma Friend, 2009; Personal interview with T.J. Gardunio, 2010.

98. Photo from Dick Leppard collection.

99. Duke Franz Ferdinand Biography, 1863–1914, Biography.com.

100. Diana Preston, *Willful Murder: The Sinking of the Lusitania* (Doubleday, 2002).

101. The Silent Film Still Archive.

102. "A look back: 80th Anniversary of the Repeal of Prohibition in Colorado," *Denver Post* (newspaper), September 26, 2013; *Denver Post* (newspaper), January 1, 1916; Personal interview with Sam Deleo, 2009; Fred Mazzulla interview with Laura Evens, March 12, 1948, Transcript one, pp. 2–3.

103. William DeGregorio, *The Complete Book of U.S. Presidents* (Gramercy, 1997); "A look back: 80th Anniversary of the Repeal of Prohibition in Colorado," *Denver Post* (newspaper), September 26, 2013.

The boxer's wife and a bottle of Lysol

104. Randy Roberts, *Jack Dempsey: The Manassa Mauler* (University of Illinois Press, 2003); Fred Mazzulla interview with Laura Evens, November 8, 1952, Reel #8, side one, pp. 18, 22–24; Fred Mazzulla interview with Laura Evens, Second transcript, pp. 5–6.

105. Cynthia J. Pasquale, *100 Years in the Heart of the Rockies* (Arkansas Valley Publishing Co., 1980); Fred Mazzulla interview with Laura Evens, Reel #8, pp. 24–30.

106. Randy Roberts, *Jack Dempsey: The Manassa Mauler* (University of Illinois Press, 2003); Fred Mazzulla interview with Laura Evens, Reel #8, pp. 24–30.

107. *Mountain Mail* (Salida newspaper), May 1, 2009; Fred Mazzulla interview with Laura Evens, March 12, 1948, Tape #1, pp. 1–3; Fred Mazzulla interview with Laura Evens, Reel #9, pp. 118–121.

108. Fred Mazzulla interview with Laura Evens, Reel #9, p. 114.

109. Ibid., Reel #9, pp. 118–121.

The Chihuahua puppy and a bottle of happy dust

110. Military discharge papers, June 17, 1918; Fred Mazzulla interview with Lillian Powers, Reel #3, pp. 112–115; Fred Mazzulla interview with Fern Pedro, Reel #10, pp. 6–9.

111. Photo, History Colorado, Fred Mazzulla Collection, Denver, CO.

112. Fred Mazzulla interview with Lillian Powers, Reel #3, pp. 112–115; Fred Mazzulla interview with Fern Pedro, Reel #10, pp. 6–9.

113. Personal interview with Dick Leppard (Laura Evens' great-grandson, 2009).

114. Fred Mazzulla interview with Lillian Powers, Reel #3, pp. 112–115; Dudley Gardner O'Daniels Obituary from Lewis and Glenn Funeral Home, Salida, CO.

115. William DeGregorio, *The Complete Book of U.S. Presidents* (Gramercy, 1997).

116. Fred Mazzulla interview with Fern Pedro, Reel #10, p. 29.

117. Fred Mazzulla interview with Laura Evens, Reel #8, side 2, p. 44; Fred Mazzulla interview with Lillian Powers, Reel #2, pp. 85–86; Real Estate Conveyances pertaining to lots 5–12, Block 5, Salida, CO.

118. Judy Nolte Temple, *Baby Doe Tabor: The Mad Woman in the Cabin* (University of Oklahoma Press, 2009).

119. Personal interview with Sam Deleo, 2009; Photo from Saladia Regional Library; Real Estate conveyances pertaining to lots 5-12, Block 5, Salida, CO.

120. William DeGregorio, *The Complete Book of U.S. Presidents* (Gramercy, 1997).

121. David E. Kyvig, *Daily Life in the United States* (Ivan R. Dee, Chicago, 2002), pp. 213–221.

122. Fred Mazzulla interview with Fern Pedro, Reel #10, pp. 9–14.

123. William DeGregorio, *The Complete Book of U.S. Presidents* (Gramercy, 1997); "A look back: 80th Anniversary of the Repeal of Prohibition in Colorado," *Denver Post* (newspaper), September 26, 2013.

124. Personal Interviews: Stanley Provenza, 2009; Tony Passarelli, 2009; Norma Friend, 2009; Helen Ramey, 2010; Jim Trujillo, 2009; Jim Allen, 2009; Chuck and Joanna Jay, 2009; Ted Argus, 2009; and Sam Deleo, 2009.

125. Charles Edward Ellis, *An Authentic History of the Benevolent and Protective Order of the Elks* (Rare Book Club, 2012); Fred Mazzulla interview with Fern Pedro, Reel #10, pp. 16–17, 22–26.

The historic president and the alien encounter

126. *Salida Daily Mail* (newspaper), June 8, 1934.

127. Personal interview with Stanley Provenza, 2009.

128. Judy Nolte Temple, *Baby Doe Tabor: The Mad Woman in the Cabin* (University of Oklahoma Press, 2009).

129. William DeGregorio, *The Complete Book of U.S. Presidents* (Gramercy, 1997).

130. Personal interview with Ted Argus, 2009.

131. William DeGregorio, *The Complete Book of U.S. Presidents* (Gramercy, 1997).

132. *Salida Daily Mail* (newspaper), October 28, 1940.

133. Personal interview with Dick Leppard (Laura Evens' great-grandson, 2009).

134. Jim Corrigan, *Causes of World War 2* (OTTN Publishing, 2005).

135. Jean Edward Smith, *FDR* (Random House, reprint edition, 2008).

136. *Duluth Minnesota News Tribune* (newspaper), June 25, 1947.

137. *Roswell Daily Record* (newspaper), July 8, 1947.

138. NASA History Program office, "A brief history of animals in space," http://history.nasa.gov/animals.html

139. William DeGregorio, *The Complete Book of U.S Presidents* (Gramercy, 1997).

140. Personal interview with Joe Stewart, 2010; Obituaries from Lewis and Glenn Funeral Home, Salida, CO: Gloria P. Martinez; Mary Humphrey; Margaret Marie Weber.

Noisy parrots and the water mill

141. Fred Mazzulla interview with Fern Pedro, Reel #10, pp. 29–30.

142. Fred Mazzulla interview with Laura Evens, May 4, 1951, Tape #4, second cassette, side one, p. 8.

143. Fred Mazzulla interview with Laura Evens, Tape #5, p. 1.

144. "Orville Wright, Cat House Tales," *Colorado Central Magazine* No. 116, Local History, October 2003.

145. Fred Mazzulla interview with Laura Evens, Tape #5, pp. 1, 2–5.

146. Personal interview with Dick Leppard (Laura Evens' great-grandson, 2009).

147. Fred Mazzulla interview with Laura Evens, Reel #6, pp. 4–5; Fred Mazzulla interview with Lillian Powers, Reel #2, pp. 77–79; Fred Mazzulla interview with Fern Pedro, Reel #10, pp. 30–32; "Orville Wright, Cat House Tales," *Colorado Central Magazine* No. 116, Local History, October 2003.

148. Fred Mazzulla interview with Laura Evens, May 4, 1951, Tape #4, continued on second cassette, side one, p. 4.

149. Ibid.

150. Fred Mazzulla interview with Laura Evens, Reel #7, pp. 11–13.

151. William DeGregorio, *The Complete Book of U.S. Presidents* (Gramercy, 1997); "Orville Wright, Cat House Tales," *Colorado Central Magazine* No. 116, Local History, October 2003.

152. "Orville Wright, Cat House Tales," *Colorado Central Magazine* No. 116, Local History, October 2003; Personal interview with Joe Stewart, 2010; Fred Mazzulla interview with Laura Evens, Reel #7, p. 57; Laura Evens Obituary from Lewis and Glenn Funeral Home, Salida, CO; Laura Evens funeral program; Funeral Photos, Fred Mazzulla collection. Colorado Historical Society, Denver, CO.

Bibliography

Newspapers

Baltimore American Newspaper, March 9, 1897, and July 5, 1897.
Buffalo Commercial, October 29, 1901.
Buffalo Enquirer, September 14, 1901.
Denver Post, January 1, 1916, and September 26, 2013.
Duluth Minnesota News Tribune, June 25, 1947.
Evening Bulletin, Philadelphia, PA, April 19, 1912.
Mountain Mail, Salida, CO, May 1, 2009.
New York Times, September 7, 1901.
Roswell Daily Record, July 8, 1947.
Salida Daily Mail, June 8, 1934 and October 28, 1940.
Salida Mail, October 24, 1913 and October 31, 1913.

Books

Bancroft, Caroline. *Six Racy Madams of Colorado.* Denver: Bancroft Booklets, 1965.
Blair, Edward. *Leadville: Colorado's Magic City.* Boulder: Fred Pruett Books, 1980.
Blair, Kay Reynolds. *Ladies of the Lamplight.* Lake City: Western Reflections Publishing Company, 2000.
Burton, Walt and Owen Findsen. *The Wright Brothers Legacy: Orville and Wilbur Wright and their Aeroplanes in Pictures.* New York: Harry N. Abrams Publisher, 2003.
Cashman, Sean Dennis. *America in the Gilded Age.* New York University Press, 1984.
Coquoz, Rene L. *King Pleasure Reigned in 1896: The Story of the Fabulous Leadville Ice Palace.* Boulder: Johnson Publishing Company, 1969.
Corrigan, Jim. *Causes of World War 2.* Stockton, New Jersey: OTTN Publishing, 2005.
DeGregorio, William. *The Complete Book of U.S. Presidents.* New York: Random House/Gramercy, 1997.
Ellis, Charles Edward. *An Authentic History of the Benevolent and Protective Order of the Elk.* Rare Book Club, 2012.
Feitz, Leland. *Cripple Creek's Red Light District.* Little London Press, 1967.
Graff, Marshall Conant. *A History of Leadville Colorado.* South Carolina Biblio Bazaar/Nabu Press, 2010.
Kyvig, David E. *Daily Life in the United States 1920–1940.* Chicago: Ivan R. Dee, 2002.
Mackell, Jan. *Brothels, Bordellos and Bad Girls: Prostitution in Colorado 1860–1930.* Albuquerque: University of New Mexico Press, 2004.

Noel, Thomas Jacob. *Colorado Revisited: The History Behind the Images 1870–2000.* Englewood: Westcliffe Publishing, 2001.

Pasquale, Cynthia J. *100 Years in the Heart of the Rockies.* Colorado: Arkansas Valley Publishing Company, 1980.

Preston, Diana. *Willful Murder: The Sinking of the Lusitania.* New York: Doubleday, 2002.

Roberts, Randy. *Jack Dempsey: The Manassa Mauler.* Champaign: University of Illinois Press, 2003.

Roosevelt, Theodore. *The Autobiography of Theodore Roosevelt.* New York: The Macmillan Company, 1913.

Secrest, Clark. *Hells Bells: Prostitution, Vice, and Crime in Early Denver.* Boulder: University Press of Colorado, 2002.

Smith, Jean Edward. *FDR.* New York: Random House, reprint edition 2008.

Sprague, Marshall. *The King of Cripple Creek* (Friends of the Pikes Peak Library District), 1953.

Swift, Kim. *Heart of the Rockies: A History of the Salida Area.* Boulder: Johnson Publishing Company, 1980.

Temple, Judy Nolte. *Baby Doe Tabor: The Mad Woman in the Cabin.* Norman: University of Oklahoma Press, 2009.

Tone, Andrea. *Devices and Desires: A History of Contraceptives in America.* New York: Hill and Wang, 2001.

Wommack, Linda R. *Our Ladies of the Tenderloin: Colorado's Legends in Lace.* Caldwell, ID: Caxton Press, 2005.

Interviews by Fred Mazzulla

Laura Evens
Lillian Powers
Leverne "Fern" Pedro

Interviews by Author

Dick Leppard, great-grandson of Laura Evens
Norma Friend
T.J Gardunio
Sam Deleo
Stanley Provenza
Tony Passarelli
Helen Ramey
Jim Trujillo
Ted Argus
Jim Allen
Chuck and Joanna Jay
Joe Stewart

Articles and Maps

Central City, Colorado: A Brief History. Gilpin County Museum.

Colorado Central Magazine No. 116. "Orville Wright, Cat House Tales," Local History, October 2003.

Colorado Railroad Map, Colorado Railroad Museum, Golden, Colorado.
Duke Franz Ferdinand Biography: 1863-1914. www.biography.com.
History of Kodak, 1878-1929, www.kodak.com.
Life Magazine. Eastern National Park and Monuments Association, 1982. Original story printed February 15, 1963.
Mitchell, Nell. "Colorado State Hospital Annex: A White Elephant?" CMHIP Historian.
NASA History Program Office. A Brief History of Animals in Space, http://history.nasa.gov/animals.html.
Ringling Brothers Route Book, 1899.
Saint Mary of the Assumption. Central City, Roman Catholic Churches. Waymarking.com.
Sherlock, Tom. "The Origin of Saint Vincent Hospital, Leadville, " http://colorado-healthcarehistory.com.
The Silent Film Still Archive.

City Directories

Denver, Colorado
Salida, Colorado

United States Federal Census

Alice Chapel Reed, 1880
Carrie Ward, 1900
David VanWinkle, 1900
John Cooper Evens Jr., 1870–1900
Lucille Evens, 1900

Birth Certificates and Final Will and Testaments

Birth Certificate: Alfred Dudley Leppard, File #21375. Laura Evens' grandson.
Will: Elizabeth Leeds (Evens). John Cooper Evens' mother; Laura Evens' mother-in-law.
Will: Ellis Leeds. John Cooper Evens' stepfather; Laura Evens' father-in-law.

Family Tree

Elizabeth Evens. John Cooper Evens' mother; Laura Evens' mother-in-law.
John Cooper Evens Sr. John Cooper Evens' father; Laura Evens' father-in-law.
Martha A. Ray. Laura Evens' mother.
Hugh M. Reed. Laura Evens' father.

War Records

Dudley Gardner O'Daniels, Military Discharge Papers, June 17,1918.
Hugh M. Reed, Civil War Record; Laura Evens' father.

Colorado Cultural Resource Survey

Architectural Inventory form #5CF406.113—"The Plaza Apartments"
Architectural Inventory form #5CF406.122—"The Laura Evens House"

Obituaries and Funeral Program

Obituary: Dudley Gardner O'Daniels, Lewis and Glenn Funeral Home, Salida, CO.
Obituary: Gloria P. Martinez, Lewis and Glenn Funeral Home, Salida, CO.
Obituary: Laura Evens, Lewis and Glenn Funeral Home, Salida, CO.
Obituary: Margaret Marie Weber, Lewis and Glenn Funeral Home, Salida, CO.
Obituary: Mary Humphrey, Lewis and Glenn Funeral Home, Salida, CO.
Funeral Program: Laura Evens.

Index